ALL GOOD THINGS

Do the Dog!

♡,
Jodie Beau

JODIE BEAU

Copyright 2014 by ©Jodie Beau

ISBN-13: 978-1495315602
ISBN-10: 1495315606

Edited by Madison Seidler (www.madisonseidler.com)
Cover Design by Michelle Preast of Indie Book Covers
www.michellepreast.com
Interior Design by Inkstain Interior Book Design
Cover Models: Lindsey Wickenheiser and Lon Meehan
Cover Photography by Jodie Beau

This is a work of fiction. Names, characters, businesses, places, events and incidents are either the products of the author's imagination or used in a fictitious manner. Any resemblance to actual persons, living or dead, or actual events is purely coincidental.

This book is licensed for your personal enjoyment only. It is not transferable. It cannot be sold, shared or given away. The unauthorized reproduction or distribution of this copyrighted work is a crime punishable by law. If you would like to share this book with another person, please purchase an additional copy for each recipient. If you're reading this book and did not purchase it, or it was not purchased for your use only, please purchase your own copy. Thank you for respecting the hard work of this author.

This one is dedicated to my parents; though I'm sure neither want to read the debauchery within these pages. I swear – this is not a true story.

PROLOGUE

Summer 1994

JAKE
Ten (and three-quarters) years old

I COUNT MINUTES. The alarm clock in Adam's bedroom, the rooster clock on the kitchen wall, the digital clocks on the oven and microwave, the grandfather clock in the living room that chimes like church bells at the top of every hour, and my *Beavis and Butt-Head* wrist watch. I have eyes on them all.

9:20 – I wake up in the top bunk of Adam's bunk bed, in Adam's bedroom, in Adam's house. Nothing in this house is mine – not the bedroom, the parents, the sister, the baseball cards, or the Nintendo games. Still, I feel more at home at Adam Humsucker's house than I do at my own. I don't remember a time when that wasn't true.

Sometimes I wish I did live here. I won't lie and say I've never been jealous of Adam. J-e-a-l-o-u-s, jealous. (I spelled that word right in the fifth grade spelling bee this year and came in third place. Boo-yah!)

JODIE BEAU

I have been. Jealous, I mean. I *am*. A lot of the time. Not because of his enormous collection of video games, his mad skills on the b-ball court, or the four-point-oh he gets every quarter without even trying. I'm mostly jealous because his family is badass. His parents are laid back and funny. Even his little sister is semi-decent. I mean – she's cool for a girl. I wouldn't mind claiming her as my own sister.

We'd just finished up the fifth grade last week, Adam and I. It's summer! Yippee! Is that Alice Cooper I hear in the background?

During the summers I stay overnight at the Humsuckers' about two or three times a week, sometimes consecutively (that wasn't in the spelling bee, I'm just real smart). Most of the time I don't even call to check in with my mom. And it's totally cool. With Mom, with me, with them.

I wake to the smell of bacon. Who can sleep through the smell of bacon? I love bacon. Roxie has a t-shirt that says, "Bacon Makes Everything Better." Truth.

Last summer, Julia wrapped bacon around chicken breasts and cooked them on the grill. Roxie asked if we could have everything wrapped in bacon from then on.

"Chicken, steaks, hamburgers, pork chops, potatoes, veggies, I'll have everything wrapped in bacon, please."

"Great," her dad said. "And when you die from heart disease, we'll wrap your casket in bacon, too."

I should make one thing clear from the start: my mom does not cook. She can pour a bowl of cereal and put some slices of bread in the toaster without burning them, but that's the extent of a home-cooked breakfast in my house.

I don't mean to make the Humsuckers sound like some perfect cookie-cutter family. They eat their share of cereal and toast. This is America; it's what we do. But when they decide to cook breakfast, they do it right. And the annual Father's Day breakfast does not disappoint.

9:26 – Everyone works as a team to get the table ready. Adam gets the milk and juice from the fridge and sets five glasses on the table. Roxie sets out the napkins and silverware. I set the plates. I eat a lot of meals here and my job is always the plates. I don't know who sets the plates when I'm not here. I never thought to ask.

9:30 – We eat. While we're eating we give their dad, Henry, his handmade Father's Day cards.

Yes, *that* Henry Humsucker, the infamous college professor who is better known as Dr. Hum. He's kind of a big deal in Ann Arbor. His classes have waiting lists. Why? Because he loves what he teaches – the same thing, semester after semester, year after year, class after class. He acts like he's learning it all for the first time. How do I know this? This all comes from the mouth of the Mrs. Boasting isn't his game. But she can't talk any higher of her husband. And when the two are in the same room together, her face can't beam any brighter either.

Dr. Hum looks exactly the way you'd think a college professor should. Longish hair, thick sideburns, wire-rimmed glasses, corduroy sports coats with patches on the elbows. Yes, I'm being serious. His coats have patches on the elbows. He makes those patches look badass.

Julia had sat the three of us kids down at the dining room table after dinner last night with a plastic tote full of craft supplies. Adam and I are at the point in our lives where crafts are not cool. If she had asked us to make homemade pinwheels or pasta creations, we would have laughed our asses all the way to the Nintendo in the den. But she asked us to make Father's Day cards. We didn't argue.

I made one for Dr. Hum and another for my own dad.

While Henry has a passion for science, learning, and Simon & Garfunkel, my dad has a passion for sports ... and that's pretty much it. Oh, and beer. Sports and beer. He's that guy. He plays on adult league flag football and baseball teams, meets up with his fantasy football league at the bar every Wednesday night, and coaches my younger brother, Shawn's, Little League team. When he isn't playing or coaching, he's watching sports on TV.

It's kind of ironic, really, that the man who lives for sports has a son with an embarrassing lack of athletic skill. I'm not sure if I'm using the word 'ironic' correctly. I've only heard it used in movies. But what I mean to say is that being me, and having my dad for a dad, well, kind of sucks. I think probably for both of us.

Dad was a football player in high school. Mom was a cheerleader. So typical. Until she broke the mold and got pregnant. While she was *in high school.* Girls back then did *not* get pregnant in high school. It was a huge scandal, or so I hear. My grandparents wanted her to give the baby (me) up for adoption, but she said that was a selfish thing to do. She felt she should pay for her mistake.

ALL GOOD THINGS

I'm really young, only ten and three-quarters. But I'm old enough to know Mom was wrong. It would have been the opposite of selfish. She's not the only one paying for that 'mistake.' But blaming her now would be pointless. It is what it is, and I'm also old enough to know *that*.

Mom and Dad stayed together until Dad's graduation. I was four months old. They have one crinkly old photo of the three of us taken on Dad's graduation day. It's the only picture I have ever seen of the three of us together.

When they broke up after graduation, Mom and I stayed with Grandma and Grandpa. Dad got a job repairing cars at a body shop. Eventually he fell in love, got married, and had two more kids: my brother, Shawn, and my sister, Natalie. Shawn plays football and baseball. Natalie is only four and already on a soccer team. Me, I play a mean game of Super Mario Bros. And I came in third place in the spelling bee. Don't forget that.

I don't get to see them often. I go to their house on holidays like Easter and Thanksgiving. Thank goodness for that, or I'd be eating turkey sandwiches with Mom. She splurges and gets the turkey lunchmeat from the deli on special occasions, but still, it's lunchmeat.

I also spend two full weeks at Dad's house every August, and we always spend Father's Day together. He is picking me up at noon today. We are having lunch before heading to the Detroit Zoo. I cannot wait. Which leads me back to the clock-watching.

9:30 – Henry gushes over his Father's Day cards while we enjoy bacon, sausage, scrambled eggs with cheese, fried potatoes, and toast smothered in soft butter. I love that the Humsuckers always have soft butter. At my house we have refrigerated sticks that don't spread for shit and end up ripping a hole in the bread. Gross.

Henry treats each card as if they're precious works of fine art, rather than a few pieces of construction paper decorated with glue and glitter.

10:09 – We help Julia clear the plates. Like setting the table, cleaning the kitchen is also a group project. We know our roles. Adam wipes down the tables, counters, and island while Roxie washes dishes. I dry and put away. Henry Ford would be proud.

10:22 – Adam thinks we should go swimming. They have a built-in swimming pool. Sure, I shrug, why not? I've got time.

10:31 – We head out back to the pool. Roxie follows us. She pretty much follows us all the time. Adam hates it, but I don't mind. The more the merrier. I'd like to think Shawn and Natalie would follow me around, too, if we lived together.

Adam performs an expert dive into the deep end. He's not on the swim team. He's just the guy who is good at everything.

Roxie does a perfect cannonball, her arms hugging her knees to her chest.

When it's my turn, I nonchalantly walk toward the pool and 'accidentally' walk right over the edge and into the water. I do this all the time, and all three of us know it's not an accident. But it makes Roxie laugh every time. And it just looks cool.

11:49 – Dried off and dressed in my best polo shirt and shorts, holding the homemade greeting card I made for Dad, I stand in front of the bay window in the living room to keep an eye outside, just in case Dad comes a few minutes early.

11:57 – Any minute now and they'll be pulling up.

12:05 – They probably ran into some traffic. No big deal.

12:16 – Starting to worry a little. Most of the time the things we worry about don't happen. I decide to worry a *lot*. That way Dad will definitely show up.

12:24 – When does 'fashionably late' become just regular late?

12:31 – Did I hear the time wrong?

12:35 – "You want to call your dad's house and see if they got held up?" Julia asks, holding out the cordless phone.

I call. It goes to the answering machine. "Hi," Heidi says brightly. "You've reached the home of the Odoms. Heidi," Dad's voice chimes in to say his name. Then Shawn says his name, and Natalie says hers. Nobody ever asked me to say my name on the machine. Because I'm not really a part of their family. I'm just a visitor. I'm a visitor at Dad's house. I'm a visitor at Adam's house. And I'm invisible at Mom's.

"He might have said one o'clock," I tell Julia as I set the phone back onto its base.

"Probably," she says with a sad smile – sad because she doubts I heard the time wrong. When adults look sad, you know it's bad.

JODIE BEAU

12:38 – I sit down on the couch next to Roxie. She's watching a VHS tape of recorded episodes of the *All New Mickey Mouse Club* on the VCR. You'd think girls her age would be embarrassed to watch the Disney Channel. Not Roxie. You should have seen the fit she threw when Julia told her they were canceling the Disney Channel from their program lineup. On her knees, crying real tears, begging, pleading, and promising to put her allowance money toward the cost of the premium channel. "You can't do this to me!" she'd screamed. "Tiffani and Chase are back this season! And I can't live without Justin and Ryan. I. Can't. Live." Two words: drama and queen. Girls are crazy.

1:10 – This *is* Father's Day, right? It must be. It has to be. Where are they?

1:22 – "Now it's time to say goodbye ... to all our company." Thank you! I don't even mind that Roxie sings the song out loud because I know this means it's almost over. By the way, Roxie sings. A lot.

1:26 – Roxie turns on a rerun of *Growing Pains* and lies down on the couch. Her feet touch my thigh, but I don't move. I'm not one of those people who freak out over feet.

I hear muffled sounds from the video game Adam is playing in the den, but I don't have the heart to join him right now.

1:31 – I overhear Julia on the phone. "Hey, Laura (my mom), did I wake you? Sorry. (Pause). He's an hour and a half late. (Pause). Yeah. He got the machine. (Pause). We'll wait a little while longer."

ALL GOOD THINGS

1:33 – Roxie has fallen asleep. I can tell by the way she's breathing. She's got the right idea. Maybe if I take a nap, Dad will be here when I wake up.

I set the Father's Day card on the coffee table and curl up on the end of the couch. I slide my feet behind hers.

I'm not positive of the time because I have my eyes closed, but someone covers us up with a blanket.

2:23 – A noise coming from the kitchen wakes me up. Roxie is on the other end of the couch looking as dazed and startled as I feel. We look at each other and smile. We know that noise. It's the food processor. It means Julia is making her famous salsa from the fresh veggies she grows in her garden.

We run into the kitchen to find a nacho bar on the island. Salsa, guacamole, sour cream, chili, queso dip, tortillas, chips, even virgin margaritas with salt on the rims. It's such a treat and I forget for a few minutes that I'm not supposed to be here right now.

3:06 – The kitchen is cleaned up again and the three of us kids play cards with Henry at the dining room table. He's been in the process of teaching us this game for several months now. It's tough and I feel a real sense of pride when my team wins. Roxie is my partner today and we win two games in a row. To win a game of Euchre, you and your partner must work together and you must trust each other. You need to anticipate your partner's moves before they're made. If you can communicate without words, read each other's expressions, you're golden. Roxie and I, we're golden today. I feel a sense of camaraderie as we win another game and high-five across the table. I really needed this.

"Good thing you're here, Jake," Henry says, "or we wouldn't have a fourth player."

That's not true. Julia would be the fourth player.

I know Henry is trying to make me feel more comfortable being stuck in the middle of their day. He doesn't want me to feel like a nuisance or a fifth wheel. I appreciate that he cares enough to bother, but it doesn't help. I begin to feel uneasy. They thought I was leaving at noon. That was the plan all along. Now I don't know what to do. Do I leave? Walk home? Do they have something special planned that is ruined by my unexpected presence? Are they watching the minutes on every clock in the house, just like I am, in hopes that I'll leave soon?

4:00 – I feel like I'm about to cry. When the card game breaks up, I ask Henry if I can take a shower.

"Since when do you need to ask?" he says as he playfully messes up my hair.

4:28 – I've kept my cool so far. The shower helped me get the tears back into my brain, or wherever they go when you don't let them out. As I head back downstairs, I'm not feeling completely okay about being stood up by my own father, but at least I'm clean. That always helps.

Walking past the den, I catch a glimpse of Adam and Henry on the couch. They're each holding a controller to the Nintendo video game system. When Adam moves a character on the screen, he moves himself in real life. When he wants his character to jump, he jumps a little off the couch. When he wants him to run fast, he tilts his whole body to the right, like that will push the character even faster. He's very animated.

Henry sits next to him and hops right along with his son. Henry is not into video games, but he plays Super Mario Bros. with Adam for the same reason he watches John Cusack and Audrey Hepburn movies with Roxie.

I walk toward the living room and put my thumb and forefinger on the top of my nose near the inner corners of my eyes. I might be able to stop tears that way.

I think about funny things as I walk blindly down the hall. *Dog on a surfboard. Dog on a surfboard wearing sunglasses. Cat on a pogo stick. Cat doing the dance to Michael Jackson's Thriller.* That's funny shit right there.

I walk into the living room. I've got it under control ... until I see that stupid Father's Day card on the coffee table.

I grab it and find the closest hiding spot. I've played enough hide-and-seek in this house to know the best hiding spots. I crawl under the plant table in the corner. Henry has all kinds of leafy plants on top; some have leafy vines that hang all the way to the carpet like a curtain.

It's dark under here and I feel safely hidden. I press my finger and thumb on my nose again and I've got it, I've got it ... and then I don't. My cry comes out as a squeak. I let go of my nose and rip the greeting card to shreds because I'm still allowed to act like a child sometimes. I *am* a child. I bring my knees to my chest and bury my face in them.

I hear a voice in the kitchen. It's Julia. I can tell she's on the phone again.

"Nope. They never showed. Never answered any calls. Do you want me to send him home? (Pause). Oh. Okay. It's no problem. We don't mind him staying here."

I am allowed to be hurt right now. I am allowed to feel unwanted and unloved. I am allowed to cry. I know that. But that doesn't make me feel any less embarrassed when I look up from my knees to see Roxie peering at me from the other side of the table.

Damn! What will she think of me now? I'm the cool kid who doesn't let anything shake him up. I'm the kid who walks right into the pool. Now I'm the pussy who cries in her living room.

On her hands and knees, she peers under the table with her big blue eyes. I don't hide. I look right back at her with my wet, and probably bloodshot, brown ones. I silently dare her to say one word about this. My sadness turns into anger. I'm angry with my dad. I'm angry with my mom. I don't want to be angry with Roxie. I don't want to lash out on her. But she's there. Mom and Dad aren't. That's the problem.

Roxie should be afraid right now. She should back away and leave the room and act like she never saw a thing. That is what I want her to do. But I'm not surprised she doesn't.

She lifts a few vines off the ground and crawls under them. She sits next to me, pulls her knees to her chest like mine, and takes my hand in hers.

"It's okay, Jake," she whispers. "I can ask my mom to take us to the zoo next weekend if you want."

ALL GOOD THINGS

It's not about the zoo. Doesn't she get that? Of course not. Why would she? She has two parents and a brother who actually like having her around. If she went away to a summer camp, they would miss her. They wouldn't hold a party to celebrate their 'vacation' the way my mom did last summer when I went to my dad's in August.

She doesn't understand. But she means well.

Having Roxie console me should have made me feel better, but all it did was make me cry harder. I cry for a different reason – because she's always so nice to me. This whole family is always so nice to me, and I don't deserve it. I don't deserve them.

She lets go of my hand and puts her arm around my shoulder. I lean into her and let her comfort me like the pansy I am.

My dad is an ass. My mom is a jerk. But I change my mind about Roxie. I'm glad she's not my real sister. Because I just noticed for the first time how blue her eyes are. She's actually kind of amazing.

MAY
2005

safe ' ty net `
n.
1. a protective net suspended under a person working at a height.
2. something that provides protection or security.

Random House Kernerman Webster's College Dictionary, © 2010

CHAPTER 1

ROXIE

Looking back, I should have seen the signs. There were always signs. A person doesn't go from good to bad in the blink of an eye. It might seem that way at the time – it certainly seemed that way to me – but that wasn't how it truly happened. In all actuality, our relationship started going sour from the moment we met. It happened slowly, eroding like rocks along a beach. But the end was always there, simmering before the boil, smoldering before the burn.

Warning signs, red flags, whatever you want to call them, they were there. I overlooked them. All of them. Every. Single. One.

Now I couldn't help but look back and overanalyze every minute of those seven months, as if seeing it in retrospect would change anything. It wouldn't. But I tortured myself anyway.

At first I kept reliving my bad decisions in my head. When I began to feel overwhelmed by the high amounts of stupidity I saw in my memories, I started a list. I liked lists. I found an old high school notebook in my nightstand and wrote down each instance of foolishness I'd displayed since September. Reliving my mistakes in my head wasn't enough. I needed to see them in physical form. I needed to feel the ink (preferably blue) gliding smoothly across the paper as I bulleted the list with little broken hearts and dotted my Is with sad faces.

For the last few days I'd been feeling like one of those annoyingly dumb characters from books and movies who wouldn't see the truth if it fell from space like a meteor and flattened their house. You know the kind – the character who has you screaming, "Come on! No one in real life is that stupid!"

I had a list that said otherwise.

The notebook was helpful for a while. The more I wrote, the more I started to feel like myself again. But it wasn't enough. I needed to be able to organize and reorganize my thoughts and self-wallowing. I needed a spreadsheet.

As I sat on my bed feeling sorry for myself, I pulled my laptop onto my knees, opened up Microsoft Excel, and started a new document. I titled it *Shit I Should Have Seen* and chose Courier New as the font – a dramatic font for a dramatic person. Some people cut themselves. Some people threw up. Others reached to drugs, alcohol, or promiscuous sex. Me, I organized.

ALL GOOD THINGS

I hit caps lock. It was best if I used all caps. They were louder. If I ever forgot what an idiot I was, I would see a reminder screaming at me from the monitor. YOU ARE DUMB AS FUCK.

I met him at the beginning of my junior year at the University of North Carolina – Chapel Hill. It was September, 2004, and I was at a dueling piano bar in Raleigh. This was a time before smart phones and social networking took over our lives. If you asked someone if they had a Twitter, they'd think you were referring to a sex toy. Jennifer Aniston and Brad Pitt were still America's sweetest couple, and Justin Timberlake had yet to bring sexy back.

I missed three warning signs that night.

Prohibition was famous for their dueling piano show, especially on college nights when the underage were allowed in for a small fee. I had never felt completely comfortable in nightclubs – like I was on display in a meat market and was surrounded by better cuts of beef. I was a sirloin surrounded by filets and New York strips. There was always someone prettier than me, or skinnier, or with better shoes, a smaller waist, wider hips, a curvier butt, brighter eyes, less freckles, shinier hair, or a better complexion. Most people went to bars to socialize, dance, and find someone to hook up with. I wasn't the kind of girl who hooked up with people I just met, I had a hard time socializing when no one could hear a word I said, and my dancing was awkward and embarrassing.

So what did I do at bars? I compared myself to other girls. No need to worry. I wasn't entirely insecure. I did sometimes come out on top. On some nights, when I took extra time with my hair and makeup, I could be a fine piece of flank steak. But even so, hanging out in bars was not my self-esteem's idea of a good time.

Prohibition was different. It was a place with a purpose, not a typical skankfest filled with tricks in tube tops grinding their asses all over every guy on the dance floor. Everyone in Prohibition had a common ground – the show. It wasn't about hooking-up; it was about the camaraderie, the friendly competition, and the battle between North and South (which they were still holding a grudge about below the Mason-Dixon).

It was after midnight. The show was at its peak, and the crowd at its most enthusiastic (spoiler alert: totally wasted). It was time for the night's biggest and most popular performance: – "The Devil Went Down to Georgia." Just a few notes of the Charlie Daniels Band's classic was enough to get the crowd on their feet. *This* was why people came to Prohibition. Being in a room with that much energy gave me an adrenaline kick unlike anything else. I couldn't get enough. And that night I found something else I couldn't get enough of: Jim Crowley.

A guy jumped up from the crowd and climbed onto one of the pianos. At first I thought he was an overzealous spectator. It took me a few seconds to notice he was holding a fiddle. A fiddle! And boy did he know how to play it. His hands moved faster and faster, keeping up with every note, right on key. I didn't know human hands could move that fast, and with such precision, too. It was the most magnificent thing I'd seen in my entire twenty years.

ALL GOOD THINGS

Now would probably be a good time for me to confess to being an exaggerator, if you haven't caught on yet.

The crowd was wild. The guy with the fiddle had the girls screaming as though Usher was on the piano modeling boxer briefs. And I was as guilty as anyone. I was two drinks away from throwing my panties on stage.

This guy was gorgeous. Even three tables away and in the low light of the bar, I could tell how blue his eyes were. His dark buzz cut and olive skin made his piercing eyes all the more prominent. I could see the bulge of his biceps under the tight sleeve of his vintage *Gremlins* T-shirt. *Whoa, what?* He played the fiddle *and* liked eighties movies? Be still, my fortune cookie. Um, I mean, *heart.*

I'd never known a guy who played a fiddle before. I had no idea the instrument could be so sexy. And the way he commanded the crowd – he had such confidence, such a presence on stage. Every eye in the bar was on him and he knew it. He looked up in my direction and gave a half smile, causing me to squeal like a teenager. There were at least seventy people in my direction, and certainly the spotlights were blinding him, and there was no way the smile was for me. But it didn't matter. I wanted him. Case closed.

I'd be the first to admit I had an overactive imagination. Physically, I was in a bar in North Carolina watching a dueling piano show. Mentally, I was in a comfy suburban home, in a living room decorated in silver tinsel with a twinkling Christmas tree in front of the bay window. A crackling fire in the marble fireplace warmed the room, and four stockings hung from the chimney 'with care.'

I sat at an imaginary piano playing "Oh Holy Night," even though, in reality, the only thing I could play on the piano was about four notes of "Happy Birthday."

Two cute kids with olive skin and baby blue eyes sat on the piano bench next to me in their red velvet holiday outfits. When Guy-Who-Plays-Fiddle walked into the imaginary room in a red and gray argyle sweater vest, he carried a tray of mugs filled with steaming hot chocolate. He set the tray on the piano and the family began to sing. And they lived happily ever after. The end.

I could *totally* see it happening.

When the song was finished (the one in real life), Guy-Who-Plays-Fiddle bowed to the standing ovation and casually hopped off the piano. He quickly disappeared into the crowd toward the bar.

The piano players segued into a fast-paced TV show theme song duel. Ordinarily this would thrill me because I do love TV theme songs, but I was in some kind of fiddle daze. When I snapped out of it I told my roommate, Sera, and her former high-school sweetheart – slash - current N.C. State boyfriend, Seth, I was going to the bar for a drink (of soda).

The bar area in the back was not crowded. Most of the patrons were staying close to the stage to watch the show.

He was sitting at the end of the bar staring into a glass of ice water.

I didn't do crowds well, but I did men well. Around other girls I felt inadequate. When there weren't any other

ALL GOOD THINGS

girls around, I was as confident as a Victoria's Secret Angel. This guy was going to want me. He was going to be mine. I would make sure of it. Because that's the kind of person I was.

Was. That's the kind of person I used to be – before a guy in a *Gremlins* shirt hopped onto a piano with a fiddle. What kind of person was I now? I wasn't sure. Confident? Ha! That was a joke. Damaged? That was more like it. Pathetic? Sounds about right.

"Hi," I said in my best sweet-and-shy voice. "That was amazing what you did up there."

"Yeah?" he asked, like he wasn't sure. "Thanks. This is only my third night playing here. I'm used to working in a more subdued environment."

Subdued. He used a big word. In addition to being talented and sexy as hell, he was smart, too. And he had a Southern accent that nearly turned my knees to jelly. Bonus!

"I come here all the time," I told him, "and that was the coolest shit I've ever seen."

"Thanks," he said with a smile, showing off a mouth full of white teeth (good dental hygiene!). "My name is Jim."

"I'm Roxie."

"The name on everybody's lips?"

Hold on a second! He was gorgeous, smart, musically talented, good with his hands, liked '80s movies, brushed his teeth, AND knew a line from a musical? Was this too good to be true? Yes! Yes, it was. Why didn't I see it?

Instead of questioning my luck, I burst into a song and dance routine straight from the musical *Chicago*, complete with flapper moves and a scratchy, raspy voice. Being named Roxie, I'd had years of practice . There was once a time in my life when I hoped I'd marry a man whose last name was Hart just so people would be more likely to burst into show tunes at the mention of my name. Oh, who was I kidding? I *still* hoped to marry a man named Hart. That would be bad as hell.

Jim looked highly impressed. The bartenders were amused. I got a round of applause when I finished.

"I didn't think you'd know where that line came from," he said.

I shrugged and leaned back against the bar on my elbows like it was no big deal. The look of casual confidence was one I had worked hard to perfect, which meant it wasn't casual at all, and most of the time it wasn't confident either. But most people believed it, which was all that mattered. Fake it 'til ya make it, right?

"I didn't expect *you* to know the song either," I said.

"I was in my high school orchestra. I know *Rent*, too."

Shut the front door! I mean, open it. Open it wide, and let his man in!

"What about *Annie*?" I asked.

"No, we never did *Annie*."

Good thing or I may have unzipped his pants right there in that bar.

Never before had the expression 'Too good to be true' been, well ... true.

ALL GOOD THINGS

"That's too bad," I said with a coy smile, also something I had practiced until it was perfectly believable. "Can I buy you a drink anyway?"

And this was where I took a wrong turn. I didn't know it then, but eventually that road would lead me right over a cliff. His list of charming qualities had gotten so long that I was blinded into oblivion. The next seven months were filled with bright, flashing signs. Do Not Enter. Wrong Way. Outlook Not Good. Beware of Dog. Watch Your Back, Girl.

But I didn't see them. I drove right on past.

Until now. Now I saw them. But now was far too late.

CHAPTER 2

"**H**EY, LITTLE GIRL."

I was sitting on my bed, laptop on my knees, listening to "Here Without You" by 3 Doors Down. It had been on repeat for nearly an hour. Because that kind of music was totally going to cheer me up and definitely did not make me want to stab myself in the neck.

It had been one week since I'd found out the truth, five days since I'd taken the last final exam of my junior year at UNC, four days since I'd arrived back home to Ann Arbor for the summer, and two days since I'd brushed my hair.

The word 'moderation' had never applied to me. When I did something, I went all the way.

When I heard the familiar voice and the nickname he'd been using since childhood, I looked up to see Jake Odom standing in the open doorway to my bedroom. Leaning with his right forearm pressed up against the doorframe, he did the cool and casual look better than I ever could. He looked stylish without trying too hard in a white button-up shirt, khaki cargo shorts, and the cleanest pair of Nike tennis shoes I'd ever seen outside of a shore store. Guys and their shoes...

Jake, with his ever-present smile, and warm and friendly brown eyes, could bring me out of my darkest moods. Suddenly my room was a little brighter, a little warmer, a little lighter. Jake had that way about him. I was pretty certain his smile could change the world. It sure changed mine.

Jake Odom. *Sigh*.

Jake had been my brother's best friend since they were five and I was three, and I could count on one hand the times I'd seen him upset. I didn't know how he did it, but Jake was always happy. He didn't let anything get him down. Whatever kind of shitty luck the world threw his way, he ducked and kept on moving. He wasn't one of those woe-is-me whiners (ahem). He just accepted whatever it was, as it was.

I didn't know if he smiled so much because he was genuinely happy, or if he thought smiling would eventually make him happy. I used to believe his happiness was sincere because I didn't think there was any way someone could be that phony all the time. Even *I* let my guard down and dropped my act every once in awhile. But then I found out about Jim, and now I didn't know what to think. Or what to believe. Or who I could trust, if anyone. Maybe everyone and everything I'd ever believed in was a complete lie.

"What are you doing?" he asked from the doorway.

"I, uh..." I was caught off guard. All I could think about was what a mess I must look right now. I sat up straighter, closed the laptop, and set it on my nightstand. I pulled out my ponytail and rewrapped it, hoping the grease would give me the slick-backed look of a supermodel on the runway. Not likely.

"What are *you* doing?" I asked to flip the subject onto him.

He slowly entered the room. "I'm trying to figure out why you've been home for four days and no one has seen you."

I hadn't seen Jake or any of my other friends since holiday break back in January. Even though he was mostly Adam's friend, he had kind of become my friend by default throughout the years. He was pretty much another member of the family and I could see why he would have noticed my reclusive behavior. I used to be a pretty social person.

Jake plopped down on the foot of my bed. He sprawled out on his side and bent an elbow to prop up his head.

I scooted as far back toward the headboard as I could get and prayed I didn't smell *too* bad.

There was a very tiny bit of history between the two of us. We had kissed twice. The first time I was fourteen, and it was a teenage disaster. The second time I was seventeen and visiting him at his university. It was only one kiss, but it was way too hot to sweep under the rug. I knew it happened. He knew it happened. We were both in a silent agreement that it was best if it didn't happen again. My reason for not pushing the issue was that he was too important a person in my life to risk losing if things didn't end well. And though we'd never actually talked about it, I assumed his reason had something to do with my brother, and probably my father, kicking the shit out of him. But that didn't mean I wasn't aware of his charm or good looks. And it certainly didn't mean I was comfortable being around him in this disgustingly miserable state.

"You were supposed to come to The Bar and fill out an application," he said. He sounded disappointed in me. I hated it. I had always cared way too much what people thought of me, but with Jake, I cared even more.

The Bar was the sports bar where he worked as a bartender and assistant manager. Clearly not an original name for the place, but very popular with the twenty-something crowd. He'd promised me a while ago that he'd get me a job for the summer. It was a great opportunity. The wait staff there made tons of money. I should have been thankful instead of sitting in my room whining like a spoiled brat.

"I've been busy," I explained.

"Doing what?"

"Organizing," I said quickly, probably too quickly because he narrowed his eyes like he was on to me. "I had to unpack and organize my closet and drawers, you know, that kind of stuff."

He looked around the room. His eyes first went to my closet. The folding door was open and the color-coordinated scheme of my tops was visible. There were three shelves of pants – jeans, khakis and lounge pants – all stacked ombre-style from lightest to darkest.

He looked over at my dresser where sixteen bottles of perfume were lined up as neatly as pieces on a chessboard, to my bookcase where the books were alphabetized by author, my desk where my CDs were organized by release date, and my vanity where nail polishes and lipsticks were in rows as even as corn stalks.

And he knew. He was possibly the one person in my life who always saw me for who I really was. I didn't fool him. He didn't buy into my fake-it-until-I-make-it routine. He knew I wasn't as confident as I pretended to be, that I didn't have all my shit together, and that just because I was smiling, didn't mean everything was okay. If I weren't so self-absorbed most of the time, I'd probably see the same things in him.

His smiled faded. He looked concerned. "What's going on?" he asked seriously.

I smiled. It wasn't even totally fake because I'd started to feel better the moment I'd heard his voice from the door. "Nothing. I told you. I've just been getting settled in."

He didn't believe me, but he didn't push either. "You're going to have to leave things as they are because we have plans tonight."

I shook my head and hugged my knees to my chest. "Who's we?"

"We," he repeated. "You, me, Adam and Janelle, Allison and Braham, whoever else they invited. Some people from work. A bunch of people."

ALL GOOD THINGS

Allison had been my BFF since second-grade. Braham was her husband. They were childhood sweethearts who started having children of their own when we were in high school. They had three so far – ages four, three and one. With three kids under five, they didn't get out much. Hearing they were involved in Jake's plans piqued my interest.

"Who is Janelle?" I asked.

"Some chick your brother's been bangin'," he said matter-of-factly.

I scrunched up my nose and lightly kicked his knee. "Gross. I don't need to hear shit like that. Saying it's his girlfriend is just fine."

"It's not his girlfriend," he argued. "It's some chick he's been bangin'. That's all."

"If he's inviting her to social events, introducing her to family members, and banging her, as you so eloquently put it, on a regular basis, she's his girlfriend. Call it what it is." I rolled my eyes. Guys and their irrational fear of labels was one of my pet peeves. "Now where is it these people are all going?"

"Your 'Welcome Home' party. Tonight. At the apartment."

He meant the apartment he shared with my brother. They had moved in together when they finished school last year. When I said they "finished school," what I meant was that Adam got his BS and started med school at U of M, and Jake got bored and withdrew after taking four years of classes and realizing he wasn't even close to getting a degree. He said he'd go back someday to a school closer to home. But then he started tending bar and realized he loved it. He might change his mind about going back to school. It didn't matter to me either way. College degrees weren't for everyone. As long as he was happy, I was happy for him.

"We rented the pool area for the night," he explained. He sounded excited about it. "It's got a tiki bar. I've been waiting all winter to use it. But first you need to come up to The Bar with me to meet the boss. Get ready, Little Girl."

He pushed himself up, patted my knee, and stood.

"I'll be back to pick you up at seven," he said as he headed toward my bedroom door. "Try to look nice. And by nice, I mean slutty."

CHAPTER 3

When Jake left the room I pulled the laptop back onto my knees. I hadn't even had a chance to start the list yet. Where was I? Oh yes, the part where I went from being smarter than the average coed to being totally brainless all because of a good-looking guy with incredible eyes. *Moron!*

No, he didn't need a drink, Jim told me. He was working, and he didn't drink while working. This was only his first week on the job, and he needed to stay focused.

"Not a bad way to spend a few hours a week, though," he said with a cool shrug, as if he couldn't care less whether he had a job or not, as if Prohibition was lucky he worked there and not the other way around.

```
Warning Sign #1: A sense of entitlement.
```

He told me he was a student at UNC-Chapel Hill, which was pretty coincidental since it was forty minutes away. I didn't often run into fellow Tar Heels on Wolfpack territory.

"Omigod!" I practically squealed like a total flake. "Me too! I'm a junior. Social Work. What about you?"

"Oh, um, I'm, uh ..." he stumbled.

Warning Sign #2: Why the hesitation?

"I'm a junior, too," he finally got out. "Music major."

Ah. That made sense.

"What are you doing in Raleigh?" he asked me.

I explained that my roommate's boyfriend went to N.C. State. She came to visit him often. Sometimes I tagged along for some 'strange.'

Just kidding. I came for the piano show.

"So you're staying in Raleigh tonight?" he asked.

I nodded.

"You don't have to," he said, his eyes settling on my cleavage with a smirk.

Warning Sign #3: Not exactly a class act.

"I'm sober," he told me, pointing at his glass of Coke on the bar. "I can drive you back if you want."

It was tempting. Those eyes. They were killing me. Killing. Me. But I knew Sera would never allow me to do something so stupid as to leave with a guy I just met.

"I really don't feel like being featured on an episode of *Dateline*," I explained. "But Seth and his roommates throw killer after-parties if you wanna hang out."

His eyes moved down from my chest to my stomach until his gaze landed on the waistband of my jeans and settled there for a moment. I got the idea he was silently telling me he wanted to get into my pants. And oddly enough, I was okay with that. This guy was made to make women scream, and I was practically raising my hand and saying, "Pick me! Pick me!"

"Yeah," he said with a sly grin and a small nod. "Sounds good, Roxie."

"Great!"

"I have to get back up there for Dave Matthews," he explained. "I'll find you after."

With that, he disappeared back into the crowd.

I rejoined my friends at the side of the stage just in time to see Jim hop onto the piano and begin "Ants Marching" by Dave Matthews Band.

This performance was even better than the first. He didn't have to move his hands quite so fast, which gave him more time to practice his sexy moves and facial expressions. Not that he needed practice. The guy was good.

When the song was over he found me in the crowd, as promised, and sat down at our table. It was too loud for us to have any kind of conversation to get to know each other, but he kept making quiet moves that made me feel like we were old friends. He would nudge my foot with his, press his knee into mine, and give me a smile that made me feel like we were sharing a secret. I liked secrets. A lot.

He followed us over to Seth's apartment when the bar closed. We played drinking games until dawn and fell asleep together on Seth's living room floor. Even then he wasn't a big talker, but his quietness was enigmatic and only intrigued me more.

I had never felt such a strong sexual attraction to a stranger. I was a let's-get-to-know-each-other-before-we-see-each-other-naked kind of girl. I'd read in magazines it was considered acceptable and non-whorish to sleep with a man after three dates. With me, I needed about ten.

This guy, though? He made me want to break the rules. I wanted to see if his abs were as hard as his arms. I wanted to know what else he could do with his hands besides play a fiddle. I wanted to know if he tasted as good as he smelled. And I knew I didn't have the willpower to wait two more dates to find out.

I let him drive me back to Chapel Hill the next morning. I felt I was less likely to be murdered by a serial killer in the daylight. We stopped at a Waffle House for breakfast. It was my idea. I thought I could count that as another date closer to touching his penis.

When he pulled into the parking lot of my off-campus apartment complex, I fought the urge to invite him in. Sera was still at Seth's, the apartment was empty, and *Cosmopolitan* would not approve.

We exchanged cell phones and entered our numbers into each other's contact lists. He promised to call me soon.

I had my hand on the door handle, ready to get out, when my phone began to ring. "Naughty Girl" by Beyonce.

Sera had just learned how to download songs and set them as ringtones. She had chosen that song for me as a joke, because I was the good girl in my group of friends.

I looked up into those killer eyes and felt the little bit of self-control I still had melting into a puddle on the floorboard.

"What do you say, naughty girl," he asked with a cocky grin. "Is it too soon?"

What was the worst that could happen? Assuming he wasn't a serial killer and we took precautions to avoid STDs and pregnancy, what was really the worst that could happen?

Worst-case scenario: It's awful and awkward, and he leaves and never calls me again, and I'm too embarrassed to go back to Prohibition for at least a month.

Best scenario: One amazing morning turns into many amazing nights and eventually a cute family of four singing Christmas carols at a piano.

Most likely scenario: We have a lot of fun and continue to hook up sporadically throughout the school year, especially when I'm drunk.

And in any scenario: Dude. *Look* at him!

"More like not soon enough," I replied breathlessly. Nothing had even happened yet, and I was already gasping. What was this guy doing to me?

"Does that mean I can come in?" he asked.

"Only if you promise to fuck me." Whoa! Did I really just say that? Who the hell *was* I? Last night I was a normal college girl with self-esteem issues and social anxiety. Now I was acting like a porn star.

And I liked it.

His eyes practically bulged out of his head, and for a second he looked like he might be afraid of me. Our positions had reversed. I was now the predator, and he was the prey. I was the one in control, and I wasn't going to be played. If anyone was playing anyone, it was me. That might not be the truth, but thinking it *was* made me feel better about what I was doing.

"Um ... I can do that," he said, his voice a little shaky. I guess this was what they meant when someone referred to making a grown man quiver.

He came inside. I mean, inside the apartment, not inside me. Like Julia Roberts in *Pretty Woman*, I was a safety girl.

Even now, after all that happened, I didn't regret that afternoon. I didn't regret any of the sex we had during our time together because it was the one thing I could always count on. It never disappointed. It was the very reason I missed all of the signs. I was distracted. That was my excuse.

We became boyfriend and girlfriend right away. No game playing with us. Jim was a local. He lived with his parents and commuted to class. He spent a lot of time at my apartment and stayed overnight with me about three or four nights a week. I wanted him there every night, but he said he liked to stay at home a few times a week to catch up on his studies. I was as distracting to him as he was to me.

ALL GOOD THINGS

Warning Sign #4: I never actually saw him study. I never saw any books either. How could I miss that one?

It wasn't long, maybe two weeks, before he had a toothbrush in the bathroom and a drawer in my bedroom. This was serious. The first serious nearly live-in boyfriend I'd had in my adult life. I thought it would last forever. Because I was ... what? Dumb as fuck.

We drove out to Raleigh three nights a week for his shows. It was pretty much known that I was the fiddle player's girlfriend, and I couldn't have been prouder to be seen by his side. My boyfriend was the sexiest guy in that bar. Having someone others wanted did wonders for my self-worth.

We did a lot of normal things on campus. We ate meals together in the cafeterias (he had to pay for each meal himself because he didn't have a meal plan. I didn't think it was too odd since he was a commuter). We went to parties, poetry slams, movie nights, you know, all that fun college stuff.

Warning Sign #5: All the time we spent on campus and nobody we crossed paths with ever said hi, waved, or nodded a hello to him the way they did with me.

When it came to doing anything off-campus, besides going to Raleigh for work, he would have nothing of it. I tried getting him to take me to the movies, art shows, restaurants, even the grocery store, and he made an excuse to get out of it every time. Or he distracted me. Yeah. Like *that*.

```
Warning Sign #6: He didn't want to be
seen with me around town.
```

With us, it was a constant push and pull, fight and make-up. We were passionate. We broke things. We threw things. We knocked things over. Sometimes in good ways, sometimes not. I didn't know any better at the time, and I thought this was normal relationship stuff. I thought it was common for guys to be so jealous and suspicious of you that they thought you were sleeping with every guy in the state.

My only serious boyfriend prior to him had been my high school boyfriend, Riley. He had never acted jealous or possessive, and I had eventually caught him in bed with another girl. Since Riley didn't act jealous, and clearly didn't care about me, in my head I thought possessiveness and jealousy must equal love. When Jim turned into a pouting child every time I spoke a word to another guy, I swooned.

```
Warning Sign #7: It's called projection,
you moron.
```

His jealousy only got seriously out of hand once, when he saw me talking to a male classmate about an assignment after class. He got so angry he kicked a brick wall and broke a toe. But he promised it would never happen again. I believed him.

ALL GOOD THINGS

```
Warning Sign #8: Violent tendencies. If
there was ever a time when I really
needed to open my freaking eyes, it was
then. But I didn't.
```

    Sera and Seth gave me a stern talking-to after that incident. They said they were keeping an eye on Jim since *I* clearly wasn't. I didn't take them too seriously. Sera was generally known as a voice of reason and was cynical of all men. She was the Miranda to my Charlotte. And Seth was like a Boy Scout leader until high school. Wearing ripped jeans was as close to dangerous as he'd ever been. The two of them had been together so long and had such a great amount of trust between them; she could give a guy a lap dance right in front of him and he would think she was just being friendly. So what did they know, right?

```
Warning Sign #9: My friends didn't like
him.
```

    I closed the laptop feeling accomplished and satisfied with my list so far. I knew how everything was going to happen and how it all would end. I knew typing the list into Excel when I already had it in my notebook would seem redundant to anyone else. For me, it was therapy. Seeing it on the screen really drilled it into my head, and I felt that was what I needed. I thought the more I went over it all, the more I saw my mistakes in front of me, the less likely I was to repeat them. And wasn't the silver lining of making mistakes the fact that you learned not to repeat them? I hoped by obsessing so much over this broken heart of mine and how it came to be, I would learn an invaluable lesson that would prevent me from ever feeling this kind of pain and regret again. Roll your eyes at me if you want, but that hope was all I had.

CHAPTER 4

I MANAGED TO pull myself off my bed and into the shower. All I wanted was to put on a pair of sweatpants, get under the covers, and watch *Scrubs* until I cried myself to sleep, which was what I had done every night since *that* night. But I figured if I tried to get out of Jake's party, either he or Allison would come over and drag me there by my dirty-ass ponytail. And besides the party, Jake had already told his boss I was coming in to meet him and I couldn't let him down and embarrass him by not showing up. I needed to be grateful for the good people I had in my life and stop obsessing over the one bad one who was no longer a part of it.

I would go to the bar to see about a job. I would go to the pool party at my brother's apartment. I would dress slutty per Jake's instructions. But that didn't mean I had to like it.

Jake pulled into our driveway in his beat-up Ford pickup truck a few hours later. The windows were rolled down and I could hear the "Numb/Encore" mash-up by Linkin Park and Jay-Z coming from the speakers. It was a nice change from the country music everyone listened to in the South.

He let out a construction worker kind of whistle as I walked down the driveway in my "slutty" outfit – a super-short faded denim miniskirt that barely covered my butt cheeks, a halter top that gave me some bomb-diggity cleavage, and wedge sandals with straps that twisted up my calves. I'd bought the outfit for a Pimps & Hoes party at school, but never thought I'd wear it again. I couldn't imagine going to apply for a job dressed this way and I couldn't help but wonder what kind of person I was trying to work for.

"So is this guy some creepy older dude who preys on naïve girls?" I asked once I'd gotten into the truck and he'd pulled out of the driveway. "Because I don't know how comfortable I would be working for someone like that."

He snickered. Yes, he actually snickered. "He's not old or creepy, and you are not naïve. Even if you pretend to be."

Hmm ... don't be so sure of that, Jake.

I met Zeke, the owner of The Bar, a few minutes later. He was younger than I'd imagined. He was in his thirties and attractive, in a pretty boy kind of way. I knew by looking at him that he was the kind of guy who got pedicures. I didn't really go for that type. I preferred guys who rolled out of bed and went straight out the door over the guys who had more beauty products than I did. But he wasn't an older perv, which was what I'd expected when Jake told me he liked a scantily-clad staff. He was just a businessman who knew what worked.

All of the chairs in the bar had been placed on the tables, probably so someone could mop the floor. Zeke was in the process of placing them back on the floor when we walked in. He didn't give me a creepy feeling at all and barely gave me a onceover before going back to the chairs.

"Jake said you have experience," he said.

"Yes," I replied. "I waited tables all through high school and the last two summers."

"Go ahead and grab her a uniform," he told Jake while turning a chair onto its legs. "And show her where the schedule is posted."

Does that mean I have the job?

Jake led me through the kitchen and into a messy office. He picked up a cardboard box off the floor and set it onto the desk.

"Here are the shorts," he said. "Find a couple in your size."

They were short, black polyester shorts with flap pockets on the back. I grabbed two size tens and made a note to hit the thigh machines at the gym ASAP.

Jake set another box on the desk, this one filled with vibrant colors.

"Here are the shirts," he said. "You can pick three. Any color you want. Zeke likes 'em to be tight."

The shirts were wife-beater style tank tops with The Bar's black logo printed on the front.

I picked up a sunshine-yellow one and held it up. It was a medium and looked like it would fit an eleven-year-old ... maybe.

"Are you kidding me?" I asked Jake.

He shrugged.

I picked hot pink, bright orange, and turquoise, all in size large. "I should probably try these on first. Is there a bathroom?"

"No. We don't have a bathroom here," he said, sounding dead serious as we walked out of the office.

He led me down a hallway filled with cases of empty beer bottles and an ice machine. At the end of the hallway was a simple bathroom with a toilet, a pedestal sink, and a dusty mirror.

"This is the employee bathroom," Jake told me. "Zeke prefers us to use this one when possible, but I'll take you up front to change since there's more room up there."

I followed him back out into the dining room where he showed me the public bathrooms. The chairs were all on the floor now, and I saw Zeke behind the bar. It looked like he was weighing liquor bottles.

"Make sure you come out and model for me when you're done," Jake said before I went into the bathroom.

This bathroom was anything but plain. It had four stalls with floor to ceiling walls, basin sinks, and a tiled countertop filled with a variety of beauty products – good stuff, too. I should have expected such from a guy like Zeke.

ALL GOOD THINGS

I came out a few minutes later in my hot pink tank top and shorts. Jake stood in front of me with his arms crossed and looked me up and down. I did a quick turn for him.

"Can you turn around again?" he asked.

I did another turn, and he still didn't look satisfied.

"Again," he said.

Confused, I made another turn, slowly this time. The staring and scrutinizing was making me uncomfortable and self-conscious.

"You can stop now," he said, when my back was toward him.

I turned around and found him slowly nodding his head in approval. I gave him an exasperated look. "Very funny."

He walked toward me in two slow, determined strides. He stopped when his chest was about an inch from mine. I took a deep breath. I loved the smell of Jake. It was warm and cozy, like laundry detergent and dryer sheets. He'd always smelled like fresh blankets out of the dryer. Every time he was close to me I wanted to wrap myself up in him and take a nap. He smelled like home.

I nervously looked up into his eyes and saw a mischievous look. He slid one hand around my waist without breaking eye contact. I wanted to back up or look away, but I refused to be the one to show weakness. I forced myself, and my eyes, to stay put and call his bluff.

His touch gave me goose bumps in the best way, but also made me anxious. What was he doing? Was he going to kiss me? No. This was not part of the plan. I couldn't deal with this right now. You better not kiss me, Jake Odom!

I felt his hand on the small of my back just above the waistband of my shorts. My heart pounded so fast I could hear it throbbing in my ears. I hoped he couldn't hear it. How embarrassing would that be?

He stuck a finger into the back of my shorts, and I flinched.

I stood there with my mouth hanging open as he laughed loudly.

"What?" he asked, innocently. "Your tag was out."

I felt a tad disappointed that he wasn't trying to kiss me, but I shook it off quickly. I didn't want him to kiss me anyway. So there. "You don't think the shirt is too tight?" I asked self-consciously, wondering if I could make it a whole shift without breathing.

Sera once tried to give me sucking-it-in lessons. She's so good at it that she can go to a party, eat, drink, talk, and even laugh, all without unclenching her abs. The experiment had been a total failure on me though. I could make it about three breaths before I lost it. Eating and laughing, definitely out of the question.

Jake shook his head and gave me the kind of sneaky grin he was famous for. "I think it's perfect."

"I second that," Zeke called out from behind the bar.

I changed back into my streetwalker clothes, and Jake led me back into the kitchen to show me where the schedule was posted on the wall.

He pointed to my name at the bottom of the servers list. "You start Monday. I'll be here, too."

ALL GOOD THINGS

That was a relief. I was always so nervous on my first day at a new job. I'd been waiting tables since high school, but this would be my first time working in a sports bar. I wasn't sure I'd know how to handle the belligerent drunks. Having Jake there would make things easier. It always did. Jake was my safety net.

When we got to Jake and Adam's apartment there wasn't anyone there. Jake said everyone was probably at the pool.

"You can change while I load up the cooler," he suggested. "You did bring your bathing suit, right?"

I nodded my head and tilted it toward the tie-dye tote bag hanging from my shoulder. "You didn't think I was gonna walk around looking like a ho all night, did you?"

He shrugged and opened the fridge. "I was kind of hoping so," he said with a smirk. "But as long as you replace it with a bikini, I'm cool."

"That's disgusting, Jake," I told him, even though I was flattered by his flirting. "You're practically my brother."

He closed the refrigerator door and looked at me intensely. "But I'm *not* your brother."

As I've already mentioned, Jake was always smiling. He was always the one telling the jokes, pulling the pranks, goofing around and making everyone around him laugh. But this was the most serious I'd ever seen him look. It was also the sexiest I'd ever seen him look.

Something came over me. There was a flicker of desire, maybe even a touch of something deeper. It only lasted a moment, but it was long enough to give me brief glimpses of what could be if Jake pulled me into his room, ripped off my slutty clothes, and pounded into me with the fervor of eight years worth of pent-up desire. I nearly gasped out loud just thinking of it.

Thankfully, I didn't. I maintained my poker face. I'd done this a lot in the past, and I was accustomed to these kinds of 'moments.' The sexual tension between Jake and me was like the Whac-a-Mole game at arcades. It kept popping up at random times, and I had to knock it back in the hole with my imaginary mallet.

Whack!

Eventually Jake smiled, and the moment was broken.

"You can change in my room if you want," he said, the fiery look in his eyes gone and replaced with the friendly gleam I was used to. It was like nothing out of the ordinary had happened at all. We moved on, like always.

"I'll just use the bathroom."

ONCE I'D CHANGED into my bikini, cover-up, and flip-flops, Jake told me to walk over to the pool without him because he had to mix up some drinks. "Adam and Janelle are down there and probably Allison, too. She said she might bring the kids by to swim."

I brightened up. I needed my friend. "Can I bring anything down with me?" I asked.

"Nope. I've got it."

The grounds of their apartment complex were bright and green and smelled like freshly-cut grass. They must have a good maintenance team. As I walked toward the pool area I could smell burning charcoal. Nothing said summer like the smell of charcoal. I would probably never admit it to him, but I was grateful to Jake for forcing me out of my room. It was hard to wallow when the grass was green, the sky was blue, and I could feel the warmth of the sun on my shoulders. I even considered trying to have a good time at the party.

I walked through the gate of the pool area and found Braham and Adam hovering around the grill. It was loaded up with meats, potatoes, and corn cobs wrapped in aluminum foil. The smell of the BBQ sauce made me realize how hungry I was. I couldn't even remember the last time I'd eaten anything besides candy. I wasn't trying to starve myself or anything, I'd just forgotten to eat. I was too busy listening to depressing music and reminding myself that I was stupid.

Allison and all three kids were playing in the shallow end of the pool in their arm floaties and didn't notice me come in right away. There was a girl wearing a bikini and a pair of mirrored aviator sunglasses lying in one of the pool chairs. She looked about my age. I assumed she was Janelle since I'd never seen her before.

Adam and Braham both greeted me with hugs and high-fives. Adam and I used to fight all the time when we both still lived at home. He didn't want me hanging out with his friends, and I didn't want him hanging out with mine. But ever since he'd left for college when I was a junior in high school, he'd become more a friend than a nuisance. I actually looked forward to being around him on my school breaks, and when I was away at school I missed him.

He called Janelle over to the grill to introduce us.

"Roxie, Janelle. Janelle, my little sister, Roxie." No label. At least he didn't say, "This is the chick I've been bangin'."

Allison climbed out of the pool, looking totally put together for someone who was wrangling three children while soaking wet. Her blonde bun was in a twisty knot, and her mascara must have been waterproof because it was still in place. She was that girl people looked at and thought, *how does she do it?*

She gave me a wet hug with only one arm since she was holding the baby in the other. I didn't mind the wet spot she left on my cover-up, but when she handed me the wet baby in the soggy swim diaper, one-year-old Drew, I got a little nervous. I wasn't one of those people who cooed over babies. To me, they were just little people who smelled like poop. Always. It seemed like no matter how many times you changed their diapers and wiped their butts, they always smelled like poop. I held the little guy at arm's length while Allison gathered the girls, Kayla and Kenzie, from the pool.

"Hi, Roxie," four-year-old Kayla said as she stood at the top of the pool steps, her watermelon one-piece suit dripping onto the cement. "Happy Birfday."

I shuddered. The older kids got, the more they freaked me out. I was never sure what to say to them. "Uh, thanks," I said uncertainly, "but it's not my birthday."

"But it was," she insisted, "and you weren't here."

ALL GOOD THINGS

My birthday, the big twenty-one, was the April ninth, about a month ago. "That's right," I agreed.

"And that's why Mummy baked-ed you a cake," she said.

"You made a cake?" I asked Allison, surprised.

"Twenty-one is a big deal. Even if I'm a few weeks late, you've gotta have cake."

"It's chocolate," Kayla said.

"Chalk-wet," Kenzie, the two-year-old repeated.

We were the same age, but Allison seemed so much older. She was an adult. She did grown-up things, like bake cakes for people's birthdays. She had a mortgage and a minivan and she wore blazers when she went out to dinner. I didn't even own a blazer. I'd never even tried one on in a dressing room before.

We'd taken off on the same path back in second grade, but now we were on opposite ends of the globe. I knew she had gotten a head start on adult life, and I would never say I envied her life and wished I'd had three kids by my age, but being around her I couldn't help but feel like a child myself sometimes.

"That was nice of you," I said, feeling guilty. I should have baked her a cake on her birthday. It was back in January. I was so wrapped up in my Jim addiction that I didn't even send a card. Did I call her at least? I was ashamed that I couldn't remember. Allison wouldn't hold it against me, not for very long anyway. We wouldn't have been friends as long as we'd been if we were the types who held grudges. But I still felt like shit, as I should have. I had been a crappy friend to her when I'd been with Jim. I'd probably been a crappy person all around.

Allison waved a hand like it was no big deal. "The kids are leaving after we eat," she said quietly as she worked on deflating Kenzie's arm floatie. "I invited some of our friends and Jake and Adam invited theirs, too. We've really been looking forward to getting you back."

I felt guilty *again* because I wasn't sure if I was happy to *be* back. After three years, North Carolina was starting to feel like home. Besides being heart-broken, I was also a little bit homesick. I loved seeing my family and friends, but there was a piece of me that felt out of place here. Yep, it was official. I was an ungrateful bitch. I did not deserve any of these people.

"When Jake said it was a 'Welcome Home' party," I confessed to Allison, "I thought he was just using that as an excuse to throw a party. I didn't really think it had anything to do with me."

"Don't be silly. They can have parties anytime they want. And believe me, they do. This is all about you tonight."

Jake walked through the gate then, right on cue. I caught his eye and he smiled at me as he wheeled a big blue cooler over to the tiki bar to get everything set up.

"You should go get a drink," she told me and nodded toward the bar. "He's got all kinds of concoctions."

I walked over to the bar to see what all Jake had going on.

"What would you like to start off with?" he asked me. "We've got butterscotch pudding shots, berry sangria, and mango martinis. Or would you prefer beer? We do have some Miller Lite if you want beer instead."

"You made all of my favorite things," I said quietly, more to myself than to him.

"Well, yeah. It's *your* party."

I couldn't think of anything witty to say, so I awkwardly muttered a thank you.

"You're welcome. So what's it gonna be?"

"I guess I'll have a beer."

"Oh," he paused, clearly thrown off guard. "Okay." He reached into the ice bin to grab one.

"Jake!" I said loudly. I reached for his arm and pulled it out of the ice bin. My hand may or may not have stopped on his for a beat too long. "Did you really think I was going to drink beer after you made all my favorite drinks?"

"No," he said. "But I was willing to play your game."

"I'll have two pudding shots and sangria to start. I'll save the martinis until after dinner."

"Sounds like a good plan," he said. He slid two plastic soufflé cups with lids and a small plastic spoon across the tiny bamboo bar and started filling a plastic cup with fruit for the sangria. "Just make sure you do the shots over here so the kids don't see. They won't understand why you can have pudding and they can't. It'll cause a domino effect of tantrums."

I raised my eyebrow. Since when did Jake know anything about kids? "Good point," I told him.

He handed me the cup of sangria and held up his beer to toast. "Welcome home, Roxie Humsucker."

I smiled at his reference to the eighties movie. I'd had a poster from the movie, *Welcome Home, Roxy Carmichael*, on my bedroom wall back when I was a tween. I'd taken it down when I was about fifteen and replaced it with a *Say Anything* poster of John Cusack's iconic boombox moment. That one was still on my wall, along with a matted photo of Audrey Hepburn in *Breakfast at Tiffany's*, and a poster of the cast of *Dawson's Creek*. Capeside for life, yo. Joey & Pacey 4Ever.

"Thank you, Jake Odom."

We clinked our glasses and each took a sip of our drinks.

"Dinner's ready!" Adam called over. "Come and get it."

When Allison and Braham were done making plates for the kids, the rest of us joined them around the patio tables.

Both Adam and Braham were masters of the grill so it was no surprise that all the food was tasty. Jake's drinks in my belly were soothing me with a calming, comforting burn. I looked around the table as I ate, at this group of people who loved me even when I didn't deserve it. As they talked and laughed together, I felt blessed. For a moment I even thought I was going to be okay.

CHAPTER 5

NEWSFLASH: I WAS a bad drunk. Everyone has that one friend that needs a babysitter when drinking. That's me. I was that friend. Embarrassing, but true.

I didn't drink often, but when I did, I didn't know when to stop. It wasn't because I was a total lush – but I got so uncomfortable around crowds and used the alcohol to loosen up. Sometimes (okay, fine, *most* times) I got a little *too* loosened up. On bad nights I ended up fondled by strangers, passed out on a bathroom floor, or carried out of a bar by bouncers. On better nights you'd find me telling a whole group of complete strangers my theory that oral sex was the answer to World Peace. And on no morning-after had I ever woken up and thought to myself, *Wow, what a respectable young woman I was last night.* Nope. Never.

I'd embarrassed myself on too many occasions to count, and I was hoping not to add another at my own 'Welcome Home' party.

"Can you do me a favor?" I asked Jake after my second martini. It was approaching nine, not even dark yet and I was already buzzing. Allison's parents had taken the kids for the night, and the guests had started arriving shortly after dinner. There were around twenty so far. These were people I'd gone to school with and known practically my whole life. I was more comfortable than I would have been at a bar or party filled with strangers, but not so comfortable that I was okay with showing my ass. (FYI: In the South, the term "showing your ass" meant making an ass out of yourself. If I was to use the term here, my friends would think I planned on pulling my pants down and showing my butt to the party guests.)

"What's up?" he asked from behind the bar. He'd been there ever since dinner, making everyone's drinks.

"Can you please start making my drinks a little weaker? Or a lot weaker? It's still early, and I'd like to have some of my dignity left in the morning."

"That's not going to be very fun for the rest of us," he said with a straight face. "These people didn't come here tonight to welcome back their prim and proper weak-drink-drinking friend. They came for the show they've learned to expect."

It wasn't very nice, but it was funny. I was buzzed enough to laugh at my own expense. "I don't want to pull out all my tricks on the first night," I replied. "I need to save some for the next party."

"No shit, you've got tricks now? I should have charged a cover."

I laughed and shook my head at him. "Can you please just have my back tonight?"

He slid another martini over to me. I took a sip of the noticeably weaker drink and smiled. "Thank you."

"No problem. I've got my money on you keeping your bikini top on until at least midnight. If we work on it together, we can split the pot."

I sipped my martini and hoped he was kidding.

I WOKE UP the next afternoon with no hangover and, for the first time ever, no regrets. I'd kept my clothes on *all* night and did not injure myself, let anyone touch my boobs, or mention the word *fellatio*. Because Jake had an idea of how much I could drink without losing my shit, I was able to achieve a comfortable level of buzz and maintain it throughout the night. Having a bartender as a friend had its perks.

I ran downstairs, grabbed a cup of coffee and a granola bar, and went back up to my room. I'd had a good time last night and had been able to push Jim out of my mind for a few hours, but it was time to get back to business. I needed to work on my spreadsheet.

IT WAS OCTOBER, and we'd been dating a month. We were shopping for Halloween costumes, which was more important to me than shopping for swimsuits or formal gowns. Halloween was kind of a big deal for me. It was the one day of the year when I could show my personality and creativity and feel just as good, if not better, than everyone else.

When looking back on their lives, some people remembered birthdays or Christmases or First Days of School. I remembered Halloweens.

As a rule, I didn't buy costumes at costume stores. I made my own and aimed to be the most original. I'd always been very successful with costumes. I was the one to beat in the costume contests.

Except for one time. There was once an, um, *episode* regarding my Halloween costume.

It was third grade. I'd put a white collared shirt under a black dress Mom and I found at the Salvation Army. I'd added white tights and a pair of clunky black shoes that every girl had back then. My mom helped me put my long brown hair in twin braids. I thought my costume was clever and held my head high that morning as I walked the three blocks to school with Adam, Jake, and Allison.

Adam and Jake had dressed in backward baseball jerseys and jeans like the rap duo Kris Kross. Allison had dressed as Ariel from *The Little Mermaid*. It was going to be the best Halloween ever (which I said every year, by the way).

When we arrived at school my day was ruined. Another classmate had also come to school dressed as Wednesday Addams (insert *Home Alone*-style scream here). I would have been okay with it if I'd been the better Wednesday, but I wasn't. She looked better than me.

Paula's hair was a darker brown than mine, she had applied powder on her face to make it look white, and her mom had done her eye makeup to make her eyes pop. She looked just like Christina Ricci in the movie. She was the star. I was the bad imitation. The stunt double. The wannabe. The joke.

I ran from the classroom into the hallway. Allison ran after me. Well, actually she kind of piddle-paddled after me since her legs were trapped in her mermaid's tail all the way down to her calves. The sight of her hopping along the hallway with her red wig bouncing on her head would have made me laugh if I wasn't crying.

"What's going on?" she asked as she followed me toward the bathroom.

"Did you see her?"

"Who?"

"Paula!"

"Oh." She paused. "Yeah. I saw her. Isn't it cute that you two are dressed alike?"

"CUTE?"

Her smile was replaced with a look of uncertainty. "Yeah. Cute. When she said she was dressing up as Wednesday Addams, I thought you two would look cute. It's just like when you and I wear our matching Hypercolor t-shirts. Right?"

I turned around abruptly and spoke through clenched teeth. "Wait a minute. You *knew* about this?"

She took a hop back from me and looked scared. "Yeah."

"Do not ever speak to me again," I spat out before I threw myself into one of the stalls and slammed the door.

I was so angry. I was angry with Allison for not telling me someone else had picked the same costume. Either she wanted me to be humiliated, or she just didn't *get* why I would be humiliated, and I was mad either way. I was also mad at my mom for not letting me wear eyeliner. I was mad at myself for not thinking of the face powder and simply for not being a good enough Wednesday Addams.

I was not proud of the way I acted that day. But kids did stupid things, and I was no exception.

Once I stopped crying I stayed in the stall for about ten minutes trying to formulate a plan. If I left school I'd miss the parade and the candy, and I'd have to hear about it from everyone else later. I would be left with a gaping hole in my life's memories where my third grade Halloween parade should have been. I'd also probably get detention for skipping school.

But I was too embarrassed about my meltdown to leave the bathroom. I couldn't just return to class and act like everything was normal. I wasn't sure what Allison had gone back to the class and said. What if she told them I was in the bathroom having a diva moment? How could I go back into that classroom and face the eye-rolls? I began to have a complete internal breakdown and started to wonder if it was possible for me to switch schools.

"Roxie? Are you in here? It's me, Paula."

I lifted my feet off the floor so she wouldn't see them under the stall door. What did she want?

"Don't make me get down on my knees in this disgusting bathroom and get my tights dirty," she said.

I didn't move.

"Listen, Allison told me you were embarrassed because we both dressed as the same person. But I know a way we can change our costumes."

"How?" I asked.

"HA! I knew you were in here. Have you ever seen *The Shining*?"

"No."

"I didn't think so. It's a scary movie. Like *really* super scary with, like, blood and axes and stuff. My brother let me watch it when my parents went out to dinner one night, and I didn't sleep for two days."

"Okay."

"Anyway, there are these really creepy twins in the movie. They have brown hair and wear dresses, just like us. If we tell people we're the twins from *The Shining*, and that we have seen an R-rated movie, they will think we are, like, so totally cool. Wednesday Addams is cool and all, but she has nothing on *The Shining* twins."

"Okay." It was either that, or move. And I had a feeling my parents weren't going to go for that.

I came out of the stall, and the two of us took out our braids. We stood together in front of the giant mirror; matching brown waves, white collars, black dresses. Indeed, we looked creepy.

"Whenever someone asks who we are supposed to be we need to hold hands and say, 'Come play with us, Danny.' Can you do that?"

I nodded, and she took my hand and pulled me from the bathroom.

She had been right. Our classmates thought our costumes were brilliant. Paula and I were like, *so totally cool* that day.

Even though it had worked out in the end, I still considered that Halloween a failure, and choosing a costume had filled me with anxiety every year since. I had since typed up a lot of Halloween costume spreadsheets in my lifetime.

For a child, Halloween costumes were about being fun and playful. In college, Halloween costumes were about being sexy. It seemed like every costume at the costume store consisted of a cute, flouncy skirt and a pair of thigh-high socks. Because all nurses wore skirts and thigh-highs. So did ladybugs, bumblebees and police officers. And don't forget about sweet and innocent Strawberry Shortcake and Spongebobbie Squareskirt. (Insert eye-roll).

I thought the whole scene was absurd. For my freshman and sophomore years at UNC, I rebelled. I did what I'd always done. I created my own costume with the goal of being original. But this year was different. I had a boyfriend now. I didn't care so much about being creative. I just wanted him to think I was sexy. I wanted him to be proud to be seen with me. I didn't want to be the only one at the Halloween parties who didn't look like she was wearing lingerie.

We had stopped at a costume store in Raleigh before his shift at Prohibition started. I had figured out by now that he wasn't interested in hanging out with me in

ALL GOOD THINGS

Chapel Hill. Instead of asking questions as to why that was, I just adapted. I planned any public excursions for Wednesdays, Fridays, and Saturdays in Raleigh. *Moron!*

I wasn't happy with myself for being in a costume store, no matter what city it was in. I felt like I was betraying myself, and everything I stood for, by shopping at a costume store, but I found a costume I liked enough. It was an orange, white, and yellow dress that looked like a piece of candy corn. It wasn't too skanky or too overdone. But it was also $60.

"I don't know," I said, more to myself than anyone else, as I twirled in the mirror outside the dressing room for about the fifteenth time. "It's a lot to spend on something I'm only going to wear one time."

"Yeah," Jim said. I could see him in the reflection in the mirror. He was doing something on his phone and looked bored.

"But we're going to at least three Halloween parties on campus and then there's the one at Prohibition," I said, trying to factor the cost of the costume per party. "And what about your friends?" I asked. "Are any of your friends having Halloween parties?"

"Umm..." I was getting used to his hesitation habits by this point. "No, none of my friends are having any parties."

```
Warning Sign #10: I haven't met any of
his friends.
```

I turned around from the mirror to look at him face-to-face.

"Are you sure? You know how guys can be so last minute sometimes."

"I'm sure."

"You could invite them to some of the other parties we're going to, you know. I would like to meet them."

"Oh, well, um, you know..." He was looking at his phone, probably to avoid eye contact. "They're not really into playing dress-up."

"Hmm." I went back into the dressing room and took off the costume.

He must be ashamed of me. I wasn't good enough to meet his friends. Fine. But I wasn't going to betray myself and spend as much as my phone bill on a costume just to look good for him if I wasn't good enough for him without it.

He might not have been proud to be with me, but I was proud to *be* me when I walked out of that store. I could have easily done the desperation thing and bought the sexiest costume I could find. I could have begged to meet his friends. I could have pouted and whined and asked if I wasn't pretty enough. But I thought I acted with class. I was still a moron, but at least I was a classy one.

I ended up dressing up as Dora the Explorer. I already owned a pink t-shirt, and I found some orange shorts and the purple backpack online. I added some knee-high socks to make the costume more acceptable by college party standards. I also won the Cutest Costume prize at one of the parties. Take that, Jim.

I spent the next several weeks casually asking him to invite his friends to different events and parties, and he always had an excuse. One night he had a little too much to drink and confessed to me that he didn't have any friends. The only friends he'd had in high school were in the orchestra, and they had all gone on to colleges out of state and drifted apart. He even cried a little, and I held him and smoothed back his hair.

"It's okay, baby," I said. "I can share mine."

THANKSGIVING WAS ANOTHER disaster.

I never intended to go home for Thanksgiving weekend. It was too expensive of a trip and too short to make it worth it. I planned on staying at school like I had the past two years. Thanksgivings at UNC definitely weren't as cool as the Thanksgivings they had on shows like *Felicity* and *Friends*. You know the type: a big group of friends all bring a dish and gather around a big table filled with smiles and laughter and that whole sense of creating a family of your own. It was all right at UNC, but it wasn't like *that*.

Having a boyfriend this year, a very serious boyfriend, who had a drawer in my bedroom filled with his boxer shorts, meant this year would be better. He was a local. Surely he would invite me to dinner. Thanksgiving was the perfect time for him to introduce me to his family. I was sure he would be honored. Why wouldn't he be? I was quite a catch. I was smart, sophisticated, sweet, and even semi-pretty. My hair was always soft, I always smelled good, I never got pimples, and I had a great rack, not to mention a great future ahead of me with an education from one of the best schools in the country. I might not have frat guys putting posters of me on their ceilings, and I'd never been asked to be in a Hottest Girls on Campus calendar, but what parent wouldn't swoon over me? Right?

I went a little bit Elle Woods from *Legally Blonde* about it. I spent hours shopping for the perfect outfits. I bought two – one for summer weather and one for fall weather – because you never knew what you were going to get in North Carolina in November. They only had two seasons: spring and hell.

I wasn't old enough to buy wine, but I found a kitschy centerpiece at a boutique shop to give his mother as a hostess gift. He hadn't technically asked me to come yet, but why wouldn't he? If I was good enough to have sex with several times a day for the last two months, surely I was good enough to meet the parents.

I started to get a little nervous on Monday when I realized he hadn't mentioned it. By Tuesday I was on pins and needles.

"Baby?" I asked on Tuesday night when we were snuggled up in bed. "I forgot to ask you what time dinner is on Thursday."

"Huh?"

"You said you were having Thanksgiving dinner at your parents', right? What time should I be ready? I need to know how much time I have to prep. I want to make sure I look my best, ya know?"

"Ummm ..." That was his word of choice. "I thought you said you were going to have turkey in the cafeteria."

ALL GOOD THINGS

"Well, yeah, that's what I usually do, but it seems silly for me to have to suffer, alone, with processed turkey and powdered mashed potatoes, while you're enjoying a home-cooked meal with your family."

"Oh. Um ... I thought I told you. My brother is coming in from Arizona and bringing his girlfriend. They've been dating two years, and this will be the first time we meet her ... and my brother would be so upset if you overshadowed her. And my mom, I don't think she could handle meeting two girlfriends at once."

```
Warning Sign #11: Why can't I meet his
parents?
```

"Oh," I said sadly, trying to remember if I'd saved the receipts for my new outfits.

"Hey," he said quietly, "when it's your turn to meet my parents, I don't want any distractions. And I don't want anyone else in the way. I want it to be all about you, okay?" He kissed my forehead, and I smiled and didn't ask about meeting the family again.

"You're not supposed to be doing homework in the summer."

I jumped at the sound of his voice, slammed the laptop closed, and looked up to see Jake standing in my bedroom doorway again. I needed to start closing my door.

"It's not homework. It's just ..." I changed the subject. "What are you doing here?"

"Laundry. I come over every Sunday to do my laundry while your parents are out brunching with friends."

Brunching with friends? How sad that my parents had a more active social life than I did. But they were happy and still in love after being together nearly thirty years. Happy people had brunch. Unhappy, bitter people like me, we had brooding.

"The washing machine isn't in my bedroom," I said like a smartass. I gave him a slight smile in hopes that I came off only a teeny, tiny bit bitchy and not full-on Cruella de Vil.

"No, it's not," he said. He put his hands in the pockets of his cargo shorts and leaned against the doorframe. "*You* shouldn't be either. It's a perfect eighty degree day outside."

I shrugged and nudged the computer to the foot of the bed with my toe. "It's too early for all that brightness."

"Hangover?"

"No," I said quickly. Too quickly. A hangover would have been a good excuse for wasting another day away in my room. I should've taken the out when I had it.

"My clothes won't be dry for another hour. I'm going to get some breakfast," he said.

I nodded. "Okay then."

He lowered his head at me like he was waiting for me to say more. "Are you gonna make me go by myself?"

Grrr. Could a girl just have some time and space to grieve properly? How was I ever going to get over this if I kept putting it aside to do other things? I needed a pause button. I needed to get all of this in my spreadsheet. I needed to find out why I was so stupid before I went on living life and eating breakfast like everything was normal!

I wanted to tell him to leave me alone and do what he would normally do on a Sunday during the school year when I was in Chapel Hill. But I made the mistake of looking at him. His soft eyes looked hopeful, and his smile was kind. And that was the problem with Jake. I couldn't look at him and say no. He was like a puppy saying, "My owners aren't very nice to me. I only eat frozen meals, and I never get hugs. Please throw me a bone and restore my faith in humans."

It was just an hour. I could do an hour. And then it was back to the ex file.

I stood up and yawned. "Fine. But I'm wearing my pajamas."

"Great. We'll stop at Wal-Mart afterward."

I MET HIM at his truck after I brushed my teeth, washed my face, and threw my hair up in a messy topknot.

The bright sunshine was uplifting, and when Jake smiled at me I even felt beautiful for a second. I was rockin' sloppy hair, no makeup, and cropped sweatpants, and he could still make me feel good about myself, just by the way he looked at me.

That was great and all, and I loved that about him, I really did. But his goodness only made my badness more noticeable. When he looked at me the way he looked at me then, I felt ashamed. Jake loved me. I'd always been his favorite girl. But I knew I didn't deserve it, and seeing that look was a reminder that I wasn't good enough. Just a few minutes ago I'd compared him to a puppy. I was an awful person. Jake had never been anything but good to me. He wasn't a puppy. If anyone was the puppy around here, it was me. I was pathetic.

"Jake?" I asked as he backed out of the driveway.

"Yeah?"

"I'm glad you're my friend."

He looked shocked. I guess he wasn't used to me randomly blurting out nice things. He looked like he was waiting for the punch line.

"Um ..." He paused, giving me time to take it back, or find a way to ruin the moment with sarcasm or bitchiness.

I didn't.

"Thanks? I guess?"

He drove to a popular local diner that served breakfast all day for less than five bucks. We used to hang out there after parties when we were in high school. The place hadn't changed any with the exception of an espresso machine and a new café menu.

We sat across from each other in an old-school laminate booth and an old-school waitress with crimped blonde hair came over to take our order. She'd been working there for as long as I could remember, and her eighties style was another thing about the place that never changed. I appreciated it.

Jake ordered coffee.

"I'll have a caramel latte," I said to the server, pronouncing it CARE-uh-mel. Growing up in the Midwest, I'd always pronounced it "CAR-mull." After living in the South for a few years, I'd adopted their pronunciation into my own vocabulary. I thought it sounded classy and elegant, even sexy under the right circumstances.

"Care-uh-mel?" Jake repeated when the waitress walked away. He raised an eyebrow, mocking me.

"That's how they say it in the South," I explained. "Carmull is harsh. Care-uh-mel is soft and romantic. When I hear a guy say it, I want to lick care-uh-mel off his chest."

"Care-uh-mel!" he said quickly and unbuttoned the top button of his shirt.

"Nice try," I replied with a smile.

BEING AT THE diner reminded me of the last time the two of us had sat in a booth together. I was a senior in high school and had caught some skank in my boyfriend's bed. Rather than stay in Ann Arbor and fend off my gossipy classmates' phone calls all day, I'd run off to Jake and Adam's college to get away from the whole mess.

It had been very cold that day and I'd left the house in such a hurry that I'd forgotten my winter coat. When I'd gotten out of my car, he'd unzipped his hoodie and let me get inside it with him. He'd zipped it up behind me so the two of us were wrapped up in a soft, cotton cocoon. As he gently moved his hands up and down my back, I'd felt the tension that had been building in me all day start to diminish. It was a feeling similar to the one I felt after sinking into a hot bath. My muscles started to unravel themselves. My heartbeat and breathing slowed down. I think I might have even released a quiet sigh without meaning to. It was as if every part of my body said a collective, "Ahhhh."

Jake was my tranquilizer. And my anti-depressant. I ended up relaxing so much inside his hoodie that, before I knew it, I was snuggled up into him like he was my boyfriend. For a few minutes, it felt right. It felt like everything was as it should be in the world. Until I realized what was happening and pulled away quickly.

I wanted him. I fucking wanted Jake Odom! I looked down to evade his eyes. I was embarrassed. And scared. I was scared he would see something different in my eyes now that I knew I felt something different in my heart. And in my pants.

When he unzipped the jacket and we broke apart, I felt empty without him, like there was a hole only he could fill. I never knew the hole was there before. I'd been living my life without any knowledge of it. Kind of like when I was in eighth grade and learned about tampons.

Wait! It goes where?!

Luckily, I'd gotten my feelings and hormones under control real quick. Even though he'd kissed me later that night, we'd had coffee together the next morning and managed to whack that shit right back into the ground.

This coffee date was similar in some ways, one being that another guy had just betrayed me. Ugh! Guys seriously suck.

But it was different in ways, too. This time there wasn't any sexual tension charging the air between us. I had adapted to living with a vacant spot inside of me. My feelings for Jake had been stored in a lockbox a long time ago. As for any feelings on his part, I wasn't sure if he'd had any at all. Real feelings, I mean. Sure, he probably wanted to stick it in me. But he was a guy, and guys were notoriously horny creatures, so it may have been just a physical thing for him. Either way, it was in the past, and now we were just two people getting some breakfast.

"So what's going on?" he asked while we waited on our food. He asked this in the same tone he'd asked the day before in my bedroom. This wasn't a rhetorical question used as a greeting. He was on to me, and he wanted an explanation.

"Nothing much."

"Roxanne," he said in a warning tone.

Ugh! I hated when people called me that. No offense to anyone named Roxanne. I'm sure it's fitting on you. But there were two things that came to my mind when I heard the name.

1. A prostitute.
2. A guy with a very long nose.

Having a last name like Humsucker was bad enough. I *had* to have a nice first name, one that brought to mind images of surfer girls, beach towels, and flip flops ... and flappers who killed their boyfriends, but, whatever.

Jake knew I hated being called Roxanne. He liked to use it against me when I was pissing him off. I guess that meant I was pissing him off now.

I put my nose in the air and turned my head slightly to the left, letting him know I wasn't going to be bullied into speaking.

"Are you upset because you miss your boyfriend?"

I snapped my head back to glare at him. Nobody knew what happened with Jim. I was too embarrassed to tell anyone, even Allison. I had been talking about him nonstop since September. I'd told everyone at home that he was *the one*. I even told them I was expecting a proposal after graduation. Now, when they asked questions I just said he was staying in Chapel Hill for the summer, which wasn't a lie. But even if they didn't know how he'd betrayed me, they did know he wasn't here in Ann Arbor. They must've thought I was miserable because we were apart for the summer. That was the first time it dawned on me that I would have been sad and missing him for the summer no matter what. Somehow this made me feel slightly less angst-y. Just slightly.

"Yeah," I admitted quietly.

"How'd you guys leave things?" he asked. "Are you on a break, or are you doing the long-distance thing?"

"Um," I borrowed Jim's favorite word. "I guess we're on a break. We're supposed to enjoy our summer with the option of renewing in the fall."

"Like a leased apartment, huh?"

"I guess."

The server brought over our omelets and hash browns. I covered my food with ketchup while he covered his with pepper.

"You're not keeping in touch with him at all?"

I shook my head.

"I thought he was supposed to be *the one*."

"Jake," I said annoyed. "I really don't need you to make me feel stupid. I can do that on my own."

"Okay, sorry." He sounded like he meant it. "Maybe he still is the one. Maybe you'll renew your lease in the fall and live happily ever after."

I shrugged. I knew for certain that was not happening, but I wasn't ready to say it out loud yet. I really *had* thought he was the one. I'd had everything planned in my mind – our wedding, our kids, our house, our Tuesday night bowling league...

"If so," he continued, "this could be your last chance to sow your oats."

I'd learned in my Human Sexuality class that men were biologically programmed to sow their oats. They were born with a primal urge to spread their seed to as many people as possible. This meant they couldn't be blamed for their actions since it was a natural instinct of which they had no control. Then again, the textbook was written by men, so who knew if that was the proven truth or just an excuse for men to whore around?

Women, on the other hand, were supposedly biologically programmed to find the best father figure for their future children. Since I wasn't sure I even wanted children, I didn't know where that left me, but I wasn't feeling any urges to sow my oats or find myself another nice provider for future offspring just yet.

"You said you're supposed to enjoy your summer. When is that supposed to start happening?" he asked.

I stopped chewing and glared at him again. He always saw right down to the core of me and called me out on my bullshit.

"I just need a few days to-"

"Organize," he interrupted. "I know. That's what you said. I think what you really need is a summer fling."

Jake was the master of the fling. He went through girls the way I went through hair conditioner – liberally and quickly.

"I'm not even sure what a fling is, Jake."

I was a relationship kind of girl. I did not have flings.

"It's longer than a one-night-stand, but not as serious as a relationship."

"I get that part. What I don't understand is why. If I like a guy enough to keep seeing him after one night, why don't I just ... keep seeing him? It seems silly to blow through a bunch of guys for fun when I could have something special with just one."

"Whoa!" He put a hand up to stop me. "I didn't say anything about blowing a bunch of guys. All I said was that you needed something casual for the summer."

"I don't know how to do casual."

"I can teach you," he said, like it was the best idea he'd ever had. "The first thing you need to do is lower your standards. You're not looking for a marriage proposal. You're only looking for fun. If he reads at a second grade level, lives in his parents' basement, and has no job or ambitions, that's okay. As long as you have fun with him. As long as he makes you laugh and feel good about yourself."

I cringed. I didn't imagine I'd be able to overlook those kinds of things, and I didn't think it would make any sense for me to do so.

"If he has no job, he has no money. How can we have any fun if he's always broke?" I asked Jake. "And if he lives in his mom's basement, I ask again, how can we have any fun?"

"I'm just using an example. I know how picky you are. Sometimes I think you might be too picky."

I covered my mouth to keep a little laugh from escaping my lips. Yeah, I picked some real winners. If he only knew.

"In the beginning of a relationship," he continued, "when everyone is only showing their best cards, that's the most exciting part. Eventually people start to get too comfortable, and they become complacent. Like zombies. Relationship zombies."

I nodded.

"The good thing about keeping it quick and casual is that you never have to get to that part. You never have to zombify. You just move on to the next one. That means you're always at your best and so is the person you're with."

"But how do you ever find anything real that way?" Not that I knew a thing about anything real anyway. I'd had two serious boyfriends in my life, and they were both lying, cheating assholes.

"You don't. That's not the point right now. The point is for you to have a little fun so you can enjoy the summer."

I pushed my plate away. "What's your excuse then?"

He looked surprised by my boldness. "My excuse for what?"

"Flings."

"I don't know what you're talking about, Roxanne. I just have a short attention span. I get bored easily. I can't even commit to the same radio station to listen to an entire song. I have to check the other stations to make sure I'm not missing anything better playing somewhere else."

"And by the time you realize there isn't anything better on the other channels, the song you liked on the first channel is over and you missed out."

"I'm just waiting for the right one. When all the newness wears off and she stops shaving and starts wearing boring underwear that doesn't even match, and I *still* want to be around her, I'll stop. It just hasn't happened yet."

The waitress brought the check over and Jake grabbed it. "I've got this."

"You better," I said with a sweet smile. "You're the one who made me come."

"I really wish you would not say things like that," he said. He looked pained. "Now we have to sit here for ten more minutes while I imagine something disturbing. Like my mother taking a shit." He closed his eyes and tilted his head down toward the table to visualize.

I gasped. *Was he saying what I thought he was saying?* "Dude! You're so gross."

He lifted his head, opened his eyes, and gave me a wicked grin. "Just kidding." He paused. "Partially. I'm *partially* kidding. Semi kidding. Half kidding."

OMIGOD! "Are we really sitting here talking about the current condition of your penis?"

"I guess we are. Is that weird?"

I looked up at the ceiling as I thought about it. It didn't feel weird. "Is it weird that it doesn't feel weird?" I asked.

"Hmm, yeah, kind of."

"Should we go now?" I asked quickly.

"Can I carry your purse for you?"

CHAPTER 6

SHORTLY AFTER WE got home and Jake finished his laundry, I saw Allison's minivan pull into the driveway. Was this a conspiracy? Didn't anyone use the phone anymore?

"Get in the van," she demanded when I opened the front door.

I scowled but grabbed my purse and followed her outside. "Where are we going?"

"To get pedicures."

I looked down at my feet. They were still winterized with dry skin and chipped polish. I nodded. Good idea.

I climbed into the passenger seat of her mom-mobile. A quick glance in the backseat had me shuddering. In the second row sat an infant car seat and a booster seat, both stained with random liquids and littered with crumbs in the cracks. There were a few Cheerios and a Cheeto on the floorboard. What was it with parents neglecting their car seats? It wasn't just her. It was every parent I had ever known. The only place I had ever seen a clean car seat was on display in a store or at a baby shower.

Remote controls were another dead giveaway. You knew you were at a house where small children lived when the batteries were taped into the remote controls because all of the covers to the battery compartments were missing.

When I was younger I'd started a list called:

Things I Will Never Do When I Have Kids

```
1. I will never clean something off
their faces by licking my finger.
2. I will never put my daughters in
bikinis.
3. I will never use baby talk and say,
"Mommy wuvs you."
4. I will not let the car seats or high
chairs get disgusting.
5. The kids will not touch a remote
control until they are seven.
6. I will have them potty-trained by
eighteen months.
7. They will not be held all the time.
My kids will learn independence from the
start.
8. I will not feed them anything but
homemade organic food.
9. I will not allow the use of
pacifiers past six months of age.
10. I will never say, "Because I said
so."
```

11. I will not force them to finish their plates if they're full, or make them eat things they don't like.
12. I will never wash out their mouths with soap.
13. I'll never take them to visit a giant, scary-as-hell, human-sized Easter bunny. Because seriously, what the fuck is *that*?

Every childless person had a list, whether they admitted it or not. Even if they never intended on having kids, and even if it was s a subconscious list and not an actual Excel spreadsheet like mine, they'd made a list.

Mine started out when I was little, maybe around ten years old. At that time the list consisted of things like, I would never make them do chores, and I would never take away their candy.

Once I got into high school and my classmates started having kids, the list became more mature and grew a lot longer. I sat back and observed all these parents making all these mistakes, all the while making a note on my mental checklist. I was never obnoxious enough to say these things out loud, of course. Not until I transferred my list from a mental note to a document stored it in my laptop. I read it to Allison one night when I was drunk. I thought she might be offended since she had violated practically every single item on the list. All she did was laugh at me and say, "Just wait."

ALL GOOD THINGS

"My parents had to put Snoopy to sleep yesterday," Allison told me, sadly, once we were at the salon with our feet soaking in the tubs.

I frowned. Allison's family had had Snoopy, their lab mix, since we were in elementary school. It was sad, but the poor guy had lived a long, happy life.

"At least he's not suffering anymore," I said.

"Yeah."

"Did you tell the kids?"

"We told them we gave Snoopy to a nice family who lived on a farm."

I lifted my head abruptly as a wave of déjà vu washed over me. That sounded so familiar.

"You know," she continued, "so he'd have more room-"

"-to run and play with the other animals?" I asked loudly.

She nodded.

I clenched my fists tightly on the armrests as I realized several things.

```
1. I had heard this before. Twice.
2. My parents were liars.
3. My dogs were dead.
```

Our first dog, Chip, went to a "farm" when I was about eight. I could understand my parents wanting to shield me from the blow at such a tender age. But our second dog, Ramsey, he had just gone to a farm when I was in high school. I was like sixteen! I could handle the truth.

Seriously, was everybody on this planet a freaking liar? I couldn't trust anyone, not even my own parents.

"So, what happened with Jim?" Allison asked at the wrong time.

Hearing his name brought actual pain to my chest. Heartbreak was not a myth. It was a real, physical thing. It hurt to think back to that night, the night Destiny showed up at my door.

When I'd opened the door of my apartment, and saw her standing there in the hallway, my heart had clenched up in defense, like a turtle. I'd felt it harden like cement. It was like my heart knew to put on the armor before my head did. I hadn't known who this girl was, or why she was knocking on my door at one in the morning, but my heart had an idea.

"Hi," she'd said quietly. I could tell she was sweet, like me. Her voice had been soft, and her pale blue eyes filled with innocence. But something else – pain, the same kind of pain that would take over my own eyes in just a minute.

"I'm looking for my boyfriend. James," she'd said quietly.

She must have the wrong apartment, I remembered thinking. I'd hoped I could help her find her boyfriend. If the size of her belly was any indication, this boyfriend of hers was about to have a baby. Like maybe right now. But before I could tell her she had the wrong door, she looked behind me and burst into tears.

I'd turned around to see Jim. He'd looked horrified.

"Baby!" he'd said, alarmed.

I'd thought he was talking to me. He wasn't.

"Destiny? What's the matter? Is something wrong with the baby?"

"You know this girl?" I'd asked him. *Oh good. He might know her boyfriend. He might be able to find him.*
YOU ARE DUMB AS FUCK.

I'd taken a sculpting class my sophomore year, a little lightweight course to give me a break from all of the damn science classes. We'd used these tools called gouges. Like sharp ice cream scoops with heavy wooden handles, their purpose was to carve chunks out of clay.

Once I'd figured out who the girl's boyfriend was, I'd felt like someone had taken a gouge to my heart and dug the pieces out, one spoonful at a time. Many hours later when I'd finally collapsed into bed and tried to sleep, I didn't feel pain in my chest anymore. I felt numbness, emptiness. And that was how I'd managed to finish packing and make the long drive home – by telling myself my heart couldn't be broken because it wasn't there anymore. I'd left it back in Chapel Hill, on the floor of my apartment, in a big pile of gray clumps.

IT MUST HAVE come back because it hurt like hell in that nail salon. It hurt for my dogs, it hurt for Destiny, and it hurt for the innocent baby. Or maybe that was phantom pain.

I thought about giving Allison a line of crap like I'd given Jake and my parents, but I was starting to feel like I needed the support of my friend. Maybe I would feel better if I told someone.

"He didn't hit you, did he?" she asked.

"I wish," I said quietly. It was the truth. I was convinced that violence would have been easier to deal with. I had never had to deal with anyone physically hurting me, and I didn't mean to downplay it at all, but I thought a broken bone would hurt less than a broken heart. At least you knew it would eventually heal. And they've got Percocet for that. There wasn't a pill that could help me now, and I wasn't sure I would ever completely heal. I might be a cynical, spreadsheet-maker my whole life. I might never trust another man again.

"He wasn't who I thought he was. Everything he told me was a lie."

"What do you mean?"

"For one thing, he didn't even go to UNC. He worked there as a janitor. All the times he said he was in class, he was changing the trash and mopping the floors."

"How'd you find this out?"

"His girlfriend told me. His pregnant girlfriend."

She looked at me, alarmed, and too stunned to speak. I had Allison's undivided attention, as well as the attention of both women doing our toes.

"She's in high school."

All three women gasped.

"Her name is Destiny."

"How tacky," Allison said under her breath.

"All the nights he said he was spending at his parents', he was at *her* house. Thanksgiving and Christmas, he brought *her* to the family dinners. She was the girlfriend. I was the other woman."

"High school?" Allison repeated. "That's sick. Is he going to prison or what?"

"Oh yeah. That's another thing. He's only nineteen. He *just* turned nineteen. I never asked to see his ID. He always drank soda when we were at the bar, but I thought that was because he was working, you know?"An age difference of two years wouldn't be a big deal to people older than us, but at my age, it was a big deal, especially when I was the older one.

"Oh my God," Allison said quietly.

"I'm a cougar! A desperate cougar and a home-wrecker, too." I put my head in my hands, ashamed for fucking a nineteen year old, ashamed for being a home-wrecker, and ashamed for announcing it out loud in a salon. *I* was the tacky one. Destiny was just a naïve girl with a cheating bastard for a baby-daddy.

"I am hurt over being lied to and played. I am embarrassed for falling for the whole scheme. I am guilty for being the reason he cheated on his pregnant girlfriend. I even feel awful for the baby to have a shit-stain for a father."

"You pick out color?" the lady at my feet asked.

I grabbed the bottle of dark purple polish I'd set in the cup holder of the armrest. It was so dark it was almost black. I tried to hand it to the lady, but Allison reached over and snatched it from my hands before I had the chance.

"If we're going to get through this," she said, "it's not going to be with gothic-chic."

She handed the lady the bottle of hot pink polish that she'd chosen for herself.

"You need it more than I do," she said and sat back in her massage chair.

WHEN OUR MATCHING hot pink nails had dried, (just like our matching Hypercolor t-shirts in elementary school, Allison pointed out), I thought she was going to take me home, but she said we had one more stop to make.

"Don't you need to get home to the kids?"

"Braham can handle it. I think you need me now more than they do."

When she pulled into the Briarwood Mall, I knew exactly where we were going. Allison knew what I needed to make me feel like I was on top of the world. We were going to the makeup counter.

Right before I left for college we worried that our friendship would never be the same. I'd be studying Abnormal Psych; she'd be studying soothing techniques for newborns. I was afraid she'd meet a bunch of moms at the playground and she'd prefer talking to them about jogging strollers rather than hear about another of my drunken nights at parties. She was afraid I'd have too much fun doing hair and having pillow fights in my underwear with a bunch of sorority girls that I wouldn't have time to hang around with a bunch of tantrum-throwers. We were afraid we'd drift so far apart on our different paths that we'd never be able to reconnect.

In ways, we'd been right. I would never know what it was like to be a married mom of three before I could legally drink wine. Just like she was unable now to understand my breakup with Jim since she'd never had a breakup before. But we realized soon enough that just because we had different lives, didn't mean we didn't need each other anymore. She needed to hear about my crazy single-girl escapades because, "How else am I supposed to get the college experience?" And I needed to hang out with rambunctious kids once in awhile to remind me why safe sex was so important. And while we couldn't always relate to each other's lives, we could always relate to the MAC counter.

Yes, it really was nice to be home. I loved having a friend who took the lead and pulled me up when I was down, even if she was sometimes a little too honest about it.

Example: "How does this color look on me?" I asked about a bright coral lipstick.

With mascara wand in hand, she answered, "If you had the matching nail polish, you'd look like a body in a casket."

Ouch.

When we'd had enough fun with glitter and purple eyeliner, she led us to my other favorite place in the mall: Borders. The smell of books mixed with the smell of coffee – it was an insta-pick-me-up. I could grab a drink from the café and easily get lost between the stacks until I forgot all about the baby-mama drama.

"You get the drinks," she said, "and I'll get the books."

That was unusual. Allison wasn't the reader I was. She was usually the one who got the drinks while I was the one that needed to be ushered out of the building because the store had closed fifteen minutes ago, and the staff wanted to go home.

"You need this," Allison said, joining me at the table where I'd brought our mocha lattes. She slid a book across the table.

Who Moved My Cheese?

I raised an eyebrow at her. Not a self-help book. Puh-lease not a self-help book. I'd rather drown myself in romance novels about 27-year-old virgins being deflowered by Fabio, than be seen near the self-help aisle.

Things Less Embarrassing Than Reading a Self-Help Book in Public

```
1. Reading a book about how to achieve
the ultimate orgasm in public.
    2. Buying yeast infection medication.
    3. Having a really hot pharmacy tech
who happens to be in your Social Problems
class explain how to use said yeast
infection medication right at the
pharmacy window while five people wait in
line behind you.
    4. Having to leave your underwear in
the bookstore's bathroom because you peed
your pants while laughing too hard at
someone else reading a book in public
about achieving the ultimate orgasm.
```

"Don't be so Judgy McJudgerson," Allison said. "They gave this book to everyone at Braham's work when the company was bought out. It was really helpful to him. It's about dealing with change."

"Judgy McJudgerson? Is that, like, your neighbor or something?"

"Yes," she said with a straight face. "Now, this book is about a mouse-"

I interrupted her by singing my own rendition of Michael Jackson's "Ben."

"Can you please, just for once, not sing?"

She tried hard to keep the serious look on her face. But as I continued to sing I saw her cheeks bulge out like a squirrel's and I knew I had her. She was barely holding in her laughter.

"Don't hurt yourself," I said when I stopped singing.

She composed herself and got her squirrel face under control. "So there's this mouse. He goes to the same place every day to get his food. But one day he gets there and there's no cheese."

"Someone moved the cheese?" I asked.

"Yes! And he has to decide what to do."

"So what does he do?"

"I don't know. I guess you have to read it. See, the cheese is your relationship."

"I get it."

"You can sit in your room crying, stomp your feet and avoid all your friends. But you won't find food that way.

You need to keep on moving and hope you'll find cheese somewhere else."

I rested my chin in my hand. "Huh." There was a lesson to be learned from that mouse.

"I've got something else for you."

She left and returned a few moments later with a hot pink paperback. *The Breakup Repair Kit.*

"This looks fun!" she said. "It's filled with activities and recipes and funny stories. Look!" She flipped it open and pointed to one of the pages. "It teaches you how to build a Nurture Nest."

I put my head in my hands on the table. This was even worse than the cheese.

"I'm buying this for you," she said, and ran to the cashier before I could stop her.

WE FINALLY GOT back to her house in time to feed the kids dinner. Braham took off to the den with a beer. I didn't blame the guy.

Chaos ensued. I still wasn't sure how someone my age could take care of three kids. I couldn't even take care of a plant that only needed to be fed two ice cubes a week. I had killed three different orchids, and she was responsible for three human lives! How did she do it?

First, the baby, Drew, poured his apple juice into his macaroni and cheese. And then ate it. Oh, the nerve!

"Allison!" I said, alarmed. "Did you see that?"

"What?"

"He poured apple juice into his food and ate it!"

"Oh." She shrugged like it was no big deal. "I don't care what he does with it as long as he's eating."

Things I Will Never Do When I Have Kids #23: I will not let them mix their liquids into their solids. Unless they are making smoothies.

I tried not to watch Drew as he ate. But it was like a fender bender on the side of the road. I couldn't help but stare. And pray.

As I was telling Allison more about my breakup with Jim, Kenzie started choking. Not just a cough, but a serious, we-should-call-911 choking episode. My heart stopped beating for a second and I froze in fear. I knew all about choking. I'd almost lost my life to a piece of raspberry bubblegum. It was the scariest thing *ever*.

Allison acted like it was just another day in the life of a mom. In the middle of her sentence she reached over and smacked Kenzie on the back. A green grape flew from her throat, hit the wall and slid down to the floor. Kenzie took another bite, and Allison finished her sentence. If I didn't see a green grape on the floor as evidence, I would have thought I'd imagined the whole thing. *Seriously. I am never having kids.*

"I didn't say this before because you were so happy," she said, "and I wanted to give you time to figure it out on your own, but I never thought he was the right guy for you."

"You never even met him," I pointed out.

Drew got a massive amount of juiced-up mac 'n cheese on his spoon, and before it got to his mouth, about ninety percent of it had fallen onto his shirt. What a mess. Did she really do this like three times a day? My anxiety was growing stronger with every minute I spent in their house.

"No, but I heard enough about him from you. Didn't you say he kicked a wall because a guy in your class asked you about an assignment?"

"Yeah," I reluctantly admitted.

Kayla knocked her apple juice over. The puddle dripped over the edges of the table on not one, but two sides. *No.* I couldn't take another second of this.

Allison pulled a dishtowel out of thin air like a freaking magician and had the spill wiped off the table and the floor in less than ten seconds. "How long was it going to be before he kicked you instead?" she asked after she'd tossed the wet towel into the hamper in the bathroom.

"I know I messed up, okay?" I said defensively. She wasn't telling me anything I didn't already know, that I didn't already have on the list.

"All right," she said patiently. "Can you imagine being a stepmother at twenty-one?"

I cringed. No way.

"I know it hurts, and you feel stupid, but in the end you'll be glad he's out of your life. I really believe that."

I hadn't admitted it to myself yet, but I believed it, too.

"I think you need a rebound guy," she told me. "A summer hook-up."

"That's what Jake said."

"It shouldn't be hard to find one working at a bar. You'll have guys eating out of your hand." She paused. "Or drinking out of your belly button."

ALL GOOD THINGS

She was right. Jake was right, too. This was my last summer before I graduated from college, my last summer to be young and wild and free, before the "real world" caught up with me, and I was a slave to the man and Sallie Mae. I needed to stop obsessing over a shit-stain and have some fun.

CHAPTER 7

I ARRIVED AT THE Bar at 4:45 the next day in my hot pink tank top, little black shorts, and black slip-resistant sneakers. I'd spent some extra time on my hair and makeup to make a good first impression. Starting a new job was nerve-wracking and being able to go in there with confidence made all the difference in the world.

I needed that extra confidence when Zeke introduced me to Rachel, the girl who would be training me. I knew her type right away: passive-aggressive, catty, and competitive – the kind of girl who has lots of guy friends, but no girlfriends.

"Oh, you're Jake's friend," she said with the amount of enthusiasm I would expect from someone about to get a tooth pulled.

"Yes."

She looked me up and down and then up again and gave my cute updo a look of disgust, probably because she knew my hair looked better than her faux-hawk ponytail. *Whatever, bitch.*

She said all I really needed to do was follow her around the whole night and learn as we went along.

It was slow for the first few hours.

My safety net arrived at six and waved to me.

It got busier around seven when the Tigers game started. A bunch of guys came in to drink beer and watch the game. Most of them sat at the bar, and Jake was too busy to pay any attention to me. Boo hoo.

Rachel assigned me the task of asking a four-top of college-aged guys what they wanted to drink while she took an order from a couple a few tables over.

Once I had the drink order (four Miller Lites, easy), she taught me how to put it into the computer. When I hit SEND, a slip of paper printed at the bar so Jake would know I needed four beers.

Since I didn't have anything else to do, I watched Jake pull four bottles of beer from the cooler, line them up on the server's counter in a row, and pop the tops off in quick succession. He was so sexy back there. I could watch him all night. *Oh, I mean, did I really just think that? Shit.*

Whack!

"The guy with the white hat on," he said, like he was answering a question.

Uhhh. What? I didn't ask a question.

"He's been staring at your ass since he walked in the door. I can't say I blame him."

"Jake!" I squealed, embarrassed. I looked around to make sure Rachel hadn't heard. I had a feeling that would make her like me even less.

"I think the point of wearing shorts like that is to make people notice your ass," he said. "All I'm saying is, it's working."

Great. I started loading the beers onto my black tray.

"The guy in the white hat," he repeated. "He could be the one. Your summer guy."

I gave the guy in the white hat a better look. He was wearing a shirt that had an outline of Ohio on it. It read "Worst State Ever." There was a huge rivalry between University of Michigan and Ohio State. That was just one of the dozens of OSU-insulting shirts you'd see in Ann Arbor.

Hmm. I could tell he had a sense of humor. And he was cute in a preppy jock kind of way. And his glasses made him look smart. He was like a jock-slash-nerd hybrid. I could go for that. I shrugged and took off with my tray.

By the time the guy in the white hat left, he had my number in his phone.

The kitchen stopped serving food at midnight on Mondays. We wiped tables and filled salt and pepper shakers while we waited for the last of the diners to finish up. Once they paid their tabs and our clean-up was finished, we sat at the bar while Rachel showed me how to do the paperwork and turn in my money at the end of a shift.

She asked Jake to make her a drink. I assumed he knew her drink of choice since she didn't specify.

"You get one free drink per shift," she explained as she organized her money into piles on the bar.

What? Free alcohol? Free alcohol after a long night on my feet? Free alcohol after a long night on my feet while I was counting all the money I made? (Well, technically she made it, but I saw it and it was a lot). This job was awesome!

Jake placed some kind of brown drink in front of her, probably a Long Island. Gross.

"For you, Rox?"

"You pick," I told him.

A few minutes later he placed something in front of me in a martini glass. Inside the glass were four jumbo bleu-cheese-stuffed green olives on a skewer.

"I gave you extra olives," he said.

Bleu cheese and green olives. Two of the greatest things on Earth. Combined in one bite. Yum. "I love olives, and I love you," I told him.

"Olive you, too," Jake said. He was purposely trying to sound dorky. It was endearing.

Rachel rolled her eyes. *Whatever, bitch.*

When we were finished with our drinks Rachel handed Jake a ten-dollar bill for making her drinks, and gave me a twenty for being her assistant. She led me down the hallway to show me the safe where she turned in her money, and then we punched out.

She walked out the back door without even saying goodbye.

It was 1:00AM.

I WENT BACK to the bar and sat down on one of the hightop stools.

"Do you have a ride home?" he asked.

"I'm about to call Adam. He said to call him when I was off."

"Don't do that," Jake said. "He's probably sleeping. I'll be off by two-fifteen and I can take you home. I'll even make you another drink."

There were no customers in the bar. The last few baseball fans had left while Rachel and I were counting our money.

"You don't have to bribe me with alcohol," I told him as I texted Adam.

He shrugged. "I will anyway."

He set another martini in front of me before he got to work stocking the beer fridge behind the bar. It was one of those refrigerators with a glass door that were in gas stations and convenience stores everywhere. I'd never seen one in a bar before.

I took a sip of my drink. This would have to be the last one. I was already feeling the first.

I leaned back in the bar chair, crossed my legs, pulled *The Breakup Repair Kit* out of my tote bag, and began to read.

It wasn't very long before I heard a snicker. I had a pretty good idea what he was laughing at, but I played dumb.

"What's so funny?" I asked, doe-eyed.

"Are you being serious right now?"

"I'm learning how to build a Nurture Nest," I said seriously.

He burst into laughter and grabbed the book from me. He scoffed as he flipped through the pages. "Find a gay best friend?" he mocked. "A homemade face mask? How is a clean face going to help you get over a breakup? And why do you need a gay friend when you have a straight one right here?"

I grabbed the book back. "It's not meant to be taken too seriously. It's more like a distraction. I actually think it's kind of fun. I made the face mask last night, and it was amazing. I also took a bubble bath for the first time since I was, like, twelve. Also amazing."

"Are you really this upset about it?" He looked confused, but concerned. "I thought you said you were on a break. Like Ross and Rachel."

I shrugged and looked into my martini. "I'm fragile right now. I need nurturing."

"Sorry," he said quietly. "I didn't know it was that serious."

"I'm trying to make it *not* be serious."

"I already told you what to do about that. Did you give him your number?" He turned his back to me and began to stock the fridge.

"Yeah. Do you think it was too soon?" I asked as I stirred my martini with the skewer of olives.

"Too soon for what?"

"It's only my first day on the job. If I give a guy my number every time I work, I won't even remember who is who."

"So what? You're young and single. You can go out with as many guys as you want." He closed the refrigerator door and walked back over to my end of the bar. Putting his forearms on the marble, he leaned forward and looked at me sternly. "But make sure you're being safe."

I scowled and rolled my eyes. "Okay, Dad. Are you kidding me right now? I am the last person who needs a lecture on safe sex."

He started breaking down the cardboard beer cases while I took another drink of my martini.

"I have never had sex without a condom," I told him as I popped another olive in my mouth. "I am the safe sex poster child. I am the one who passes condoms out to my friends before we go out at night. They call me Mama Rox."

He stopped bending cardboard for a second but didn't look over at me.

"Really," he said. It was more a statement than a question. He looked intrigued. "Huh." Also not a question.

"I'm not taking any chances," I explained. "Can you believe I have four friends at school who have or have had STDs? Some of them last forever! And they are all normal-looking clean-cut girls who date normal-looking clean-cut guys. You'd never suspect it."

"Huh," he said again. He stacked all the flattened boxes on top of each other and then started wiping the bar with a polishing rag. "Interesting."

"Yup. So that's why I say if you're not going to wrap it, go home and whack it." Oh shit. The alcohol was already causing loose lips. *Shut up, Roxie!*

"Don't be in a jiffy," he added. "Cover your stiffy."

I giggled. "Before you attack her, cover your whacker."

"You've gotta love the word 'whacker,'" he said with a straight face.

"I do love the word 'whacker,'" I admitted.

Seriously. Shut. Up.

"Guy-in-the-White-Hat finally called," I told Jake a week later while I sat at the bar waiting for him to get off work. He was in the process of putting little rubber caps on all of the liquor bottles to keep the fruit flies out. He was facing the back of the bar, but I could see his face in the mirror behind the bottles.

"That was fast," he replied sarcastically.

I ignored the sarcasm. "We're going out on Thursday. I told him to pick me up here. I don't know if I want him to know where I live yet. Do you want me to help you with those?"

"Nah. You're off the clock. I got it."

The bar was empty again. He said that was normal for Monday nights. After the crazy-busy weekend we'd had, I didn't mind a nice calm Monday night shift. And I didn't mind a nice Monday night martini either.

"Where is he taking you?"

"Dinner and a movie."

He met my eyes in the reflection on the mirror and smirked. "How original."

"It was your idea," I reminded him as I bit an olive off the skewer. "You said to have a fling. You didn't say the guy had to be original. I think it's best if he's average. That way I won't want to keep him."

"Makes sense."

I wasn't sure where Brandon was taking me for dinner. I figured dressy casual would work at most places. I wore a strapless sundress and wedge sandals. Adam dropped me off at The Bar, but since Jake had the night off, I didn't bother going inside. I sat at a table on the patio until I saw Brandon and his white hat pull up in a white Nissan. I have no problem with white. It's clean and refreshing.

"You look nice," he said when I got into his car.

"Thanks."

I noticed the pair of blue fuzzy dice hanging from his rearview mirror weren't the typical kind of dice. One of the cubes said, "I" with a fabric heart sewn on next to it. The other cube said "Britney." *I heart Britney.*

I touched the die and held it toward him. "Britney?" I asked, wondering if he had a crazy obsession with an ex-girlfriend.

He nodded. But it was more like a half nod because he moved his head upward and didn't bring it back down. "Spears," he said without an ounce of irony in his voice. He was dead serious about this.

To show me just how serious, he pulled a photo out of his dash and held it out for me to see. The picture of cute, innocent, teenage Britney Spears on her *Baby One More Time* album cover had been cut out of a magazine. What's even weirder than keeping a photo of a celebrity on your dashboard? Keeping an *old* photo of a celebrity as a teenager on your dashboard. Unless, of course, you are a teenager. In this case, the owner of the dashboard was not. At least not that I knew of. I had checked his ID at the bar that night, but who knew if it was even real? He could totally be seventeen. Omigod, he was probably seventeen! I told myself to relax and not let my experiences of the past ruin this night for me.

"The movie starts at nine," he said as he shifted the car into gear.

Ohhhh, a stick shift! I loved to watch a guy handle a stick shift, especially when they leaned back in the seat with a carefree, I-got-this-shit kind of attitude, as Brandon did then. And especially when they had arms that made an otherwise loose-fitting t-shirt look tight.

"I was thinking we could do a real quick dinner for now, and maybe go out for drinks and appetizers after," he said.

"You already decided on a movie?" I asked, surprised. Aren't we supposed to decide on a movie together? I hadn't gone on a whole lot of dates with strangers before, but I'd seen a lot of these scenarios in movies, and I was pretty sure the guy never picked out a movie before he picked up the girl.

"Yeah. I bought the tickets a week ago," he explained as he pulled the Nissan onto the main road. "I had to. They were selling out fast. I hope you don't mind."

I reminded myself this was just for fun. I wasn't going to marry the guy. He didn't need to have the best manners because he looked like an Abercrombie & Fitch model. That was how this worked, right? With every bottle of beer on his six-pack, I must forgo a virtue I would otherwise consider important. Thoughtfulness was out. What next?

"What movie?" I asked.

"*Episode Three*," he replied.

"Episode three of what?" What was he talking about? What were the first two episodes?

He looked at me and gave me a condescending smile. I almost expected him to pat my head and tell me I was a sweet girl. "Not a *Star Wars* fan I take it?" he asked.

"No." As a film buff, I knew what *Star Wars* was, of course, but I'd never been able to get into it.

"I'll forgive you for that. But I'm going to have to convert you. Starting tonight."

Maybe I didn't want to be converted.

```
Things I'd Rather Do Than Watch Star
                Wars

1. Get a cavity filled.
2. Get blood drawn.
3. Have diarrhea.
4. Have someone wax the little hairs
out of my butt crack.
5. Have diarrhea right before someone
waxes my butt crack.
```

Before I could get any further into my list, he pulled into a gas station. Instead of pulling up to the pump, he parked in one of the four parking spots along the side. He turned the car off, meaning he wasn't even going to leave me with AC. I'd been willing to give him the benefit of the doubt over choosing a movie without caring if I was interested in seeing it. But leaving me in a parking lot with no air conditioning on a hot summer day was just more proof this guy was an inconsiderate a-hole. What had I gotten myself into? I wondered. And how could I get myself out?

Just a fling, I thought, as I gave myself a quick pep-talk. *Look at him. He's super sexy. Great complexion. Nice arms. Good style. It's just a fling. I can do this.*

He opened the door and got out. I remained seated in the passenger seat. He did the gentlemanly thing and walked around the car to open my door, but I suspected this was only because I didn't budge, and he felt forced. He wanted me to go in with him. Maybe he wanted to pick out some candy for the theatre. At least he was going to let me pick out my own. I could suffer through a movie I didn't like if I had gummi bears and Goobers.

As we walked toward the gas station, he put his hand on my lower back. Ordinarily when a guy did that I thought of it as a sweet, intimate gesture. When he did it, it felt possessive. I was uncomfortable and didn't like him touching me. At all. The night had barely started, and he'd already rubbed me the wrong way.

Just a fling.

As we walked into the gas station he removed his hand from my back and veered to the left. That wasn't where the candy was. It was where a Subway was attached to the gas station.

Uh uh. No way was he taking me to Subway for dinner. It wasn't even a stand-alone Subway. It was *inside* a gas station! No, it wasn't possible. It was over-the-top ridiculous. Nobody would even believe me if I told them.

But he *had* said we needed to hurry. He might have plans to go somewhere nicer after the movie.

Just a fling.

"Go ahead and get whatever you want," he said as we inched closer to the counter where the sandwich artist waited to take our order. "You can even get a foot long," he said with a silly smile. "That is, if you can handle a foot long."

No freaking way. This could not be happening right now. I wanted to run, but I felt trapped. I couldn't just walk out in the middle of a date, could I? That would be cruel, and while I might be bitchy sometimes, I am never cruel. I should have arranged an 'emergency' phone call from Allison.

"Find us a table," I said to Brandon, even though we were the only two people in there, and there was nothing but empty tables. "I need to use the bathroom."

My first thought was to go into the bathroom and see if they had any windows I could climb out, but I thought that might be taking it further than necessary. I decided to keep it simple. I walked right out the front door and didn't look back. When I was safely out of the parking lot, I started running. I ran to the street corner and then snuck into a residential neighborhood through a backyard.

Once I was two blocks away I slowed to a walk and pulled my cell phone out of my purse as I huffed and puffed from the unexpected exercise.

"I can't do this," I gasped into the phone. "Can you please come pick me up?"

ALL GOOD THINGS

"No fucking way," Jake said. We were in his truck and I'd just told him the whole awful story from Britney to Star Wars to Subway. "I don't believe you. There's no way a guy can be that stupid."

"I wish I was making this up," I said dryly.

"I'm sorry I picked the wrong guy for you." He really did look sorry. "I'll pick a guy with more game next time."

"Oh no," I said quickly and put my hand up to stop him. "No next time. I'm not cut out for this. If I'm hooking up with anyone this summer it's going to be someone I actually want to be around for more than a few days. I'm not overlooking flaws just to have meaningless sex."

"I was only trying to help," he said. "You were so unhappy about the North Carolina guy."

"I know. But I don't need a new guy to make me feel better."

"What do you need?"

"For one thing, I need something to eat. And I don't know what else. I feel like breaking something. I should have taken a baseball bat to his car before I left."

"Whoa! Calm down there. Taking a girl to Subway on a first date is not the classiest move, but it's not enough to warrant vandalism. I think you got your point across by walking out."

Oops. I had been talking about Jim, not Brandon. But then I remembered Jake didn't know anything about that.

"I didn't walk. I ran."

Shaking his head in disbelief, he said, "So what do you want for dinner? I take it a foot long is out of the question, but how about a Big Mac? Can you handle a Big Mac?"

CHAPTER 8

"It's not like I'm such a princess that I can't eat Subway," I explained, "but a Subway inside a gas station? And that comment about the foot long? I wanted to die."

We'd skipped the Big Mac and invited Adam and Janelle to join us at The Bar for wings, beer, and baseball. The four of us nearly died laughing over the Subway story. In a way, I was thankful to Brandon for giving me something I could laugh about for years to come. It would always make a funny story to share with others.

We were having a great time until Shannon, one of the waitresses working that night, came over to sit with us when she got cut from the floor. She was a curvy blonde who wore lots of makeup and looked like she went to a tanning booth daily. She was the kind of girl who couldn't kill one bird with two stones, but she'd been nice to me the few times we'd worked together, and I hadn't had any problem with her. That was, until she squeezed a high-top stool right between Jake and me and made herself comfortable by laughing too loudly at his jokes and making too many excuses to rub up against him and show us her cleavage. Then I had a problem with her.

I didn't like Jake's attention being on someone else. It gave me an unsettled feeling in my stomach that I had never felt before. I was always his number one girl. Now he couldn't even see me past her huge hair.

I pushed my plate of wings away with three left uneaten. She made me lose my appetite for wings. This was serious.

I tried to play it off like it didn't bother me. I smiled at her when appropriate and chimed in on the conversation when I was supposed to. But I couldn't shake the bad feeling I had. When I saw her reach over and touch his khaki-covered thigh, I had an unexplainable urge to smack her hand away and say, "That's mine, bitch."

What was wrong with me? Jake wasn't mine. Just because he'd been my friend since toddlerhood didn't mean I had to act jealous and possessive and try to cockblock him. I didn't like him like *that*. I didn't! I couldn't! I wouldn't!

Whack!

I needed to keep my head on and be casual. *Don't let them see you sweat.*

We hung out until the bar closed, but I stuck with beer to make sure I didn't do anything I'd regret, like tell Jake to go ahead and fuck this skank, and I'd pray for the safety and health of his member. That would make me seem totally psycho. And I wasn't. Right?

ALL GOOD THINGS

The other bartender, Katy, invited everyone to her house for a bonfire when the bar closed. I was torn. I wanted to go because I did love bonfires, and my coworkers were fun to hang out with. But I thought I'd be better off going home and not having to watch those two anymore. I had a feeling things between them would go from classy to trashy real quick, and I didn't feel like watching.

Shannon left before us, making a big display of hugging Jake. It was a whole body hug, not just the arms around the neck kind. "I'll see you there," she said to him, giving him a look that let us all know he could see all of her if he wanted.

I gave her the biggest, fakest smile I had in my bag of tricks and waved goodbye.

"All right," Jake said to the three of us as we finished the last of our drinks, "Who's driving? I'm pretty buzzed."

"I've only had three beers," I told them. "I can drop you guys off at Katy's if you want, but I don't really feel like hanging out tonight."

"You've only had three beers?" Jake asked, like he thought I was lying.

"Yeah. You probably would've noticed, but all that blonde hair was blocking your view."

"Sounds like someone might be a little jealous," Adam said in a sing-song voice. I knew he was teasing me, because thinking I'd be jealous of one of Jake's groupies was a joke.

Except it wasn't funny this time.

"Yeah," I said sarcastically. "Of her tanning package."

Adam and Janelle laughed.

"You guys figure it out," Adam said. "I'm gonna hit the bathroom before we go."

"Me, too," Janelle said.

They walked away together, hand in hand. Not boyfriend and girlfriend, my ass.

"More like he's going to hit *it* in the bathroom before we go," Jake said once they were out of earshot.

I covered my ears in a dramatic display. "I told you not to say shit like that about my brother. I do not wish to hear about his sex life!"

Jake leaned over the empty stool Shannon had been sitting on to get closer to me. He peeled my hands from my ears and held them down on the table. His face was only inches from mine. I was close enough to smell beer on his breath. I could easily reach my lips to his if I wanted. And I did want to. Dammit.

Whack! Whack! Whack!

I met his stare and he looked intense, serious.

"Were you really jealous of Shannon?" he asked. I thought I saw something like hope in his eyes.

I wanted to say yes. I wanted to tell him I was jealous, that the thought of him with Shannon made me want to throw up, that thinking he might one day like another girl, or love another girl, more than me made me feel like I couldn't breathe. I wanted to stop trying so hard. I wanted to stop fighting. I wanted to put down my mallet and let go. But I wouldn't.

I rolled my eyes. "Yeah. I told you. I'm jealous of her tan. I wish I didn't care so much about SPF."

He let go of my hands and leaned back. "If you *were* jealous, I was going to tell you she's got nothing on you. But since you're not jealous, I won't."

I gave him a half smile. "If I *was* jealous, I would love hearing you say that. But I'm not."

"Would you love it enough to come to the bonfire?"

"I don't know, Jake. It's two in the morning."

"And you're twenty-one, not seventy-one. But seriously, if you don't come, they'll be offended that you don't want to hang out with them, and they'll say it's because you were upset about Shannon because you've got some mad crush on me."

He really knew how to hit me where it hurt. If there was one thing I cared about way more than I should, it was what people thought of me. He knew that.

I did not want everyone at work thinking I was pining after Jake like some pathetic school girl. And he was right. It would look like that. I knew he wasn't saying it to be a smart ass. He was trying to look out for me and make sure I didn't become the target of any work gossip.

Without another word, he handed me his keys. I accepted.

WHEN ADAM AND Janelle finally came out of the bathroom (ick, I didn't even want to know what was going on in there), they said they were skipping the bonfire and heading back to the apartment. That meant it was just Jake and me. And Shannon.

If things were bad at the bar, they were worse at the bonfire. Shannon sat on his lap on a wooden bench by the fire. He made no attempt to move her. I saw the way she leaned into his chest like she belonged there. And the way he held onto her hips like he'd been touching them for years. There was a level of comfort between them that anybody could see. They were used to touching each other.

Jake and I had a high level of comfort between us, too, but it was a different kind. We had a more subtle type of intimacy. We could say anything to each other, no matter how embarrassing or personal. We could fight with confidence because we knew we'd always make up. We could tease without hurting. We could be at our best or at our worst and knew the other wasn't going anywhere. We could speak without opening our mouths. We could laugh together at things only we understood. We had almost two decades worth of memories and private jokes between us. Those were things no one could take away. If given the choice, I would definitely choose what we had over what they had. Anyone could have his present, but no one could ever take our past.

Knowing I had the better end of the bargain, I still sometimes wished I had the physical part of him, too. I wished I knew how to touch him to make him crazy. I wished he would touch my hips the way he touched hers. I wished I could lean back into his chest the way she did. And that he would wrap his arms around me from behind. She looked safe and comfortable and happy. She was confident and wanted. I wished I could feel that.

ALL GOOD THINGS

But I didn't. So when Katy asked if anyone wanted a shot of Jameson, I raised my hand. I'd said it before and I'd say it again – having bartenders for friends was a great thing.

I WOKE UP in a bed I'd never seen before, in a bedroom I'd never seen before. The walls of the room were a boring beige, and the furniture was cheap and generic, the kind of furniture one would put in a spare bedroom. The homemade quilt I was under was comfortable, but the sour feeling in my stomach was not.

The door to the bedroom was open and looked out into a plain white hallway. The house, I assumed it was Katy's, was quiet.

My phone and purse were sitting on the nightstand next to me. I reached for the phone to check the time. It was 9:34.

I sat up, cross-legged, to see if I could do some breathing exercises to calm my stomach. My knee came into contact with someone else's bare skin under the quilt. I let out a yelp that sounded like a barking dog.

Fuck!

I closed my eyes and tried to put together the events of the night before. I'd been upset seeing the closeness between Jake and Shannon. Katy had gotten out the Jameson. I had taken a shot. Maybe two. Okay, fine. I'd drunk a lot. But I *remembered* drinking a lot. I remembered nothing about being in bed with someone. I wouldn't forget something like that. Would I?

I put my head in my hands and rocked back and forth on the bed. Oh God. What did I do? Please tell me I did not have sex with some random guy. What if he didn't use a condom? It would be like losing my virginity all over again. And to a stranger. Without remembering. I felt like crying.

No. I wouldn't do that, I told myself as I tried to calm down. No matter how drunk I was, I would not do that.

I stopped the rocking because it wasn't helping my stomach and lifted the quilt to check myself out under the covers. I still had on the sundress I'd chosen for my date with Brandon. I ran a finger up my thigh until it reached fabric. My underwear was still there. That was a good sign. The odds were in my favor. I looked around the floor and didn't see any clothes or condom wrappers strewn about. And besides all of that, I didn't physically feel like I'd been reckless or violated. Things were looking up.

So who was this body under the covers next to me? The quilt was pulled all the way up over the person's head, probably because it was freezing. The only sound I could hear in the house was that of the central air blowing into the room.

I took a deep breath and pulled back the covers to reveal the mysterious person's identity.

Of course. So predictable.

"Jake!" My voice came out like a whisper-slash-yell.

I was relieved it was him, because I knew I hadn't been hurt in any way. But why was he there? Why wasn't he shacked up somewhere with Shannon Tanning?

He was on his back, one arm bent at the elbow with his hand tucked behind his head. He had taken off his shirt but left on his khaki shorts. His chest looked damn good with all of his tattoos. I didn't get to see him without his shirt very often, but when I did, I wanted to touch him. I could have touched him then, but what if he woke up and caught me? How embarrassing. He'd probably think I was a necrophiliac.

"Jake?" I asked, a little louder this time.

He opened his eyes, looked at me for a second, and then rolled onto his side toward me, tucked his hands under his cheek in a praying style, and closed his eyes again.

"Jake, wake up."

"I don't want to," he whined without opening his eyes.

"Why are we here?"

"We were too drunk to drive."

"But what are you doing in here? With me? I thought you were going to hook up with Shannon," I said. And then, with a case of verbal diarrhea, I added, "I hope you didn't have sex with her before you got into bed with me. That would be wrong in so many ways."

He sighed loudly and impatiently and got out of bed. As he walked over to the door, I couldn't help but stare at the dimples he had on his lower back, one on each side.

He quietly closed the door and headed back to the bed.

"Calm down before you wake everyone up," he said. "I did not have sex with Shannon. She was even drunker than you were. She's probably passed out on the bathroom floor right now."

So what was he saying? That he would have slept with her had she been sober? That he picked the least drunk one to get in bed with? That sleeping next to me was a consolation prize after his sure-thing started purging? And why did this bother me anyway? I had no claim on him.

He got back into bed and resumed his hands-under-cheek, eyes closed position.

I was in a bed. With Jake. With the door closed. My belly started to feel a little better. Probably because I was starting to ache in other areas. It was just ... those dimples. And the way his shorts hung so loosely without a belt. I could easily pull them off. I was wearing a dress. Easy access.

"What about me?" I asked.

"What about you?" he asked, his eyes still closed.

"Did you have sex with me?" I blurted out. I must have still been a little drunk if I was asking mortifying questions so bluntly. I hoped he was still a little drunk, too.

If he answered yes, I would only be disappointed that I didn't remember it, not that I'd done it.

He let out a short burst of laughter, almost like a snort, and opened his eyes to look right into mine. "Roxie, if I had sex with you, you would know it."

Ugh. Being in a bed with Jake was not good. Especially when he said things like that. Damn!

"We did make out for a little bit, though," he added.

I perked up. "We did?"

He laughed. "No. But you seemed pretty excited about it. Look, if that's something you'd be interested in, just let me know. If you don't tell Adam, I won't tell Adam."

ALL GOOD THINGS

"You know that's not what I'm interested in," I said defensively. "I'm just confused. I don't remember getting in bed with you."

"It's not a big deal, Rox. Katy was trying to get you to take shots with her, but you said you needed to stay reasonably sober because you had to drive us home. She told you not to worry about it because you could spend the night. That was when you two started drinking Jameson right out of the bottle. And that is how you ended up getting the only extra bed."

I was surprised his memories were so detailed considering that he wasn't paying any attention to me last night. "That explains why *I'm* here. But why are *you* here?"

"Because I wasn't going to sleep on the floor," he said with a smirk. "And I wasn't going to have you sleeping in here by yourself. If someone else came in here, you would've been too drunk to fight them off. Now can we go back to sleep, please?"

I was still sitting up, cross-legged. I wasn't confused anymore, but I was frowning. I'd spent a night in bed with Jake without knowing it. How unfair!

He looked up at my scowl. "What's wrong? And you better not tell you're mad at me for twat-blocking you."

I smiled at the memory and then shrugged as I played with one of the ties on the patchwork quilt covering my lap. "I'm a little disappointed," I answered honestly. "But not because you twat-blocked me. Because I got to spend the night with you and didn't even have the chance to enjoy it."

He smiled up at me, and I felt my heart do a little flip-flop. I think my uterus did one, too. Oh, how I loved that smile.

He patted the bed behind my back, implying that I should lie down. "There's still time," he said.

I lay back down, on my side, my back to him.

"I'm not going to touch you," he said quietly. I could feel his breath on the back of my neck. "It's not because I don't want to. It's just that I can't."

"I understand," I whispered.

"Do you?"

"Yeah. My brother would kick your ass."

He didn't respond immediately. Then he said, very quietly, "Right."

There was only an inch or two separating us, but I could feel the heat coming from his body. Being near him made my whole body feel heated, too, like I'd done another shot of whiskey.

He kept his hands off me, just as he said he would. Just knowing he was there, and hearing the quiet rhythm of his breathing, made me feel safe and comfortable and happy.

CHAPTER 9

SUMMER 1994

JAKE
Eleven years old

I'M THE ONE who brings in the mail. If I left it up to Mom, the bills would pile up in the mailbox until the post office stopped delivery. I set them on the table in the kitchen every day and let them pile up there instead, along with the cigarette butts in the ashtray. I swear that thing would never get emptied if I didn't dump it myself.

I am accustomed to seeing the envelopes come in with yellow or pink paper showing through the clear windows. I know they are shut-off notices and final warnings, but Mom acts like we're not in trouble. The table might be covered with bills, and the answering machine might be loaded with a bunch of threats, but she always seems to find a way to make it work.

She's like a superhero who masters in last-minute saves. I don't know what she has to do to get us by, but she does it. As flaky as she can be, I have to respect her for that.

I pull three envelopes from the mailbox and open the door to our small brick ranch. It's the house my mom grew up in, which she'd inherited when my grandparents died. I find Mom in the kitchen making tuna sandwiches.

"Hi, babe." Her wavy blonde hair bounces as she turns from the counter to look at me. My mom is prettier and younger than any of my classmates' moms. "I'm making lunch!"

She says this with more oomph than most people would because it's such an unusual occurrence.

"Nice," I say as I sit at the table and glace at the envelopes. Bill, bill ... and what's this? It's from the Department of Education.

I'm the only one in this household who goes to school, so I know this letter is about me. I feel a flash of excitement as I imagine what the letter could be about. Maybe they found out about my third place spelling bee award, and they'd like to recognize me in an award ceremony. Or maybe, because I'm so smart, they want me to skip a grade.

"Mom, we got a letter from the school."

"Oh?"

She sets a plate containing a sandwich and some potato chips on the table in front of me and takes the envelope.

She rips it open, unfolds the letter, and breathes out a loud sigh.

"What a relief," she says quietly. "It's so nice to get some good news in the mail for a change."

She sets the letter on the table and turns back to the counter to finish her sandwich.

I anxiously take a peek at the letter. And then I wish I hadn't.

As soon as I see the words 'Child Nutrition Program,' I know what it is. What I read only confirms my first thought. Mom's income level is low enough that I am now eligible to receive a free lunch every day at school.

I can't even think about eating this sandwich, considering I feel like I'm about to retch. How can she say this is good news? How is it a good thing that we are poor enough to get free stuff? This is awful news!

I get up and run. I run out the door and run the two blocks to Adam's.

I run straight to the back yard, right where I left him not twenty minutes ago.

Yep, just as I suspected. Adam is in the pool. He's been trying to get as much swimming in as he can before the weather turns cold and they have to close it for the season.

He looks startled when I come through the gate.

"What's the matter?" he asks. "Did you get locked out?"

I bend over at the waist and touch my knees as I try to catch my breath. I'd run all the way from my house.

Roxie comes out of the patio door just as Adam pulls himself out of the pool.

"What's wrong?" Roxie asks.

I get the words out between gasps. "Free lunch."

Roxie puts a hand to her open mouth. Even two grades below us, she knows that's not a good thing.

Adam looks down at the cement and shakes his head sadly.

"Man, that is a bummer."

Yeah. A bummer is putting it mildly. It's basically the end of my reputation.

There are two lines of kids in the cafeteria at school – those who are paying, and those who are on the free lunch list. As first-graders, this difference meant nothing to any of us. At our age, people know the difference between the two lines.

Some kids pity the ones in the free lunch line. Some get angry and repeat some nasty things they've heard from their parents.

I collapse into a patio chair feeling defeated. I am going to be in that line now. When school starts, in four days, I am going to be the butt of the jokes, the bullied, the target. They will be even harder on me because I'm new. They're tired of picking on the same kids year after year. I'm fresh meat.

I'm also a crossover. That means I'll be ridiculed by the non-frees, and universally hated by the frees. Not that I have ever joined in on the bullying, but I would be seen as an enemy nonetheless. I'll have the support of neither group. It's not right, but it's the way it is.

"It'll only be bad at first. It'll die down real soon. It always does. And you know you've got us on your side," Adam says.

ALL GOOD THINGS

"You could bring your lunch," Roxie suggests. "Then no one would even know. Just tell people you had to go on a special diet or something."

I shake my head. My mom will never put extra groceries in the house to make lunches if she knows I can get it for free at school. She is thinking of this as a victory, a blessing. If I turn around and say I don't want it, if she catches me walking out the door with a packed lunch, she'll flip.

"You know how pissed my mom would be. She wouldn't let me out of the house with a lunch."

"Then *I* can bring a lunch and give you my lunch money," Roxie offers.

It is a nice offer, but I will never take her money. I give her a look that says as much.

"Fine. Then I will bring *you* a lunch," she says, her chin in the air stubbornly. "That's my final answer."

"That's a nice offer. It means a lot to me that you would do that. But I can't let a little girl save me. I have to fight my own battles."

She frowns. I know I've hurt her by calling her a little girl when she was only trying to help.

She turns and heads back into the house. I think about going after her, but Adam shakes his head.

"She'll get over it. And everyone else will get over the free lunch thing, too. You'll make it look cool. You always do, man."

Yeah? Maybe he is right. Maybe I can be the one to break the barrier between the two groups, and we can all live happily integrated. It will be like *West Side Story*.

FOUR DAYS LATER we make the walk to school together – me, Adam, Roxie, and Roxie's friend, Allison. I keep my hands in the pockets of my jeans as I walk the few blocks to school. I try to look confident, but I'm nervous. It's the first day. Everyone is going to be checking everyone else out, like hunters looking for prey – their clothing labels, their shoe brands, their hair, their summer tans, their lunch lines. Nothing is unnoticed on the first day of school.

My new school clothes and shoes came from a store that also sells groceries. The Tommy Hilfiger hoodie Adam let me borrow will save me a little in that area. But this lunch line, in addition to the cheap clothes, is going to destroy me.

I really should have snuck a sandwich out of the house this morning. If I can blend in for the first few days, maybe a week, I can nonchalantly sneak over to the free lunch line with minimal notice. That would have been the best plan.

We walk into the school. The sixth grade lockers are at the beginning of the hall. Adam and I stop to find ours. Allison heads to the other end of the hallway to the fourth grade lockers. Roxie stays behind.

From the corner of my eye, I see her unzip her backpack and pull out a brown paper bag.

She waits until I make eye contact with her to discreetly gesture toward the bag. "Peanut butter and jelly, banana, juice box, and Cheez-Its," she says quietly.

ALL GOOD THINGS

I believe my ass was just saved by a girl. I know my smile practically takes over my whole face as I accept the bag from her hands. I playfully punch her in the shoulder. "Hey, thanks, Little Girl."

When she smiles, her blue eyes light up the hallway. "You're welcome."

JUNE 2005

CHAPTER 10

ROXIE

SOMETHING CHANGED AFTER the morning I spent in bed with Jake. There was a shift in the Jake & Roxie universe, and I had Shannon Tanning to thank. Her flirting with Jake brought out my carnal instinct and got me to give up a fight I'd been struggling with for years.

I was now admitting to myself the truth – I wanted Jake Odom. He was the best guy friend I'd ever had. He meant as much to me as my own family, and I had more fun with him than with anyone else. Above all, I trusted him, which, right now, was a huge deal.

If we could have fun together talking about caramel or condoms, imagine how much fun we could have if we stopped talking altogether. And it wasn't like I was going to fall in love with him and get hurt again. I'd known him eighteen years. If I were going to fall in love with him, I would have done it already. Friends had sex all the time. It was where the term 'friends with benefits' came from. We were both single and I was only here for the summer. Why shouldn't we join the masses? Why shouldn't we enjoy the benefits?

Worst-Case scenario: We don't have the chemistry I thought we would, and things fizzle out like a bad firework. We feel a little awkward at work for the rest of the summer, but it's only a few months. By the time I graduate and move back home, it'll be old news.

Best scenario: He fucks me real good all summer long, makes me forget all about spreadsheets and warning signs, and restores my faith in men.

Most likely scenario: We hook up, get the sexual tension out of our system and after a few weeks things calm down and we go back to being the Jake & Roxie we always were. Until it builds up again … and we need to release it … again. We could keep that shit going for years. I think I'd rather enjoy it.

Now that I knew I wanted him, I acted different. When I was getting ready for work, I wasn't thinking about impressing the other girls with my sophisticated updos and perfect smoky eye application. I was thinking about impressing *him*.

When we were at work together, I was aware of him at all times. When I went over to the bar to pick up my drinks, I got butterflies in my belly. The end of the night, when I sat at the bar waiting for him to get off work, and the drive home afterward, were my favorite parts of the day. I looked forward to breakfast and laundry with him on Sunday afternoons. When my phone lit up, I hoped to see his name on the screen. When my phone didn't light

ALL GOOD THINGS

up for awhile, I checked to see if I had any missed texts from him. When I didn't hear from him for a whole day, I hurt inside. And when I had to work and he had the day off, it was a total drag.

I had it bad. I hadn't yet written "Roxie <3 Jake" on my notebook, but that was only because I was afraid someone would see it and make fun of me. I was straight-up schoolgirl crushing on him. *Hard.*

IT WAS A Thursday, two weeks from the now infamous Subway date, bonfire, and sleepover. On Thursdays, Fridays and Saturdays, the kitchen stayed open until last call. That meant most of the employees stayed all night, not just the bartenders. Once we had the place cleaned up and restocked, we would all sit around a table counting our money, doing our paperwork, and drinking. Those who didn't have paperwork, like the busboys, bar backs, and dishwashers, just hung out and drank.

We were all seated at a round high-top table, except Jake and Katy who always counted out at the bar, when a busboy named Ben laid his empty beer bottle down in the middle of the table and spun it.

"Spin the bottle, anyone?"

Rachel snorted. "Please. The junior high just called. They want their bottle back."

Ben came back without missing a beat. "Yeah, well, 1999 called, and they want their insult back."

The dishwasher, Abe, said, "Hey, while we're at it, we should call a bunch of random strangers and ask if their refrigerators are running."

"Oh, totally!" Shannon agreed. "And then we can TP someone's house!" The other two had been sarcastic. I was pretty sure Shannon was serious.

We all had a good laugh as the bottle spun around and around ... until it stopped and pointed directly at me.

"Roxie," Ben clapped his hands together once. "Great pick," he said to the bottle. "What do you say, Roxie?"

Ben was only eighteen, but at least he was legal. He was sweet and polite. I didn't see any reason why I should deny him a kiss, and embarrassing him definitely wasn't something I wanted to do. I pushed myself up onto the table by my arms, leaned across, and kissed him on the lips. It was just a quick peck, nothing special. But he looked pleased.

"Now it's your turn to spin, Roxie," Rachel told me. For someone who was making fun of the game, she sure seemed to be enthralled by it.

The bottle spun around and around and pointed at Ben.

"Whoo hoo!" he said, throwing an arm into the air.

"You know the more times it lands on the same person, the deeper the kiss gets, right?" asked the bar-back, Chris.

I shrugged like it was no big deal, and Ben leaned over and kissed me, this time for a few seconds more than the last.

ALL GOOD THINGS

Everyone oohed and aahed like it was a spectator sport.

"I get to go again, I guess," Ben said afterward as he spun the bottle.

It landed on me again!

"There better be some tongue this time," Chris said.

Jake stepped over from the bar and snatched the bottle from the middle of the table. "We're done here, guys. Time to go home."

Rachel and Shannon exchanged pointed looks. Chris patted Ben on the shoulder.

"Maybe next time, bro," he said to Ben.

Jake walked toward the back door, throwing the bottle into the recycle bin on his way out, where it landed with a loud crash.

ONCE THE REST of us had cleaned up our mess and turned in our money and paperwork, we all walked out the back door together. Jake was sitting at one of the patio tables, leaning back in his seat with his hands clasped behind his head. The way he was sitting made the hem of his t-shirt rise. I could see his belt buckle and a little strip of his abs right above it. I took in a quick breath and did not give in to the urge I had to climb onto the chair with him. And pull up his shirt even higher. And kiss his neck. And undo his belt. Nope, I didn't do it. I stayed right where I was.

I watched the others walk out to their cars. Usually this was the time when Jake would lock the door and set the alarm.

He didn't get up.

I stood next to the table and looked down at the cemented patio floor. He must be mad at me about spin the bottle. I was probably going to get a scolding about kissing coworkers while on the clock. He was the manager on duty tonight, and I should have known better.

I dragged the toe of my sneaker across the cement in a nervous twitch. I heard the sounds of car doors closing, engines starting, and tires driving away from the parking lot.

He must have been waiting until everyone was gone. Then we'd probably go inside and sit in the office so he could write me up. Being in trouble with your boss was crappy. Being in trouble with your boss, who was also your best guy friend, was mortifying.

The only vehicle left in the parking lot was Jake's truck. The Bar was part of a strip of stores and restaurants in a popular area of Ann Arbor. By this time, the other parking areas were all empty as well. We were the last two people around, and I was glad no one else would see the scolding.

I snuck a look at him and saw he had the tip of his pinky in the corner of his mouth and seemed deep in thought. I wished his pinky were in my mouth instead. *My God, girl! You're about to get in trouble with your boss. Turn the hormones off for a sec!*

On second thought, that sounded a lot like a porn plot, so maybe I was onto something. Maybe if he asked me to sign a write-up I could convince him otherwise. Omigod. I seriously needed to get laid already.

ALL GOOD THINGS

I looked down at the ground again before he caught me watching him. I was starting to feel uncomfortable with the quietness.

"I have something for you," he said.

Yeah. Probably a written warning.

"Stay here," he said as he stood up. "I've got to get it from the truck."

I guess it wasn't a write-up after all, since he wouldn't keep that stuff in his truck.

I watched him walk to the truck and pull a box out of the bed, but it was too dark to see what it was.

He smiled at me when he got back to the patio and handed me the box. He looked pleased with himself, and I couldn't help but smile back.

It was a heavy cardboard box. I set it on the nearest patio table and opened it up. It was a set of dishes. And they were butt-ugly. If I had the need for a new set of dishes, I would not have chosen those.

"Umm, dishes," I said, trying to sound happy about it. "Thanks?"

He started laughing. "You don't know what they're for, do you?"

"No," I said, honestly.

"You said you needed to break something. And I drove by a yard sale this afternoon so I stopped to see if they had any dishes. I got this whole set for five bucks."

"You want me to break the dishes?" I repeated. The idea of smashing dishes had never occurred to me. But now that he brought it up, it sounded like it would be a blast.

"Do you want to break the dishes?" he asked.

Did I want to break the dishes? Could I say hell-mother-fucking-yes?

"Really?" I asked. Was this a bad idea? Would he think I had a screw loose if I broke them?

"Roxie, those are the ugliest plates I've seen in my life. I would love it if you destroyed them."

I picked a side plate out of the box and turned it over in my hand, examining it. "I've never broken anything on purpose before."

"Some things are made to be broken. And I think these things qualify. You want me to get it started?"

I handed him the side plate. He threw it onto the cement right outside the back door of The Bar. It broke into four pieces. The sound was so loud and probably sounded even louder because it was such an intrusion into the quiet and calmness of the night.

I timidly picked up another side plate and held it above my head with both hands. But I hesitated before throwing. What if I liked it? Would that mean I was seriously fucked up in the head?

Jake stepped up behind me. He put his right hand on my right hip and leaned in toward my left ear. "Go on," he whispered. He didn't need to whisper. There was no one else anywhere near us. But I didn't mind him being that close to me. I wished he'd say to hell with the dishes, bend me over one of the patio tables, and break me instead.

I swallowed hard and slammed the plate on the ground. It shattered into about a dozen pieces. It was loud, but the silence afterward seemed even quieter than before

I'd thrown the plate. The same thing seemed to happen inside of me. When I first threw the dish, I felt a rush of adrenaline, but it was quickly replaced with a calmness I hadn't felt before.

That was for lying to me about your age, I thought.

I picked up a dinner plate and smashed it.

That was for lying to me about your job.

Then another dinner plate.

That was for pretending you were going to class when you weren't.

Another dinner plate shattered.

That one was for lying to me about Thanksgiving.

I took a coffee mug from the box and slammed in into the cement.

For breaking your toe because I talked to a guy about homework while you were fucking someone else the whole time.

I took the last dinner plate and slammed it down harder than any of the others.

That was from your girlfriend. I wish I could throw it at you instead of the ground.

A bowl went next.

And from your poor baby. The poor innocent baby who you betrayed.

I didn't know when I started crying, but the next thing I knew, a complete set of dishes – dinner plates, side plates, bowls, and mugs – were in hundreds of pieces on the patio, and my hands were covering my face to hide the sobs.

I was angry with myself for losing control in front of Jake. This was probably an exercise I should have completed on my own. I kept my face covered because the whole scene was too intense for me to watch. I definitely couldn't bear to look at him.

I wasn't sure how long I stood there with my head in my hands, but I don't think it was very long before I felt his arms around me. It was only then when I stopped crying.

He waited until he was sure the dam was plugged, and then he asked, "Feel better?"

I took a deep breath and thought about it before I answered. The truth was that I did. I did feel better. I felt like I'd gotten all of my anger out of me, like an enema of the heart. "I feel embarrassed for crying in front of you," I said shyly, "but I feel better about the other things."

"Hey, don't worry about that. It's not like I haven't cried in front of you, right?"

I nodded, briefly remembering the Father's Day I'd caught him crying under a table in our living room when we were in elementary school.

"Are you ever going to tell me what the other things were?" he asked quietly.

"Probably not," I answered honestly. "It's too embarrassing. I just got played. That's all. I trusted someone when I shouldn't have."

We each grabbed a broom and dustpan from the janitor's closet. Cleaning the mess wasn't nearly as fun as making it, but with the two of us working together it didn't take any time at all. We were in Jake's truck within minutes, driving down the lonely roads in an eerie quietness. The term "calm before the storm" was popular, but there was also a calm that came after a storm, when the tree branches lay scattered all over the roads, vinyl siding hung from homes, and people stepped out of their front doors cautiously, to assess the damage in silent, open-mouthed stares. I guess I had torn through that patio like a storm back there. Hurricane Roxie.

He used the controls on his side of the door to roll both of our windows all the way down. It was a great summer night – not too humid, not too chilly – the kind of breeze that felt good after a long night at work. It was the kind of night I would have slept outside on our trampoline when I was a teenager. I wondered what my parents ever did with the trampoline. I should totally put it back up if they still had it.

"It's a nice night," Jake said as he stuck his arm out of the window and opened his hand to feel the air.

The weather? Really, Jake? Was there anything more awkward than talking about the weather? I mean, it *was* a nice night. I'd just thought the same thing myself. But that didn't mean we needed to discuss it.

"You should definitely do the dog right now," he said.

Do the dog? Was that a yoga pose or a sexual position? I gave him a questioning look.

"Stick your whole head out of the window," he said. "You know, the way the dogs do it."

"You want me to do it the way the dogs do it?" I repeated.

"Yes."

He reached his hand over to my seatbelt and pressed the button to release it.

I gasped and clicked it back into place quickly. "Jake! What if we get into a car accident? There are drunk drivers out here right now!"

"Do you always have to think of the worst-case scenario?"

"Yes."

"That is the exact reason you need to stick your head out that window right now."

I shook my head.

"I know you think it sounds stupid. Hey, I thought iced coffee sounded stupid when I first heard about it, too. But then somebody forced me to try it. Who was that? Oh yeah. It was you. And now it's the greatest thing about my mornings. Iced coffee changed my life, Roxie. Now let the dog change yours."

I couldn't help but smile. "Should I do a slow clap right now?"

"No, you should shut up and stick your head out the window."

I sighed.

"I'll go down a side street," he said.

I rolled my eyes in annoyed defeat. He wasn't going to let this go.

I unclasped the seat belt and used the doorframe to push my shoulders out of the open window. I faced forward and let the perfect summer breeze blow into my face and through my hair. Jake was right. It did feel good. I even kind of wanted to scream and throw my arms out

ALL GOOD THINGS

like people do in the movies when they stick their heads out of the sunroof, but I was too timid to try that on my first time. Maybe next time.

When my body was back in the truck and buckled up, I couldn't hide the stupid, goofy grin on my face.

Jake turned on the radio and "Summer Breeze" by Seals & Croft came out of the speakers. I looked at his smirk and knew.

"You planned this!" I accused.

He shrugged. "Maybe I did. But you liked it, right?"

"What would I do without you?" I asked, a rare moment of honesty overtaking me.

"You would always play it safe."

I nodded. That was true.

"What would I do without you?" he asked.

"Drink hot coffee all summer?"

"Probably. Hey, did Adam tell you he's going away for the weekend?"

"No," I answered.

"Yeah. Cleveland. It's the annual guys' weekend with the basketball team."

"Oh yeah," I said. "I remember now."

Adam had played for his college basketball team. The organization had a reunion weekend every summer in a different place. This year it was Cleveland.

"So I guess it's just me and you this weekend."

"Hmm," I said, wheels spinning.

"Or maybe I shouldn't assume you'll be around to hang out with me. You might be busy cradle-robbing with your boyfriend, Ben."

"Ha-ha. You know, he's not much younger than my last boyfriend."

"Who?"

"Jim. The guy from Chapel Hill. He just turned nineteen."

"Oh, I didn't know that."

"Don't feel bad. I didn't either."

I turned and looked out the window. He didn't ask any questions, and for that I was glad.

CHAPTER 11

Tonight was the night. I was going to seduce Jake. He had been right about one thing: I needed a guy this summer. But he was wrong to think I'd settle for just anyone. Why would I settle when I could have the best? By this point, I was 100% convinced there was no one better than Jake Odom. He made me feel like I was living in a fairy tale, in a land of make-believe. The things he did, the things he said, the way he looked at me, the ways he'd touched me on the few times he'd touched me, it didn't get better than that. And one thing I could count on was that he would never intentionally hurt me. He was like the safety net under my tightrope. He was my safety guy. Just like your safety school was the one you knew you'd get into, even if it wasn't the one with the best reputation. He was the guy I knew wouldn't hurt me. If he was the only guy I could imagine myself trusting, then it was time to stop living in a fairy tale and start living on *Cinemax: After Dark*.

I spent some extra time getting ready for work. I put on my sexiest bra and panty set and made sure everything was waxed, plucked, exfoliated, and moisturized. I even stuck a travel toothbrush in my work bag. The idea was to meticulously plan the seduction, but make it look like it happened by accident.

It was a busy night at work, and I was more of a spaz than usual. I made several mistakes throughout the night, dropping a few dirty glasses at dinner, and during the bar rush I accidentally punched in an order for two Bloody Marys when I was supposed to hit the button for two Blow Jobs. Any other bartender would have given me shit for wasting their time (and the bar's alcohol), but Jake didn't get mad at me. He just set the Bloody Marys aside, and looked the other way when I drank them.

Nobody seemed to notice, or care, that I wasn't on top of my game, and I didn't care either. There was something else I'd rather be on top of.

At closing time I sat up at the bar while I counted out. Jake set a drink in front of me without me having to ask. I drank it slowly, so as not to get too buzzed and screw up my plan by doing something embarrassing. And if I was finally going to hook up with Jake, I wanted to do it with total clarity.

"We're going to Katy's," Shannon said to us on her way out. She was the last of the crew to leave besides us. "You guys coming?"

"Um," Jake seemed like he was stalling, like maybe he was waiting for me to answer. Maybe he had the same idea

ALL GOOD THINGS

I'd had when I found out Adam would be going away for the weekend.

"Not me," I said. "I'm pretty tired tonight. But thanks for the invite."

Maybe it was wishful thinking, but I could have sworn Jake looked relieved. "Um, yeah, me too," he told her.

She gave me a look. A look like she knew my intentions. Then she tilted her head toward me and gave me a small smile. I think it was silent girl-code for *Get him, girl*. Maybe she wasn't so bad.

"Okay then. See you guys later." She tossed her blonde hair over her shoulder and walked away. I heard the back door close a moment later.

"Are you really tired?" he asked me.

I shook my head.

"You need another drink?"

YES! Desperately! I was freaking out! "Nope."

He grabbed my empty glass from the bar, dipped it into the sanitizer solution in the sink, rinsed it, and set it upside down on the drying mat with the rest of the clean glasses. I loved watching Jake behind the bar. He oozed sex appeal. The way his muscles flexed under the short sleeve of his Raising the Bar t-shirt when he poured liquor or washed glasses, gahhhh, it made me hot.

Outside of work he was my silly, goofball friend. But when he was behind the bar, he had swag. He was cool and confident. He knew what he was doing and he loved what he was doing. I wondered which Jake he would be in bed. Would he be silly or sexy? Playful or serious? Passive or aggressive? Thinking I might soon get to find out was causing my whole body to shiver with anticipation and fear.

We got into the truck and I took control of the radio, turning it to my favorite pop station.

They were playing our song! I turned up the volume so we could jam to The Bar's unofficial theme song of the summer, the catchy dance tune "Pon de Replay," by someone I'd never heard of named Rihanna. We liked to listen to it at the end of the night when we were cleaning up. It was one of those songs you couldn't help but dance to. If anyone were to sneak a peek into the windows of The Bar at night, they'd see us singing and dancing while wiping tables and sweeping floors, like a scene straight out of *Annie*.

Without missing a beat, Jake and I started bobbing our heads and singing along. We were as serious about it as *American Idol* contestants, with the over-emphasized lip movements and smoldering looks at the imaginary cameras. The seriousness only lasted about fifteen seconds until we both burst into a laughing fit.

I was thinking he'd be more playful than serious.

Remembering my meticulously planned "accident," I turned the radio down.

"Let's do something different tonight," I said. My heart was pounding, and I could feel a nervous buzz in my belly. Even though it was over eighty degrees outside, I was shivering with nervous energy.

"Like what?" he asked.

"Like … not taking me home." I hoped he didn't hear my voice shaking.

"Okay. Where do you want to go?"

This was the point of no return. If I said what I wanted to say, and he denied me, it would make things weird between us. We would never be the same no matter how many snowball fights or wrestling matches or cookie baking montages were added to our film. He would pity me, and I would be embarrassed every time I was around him. I would be the pitiful little sister of his best friend who had some childish crush on him and had once tried to seduce him. I would forever be the girl he didn't want.

On the other hand, if I was successful, if he wanted me like I wanted him, I had no doubt it would be anything less than amazing.

Either way, things would be different.

I still had a chance to change my mind. I could ask him if he wanted to grab some beer from his fridge and go to a playground or something. I could live the rest of my life never knowing what might have happened if I'd been brave enough to say what I'd wanted to say and do what I'd wanted to do.

But what the hell kind of life would that be? Nah. I couldn't do that. He was worth the risk. We were worth the risk.

"I want to go home with you."

I heard him suck in a breath real quick, and he was quiet for way too long for my comfort. I couldn't be sure, but I thought he might be waiting until he got his breathing under control before he spoke.

"Are you fighting with your parents?" he asked curiously.

"No." Leave it to Jake to need this spelled out for him. "Did you leave your sheets in the washing machine? I've done that before."

"No, Jake." I stared straight ahead through the windshield. "It's not that I don't want to go to my house. It's that I want to go home with you. Get it?"

"Umm ..."

"Oh jeez," I said, exasperated. "You're being a buzz kill. Never mind. Just take me home."

"No. We can go to my place."

"Forget it." I was probably overreacting and jumping the gun on this. I was so amped up with adrenaline and anxiety that I was bailing at the first sign of doom.

He turned the truck to go toward his apartment instead of my house.

"I said forget it. Take me home."

"I don't want to," he said. "You said you wanted to come home with me, so that's where we're going."

"It's pointless now. You've ruined the moment." As he turned onto his street I crossed my arms and stared out the passenger window, feeling mortified that this conversation was even happening.

"You can't blame me for ruining a moment I didn't even know we were having. Let's start over. Tell me to take you home with me again."

He pulled into his apartment complex, found a parking spot and put the truck into park.

"I feel really stupid," I said, looking down at my hands as I nervously pushed my cuticles back. "Can you please just forget this ever happened and take me home? There's really no way to make the moment sexy again."

He turned off the ignition. "I can make this sexy again." It was Bartender Jake speaking. He sounded confident, and he had good reason. He could make anything sexy. But he didn't *know* it, which made him even hotter.

I looked up from my fingernails warily and locked eyes with him. I may have lost my breath for a sec. He wasn't playing dumb anymore. He knew what I was coming over for, and the look in his eyes let me know he was ready and willing to give me exactly what I wanted. He totally eye-fucked me right there in the truck and that was enough to make the moment sexy again.

"Will you take me home with you?" I asked again, quietly, suddenly feeling shy.

Jake got out of the truck and walked over to my side. He opened my door and met my eyes again, then reached across my waist to unbuckle my seat belt without ever looking away. He put his hands on my hips and turned my body toward him.

"I've been wanting to get this uniform off you all summer," he said.

"Then what are you waiting for?" I asked.

He could make it sexy again.

He slid his hands behind me, grabbed onto my ass and pulled my whole body toward him until I was as close to him as I was going to get.

Then he kissed me. Jake kissed me!

It seemed like our tongues touched even before our lips. His mouth caused chaos to my entire body. All at once I was dizzy and throbbing, weak but powerful. I wanted him *rightthissecond*, but I wanted to take our time and enjoy it. I was a frenzy of contradictions.

The kiss was perfect, like it had been professionally choreographed. I had been ready for this for years, and I think he'd been ready, too. I could definitely tell he was ready now. I reached my arms around his waist to keep him close to me and there was nothing partial or halfway going on in his jeans.

Fuck! I couldn't wait. I needed this. Right *now*. We could take our time another night. This was urgent.

"Jake," I managed to get out before he moved his mouth to my neck and I nearly died right there in the passenger seat.

"Roxie," he said, in more of a pant.

"I need you," I whispered.

He pulled his face away from my neck to look at me for a second. He touched his forehead to mine. "I need you, too," he whispered breathlessly, and then took over my mouth with his again.

What we really needed was to get out of the truck and into the apartment. But I didn't want him to stop anything he was doing to get us there.

He turned around so his back was between my legs and told me to get on. He wanted to give me a piggyback ride? Um, okay. I wrapped my arms around his neck and my legs around his hips. He reached his arms behind to get a good grip and then pulled us away from the truck and closed the door with his elbow.

I couldn't help but smile all the way to the apartment building. I hadn't been given a piggyback ride since I was like five. When we reached his door he set me down, but kept my hand in his while he unlocked the door, like he was afraid I'd run if he let go. I liked it.

When we were inside he gently pushed me into the closed door and rested his forearm above my head. He pressed his forehead into mine again and I felt like the two of us were the only people in the world. When he smiled at me, my knees quivered. A lot of things quivered.

"Do you want a beer?" he whispered.

Maybe he felt obligated to offer me a drink since I was a guest. Maybe it was a bartender thing. Maybe he thought he needed to get me buzzed to make sure I didn't change my mind.

I shook my head. "No," I whispered. "I want *you*."

He lifted me up again, this time he held me "crossing-the-threshold" style. As a size ten, (sometimes twelve when I was really happy and not forgetting to eat), I wasn't exactly a tiny girl. I wasn't used to being carried around. But I could definitely *get* used to it, because it was pretty freaking cool.

He kissed me as he carried us down the hall and into his room. He didn't pause to close the door or turn on a light. He threw me on his bed (loved the aggression), and I landed with a small bounce. I ended up toward the top, with my head near the pillows. Standing at the foot of the bed, he leaned over, grabbed my thighs and quickly pulled my body down toward him. Taking control, it was Bartender Jake.

I had never been in his room before, and I took a second to take a quick look around. There was a little bit of light in the room from the glowing screen of his computer monitor.

I was overcome by everything Jake – his smell on the sheets, his clothes on the floor, his CDs stacked haphazardly and unorganized (gasp!) on his desk, right next to a framed photo of him at age six with his grandparents. I'd seen the picture before. They died shortly after the photo had been taken.

I was surprised to see there was also a framed photo of him, Adam, and me on his bookshelf. The picture had been taken at Cedar Point when we were teenagers. I remembered the day very well. My parents let us each bring a friend to Cedar Point that summer. Adam and Jake had each brought their flavor-of-the-day girlfriends, and I'd brought Allison. Their high-maintenance girlfriends had to stop at nearly every bathroom to reapply their makeup and fix their hair, which kept frizzing out in the humidity. By mid-afternoon the boys made a pact: no girlfriends allowed at Cedar Point. Then we all had a blast seeing how many different ways we could ditch them for the remainder of the day. I even convinced Jake's girlfriend to come on a water ride with me. I swore to her that no one actually got wet, that it was just a little mist of water to cool everyone down. Yep, she got drenched. And her navy blue shorts must have been new because the color from the dyes ran down her legs making her look like a Smurf. Good times.

I was also surprised Jake had a bookshelf. He reads? I would have to check out the titles later.

What else didn't I know about him?

As he lowered himself over me, I could feel his body with nearly every inch of mine. My face was still turned toward the bookshelf and the picture of us. He kissed my cheek first. Then he used a finger to turn my face up to look at him. I looked into the brown eyes that had been lighting up my world for as long as I could remember. But they looked different – scared. I was feeling scared myself. It really dawned on me then just what was going on. This wasn't hooking up with a sexy bartender from work. This was Jake! This was the boy I'd caught crying under the table in my living room. This was the guy who gave me the Heimlich maneuver when I was choking on bubblegum. The guy who rescued me countless times in high school when I was too drunk to drive. The guy who wrapped me up in his sweatshirt when my boyfriend betrayed me. As sexy and confident as he seemed to be at work, he was still just my Jake – my goofy, funny, sweet, Jake.

"You know you're my best friend, right?" I asked quietly. Even though it had pretty much always been true, I'd never actually said it out loud. Guys didn't go around claiming anyone as being their "best friend." That was more of a girl term. Even Jake and Adam never called each other that.

"Does this mean you're going to give me half a heart? Or a braided bracelet?" See? Still Jake. I knew he was teasing me, and it was funny, but I wished he had just said something nice to me in return.

I turned my head and looked at the picture on the shelf again. I felt stupid. "No. I just wanted you to know."

He pushed my face up again. "Hey," he said softly as he twirled a strand of my hair around his finger. "I was just kidding. You know you're my best friend, Rox. I'm not gonna screw this up. I promise."

I didn't know if he would keep that promise, but I wanted him badly enough to say – to hell with it. *Screw me up all you want, Jake.*

He glanced over at the photo of us on the bookshelf. I turned my head to look at it again, too. Cheek to cheek, we looked at it together. I suspected we were both thinking the same things. Were we making a mistake? Would things change for the better or for the worse? What would it be like if this didn't work? Would we be okay?

"Are you sure you wanna do this?" he whispered. "We won't be able to go back if we do."

I was sure of one thing: I wanted more skin and less clothing between us. Now. I pulled his shirt up over his head and threw it to the floor. We couldn't go back now either way. This wasn't a sweet twenty-second kiss in a dorm room like last time. I could feel his hard-on between my legs. You can't go back from that.

"I'm sure," I whispered.

He pulled my turquoise tank top over my head and kissed my bare shoulder as he reached under my back to unclasp my bra. He threw it off the side of the bed and kneeled between my legs to get a better look.

"Damn. I wish I had turned on the light."

It was better that he hadn't. Boobs didn't look good while a woman was flat on her back. The real ones fell out to the sides and looked like pancakes; the fake ones stood unnaturally tall, like grapefruits. It wasn't a good look on anyone.

"It's okay," he said. "We can make up for it tomorrow in the daylight."

His chest landed on mine again, and he ran his hands along the sides of my breasts where my chest met his.

He kissed me under my chin. Nobody had ever kissed me there before.

"I'm sure, too," he whispered. Then he unbuttoned my little black shorts and pulled them off.

CHAPTER 12

I WOKE UP in the morning filled with dread. The morning after a first time was pretty much guaranteed to be uncomfortable, whether you'd just met them the night before, or you'd known them for years. There were always so many questions. Did they mean anything they said? Did they regret it? Were they drunk? Did they like it? Did they want to do it again or did they want to get the heck out of there bad enough to chew off their own arm?

I was on my side, facing the desk and the digital alarm clock that said 10:16 in red numbers.

All through the night I'd been aware of his arms around my waist, his chest pressed into my back, his breath on my neck. His smell was everywhere. It smelled like dryer sheets and Tide. I'd felt him kiss my cheek before I'd fallen asleep, and I can honestly say I'd never felt more comfortable or more protected in all my life.

But that was then, in the middle of the night. Now there was a harsh light coming through the windows in his bedroom. There was a coldness. I no longer felt him. He was gone. He'd left the room.

Don't panic, I told myself. He probably had to pee. I decided to pretend I was still sleeping and wait until he came back. If he crawled back into bed and snuggled up to me, I would know everything was okay. If he didn't, I'd get out of there as soon as possible so he wouldn't see me cry.

Then I remembered I had no way to get home besides him. Adam was out of town, and I couldn't call one of my parents to pick me up at Jake's. They would totally know! How absolutely humiliating.

I guessed I could call Allison. She wouldn't be judgmental about it, I didn't think. But I would prefer if I didn't have to call anyone. I would prefer if Jake wanted me to be here when he came back to the room. I would prefer, very much, if he wasn't out in the living room trying to figure out how to get rid of me.

I heard him enter the room and I tensed up. This was the moment of truth. Come back to bed, Jake. Please come back to bed. It would hurt so much if you didn't, and I can't handle anymore hurt right now. Please, come back.

Chill out, I told myself. He was my safety guy, remember? Even if he didn't come back to bed, it would be okay. It was fucking Jake for Christ's sake. He loved me. He might have decided he didn't want to see me naked again, but he loved me no matter what. I didn't need to be so tense and scared. We could make a joke of it, have a good laugh, and move on with our lives. Or else he'd come back to bed and I wouldn't have to worry about it.

I heard his closet door open and close. Was he getting clothes out? Was he going to get dressed so he could take me home? Oh, the embarrassment.

I felt him sit down on my side of the bed, right on the edge by my knees. I could feel him looking down at me, but I was too afraid to open my eyes. I didn't want to see his look of pity.

I had the blanket pulled all the way up to my neck, and I felt him tug at it to pull it down. I was completely naked underneath and I quickly reached up and grabbed it to keep it from being pulled below my shoulders.

I finally opened my eyes to find him smiling down at me.

"Tense much?" he asked.

"Trying to check girls out while they're sleeping much?"

"I knew you were fake sleeping."

I sat up, cross-legged, and kept the blanket pulled tightly against my chest. "How'd you know I was faking?"

"Because you weren't breathing. Either you were faking it, or you were dead."

"Right."

"I wanted to make you breakfast, but you know I can't cook. So I went to McDonald's"

I perked up. *Please say you got me a McDonald's Coke!* "What'd you get me?"

"Sausage biscuit with cheese, and a Coke. With a packet of grape jelly."

YES! And he remembered I liked jelly with my biscuit. I freaking loved this kid!

"I freaking love you!" I said. Oh, maybe I shouldn't say stuff like that out loud anymore. I asked him where the food was before he had a chance to react to my outburst of love.

"It's in the kitchen."

He stood up and walked toward the door. When he got there he turned around and waved for me to follow him.

"Go ahead," I said. "I'll be there in a minute." I needed to get dressed first, and I wasn't confident enough to get dressed in front of him.

"I'll wait for you."

I shook my head.

"Roxie. I had my tongue in your vagina last night. I think the modesty ship has left port."

"Says the guy who is fully clothed," I argued. He had gotten dressed in a t-shirt and shorts to go to McDonald's.

"Would you feel more comfortable if I got undressed?"

Actually, yes, I would. I nodded.

He pulled off his shirt and threw it on the ground. He made tattoos look so hot. Fuck, Jake! Now I wasn't hungry anymore. All I wanted was him. Again.

"An eye for an eye," he said. "Drop the blanket."

I let the blanket drop to my waist. The room was bright. The view was much nicer when I was sitting up. I had never been modest about my chest before. My butt maybe, my thighs for sure, my belly, but never my breasts. They were my best feature and I wasn't nervous to have them exposed in complete daylight – as long as I was upright.

He took a deep breath and looked like he was in pain. "Is it okay if I'm not hungry anymore?" he asked.

I nodded. "An eye for an eye, right? I need to return a favor."

"Right now? But your Coke might go flat."

I motioned with my finger for him to come closer. When he reached the bed I unbuttoned his shorts. "This won't take long. The ice won't even have a chance to melt."

When we were done eating our McDonald's (which was still warm when we got to the kitchen, by the way), he asked if we could go back to sleep. I liked the way he said "we," like we were a team, like we were in this together.

We snuggled up and fell asleep, happy and peaceful. I really did freaking love this kid. And I meant that in the least romantic way possible. Honestly. Cross my heart.

"When I woke up this morning," I confessed later that afternoon as we ate leftover pizza in bed, "and you weren't here, I thought you were trying to think of a way to get rid of me without being a total douche."

He stopped chewing for a second. He looked guilty for making me feel that way, but I could tell he appreciated my honesty. When he swallowed his food he apologized. "I don't usually have girls spend the night here. I wasn't sure what to do. I didn't want to offer you up a bowl of Cinnamon Toast Crunch."

ALL GOOD THINGS

"I really loved McDonald's. Especially since you knew what to get me." I paused, hoping my next comment didn't sound too presumptuous. "But, just so you know, if I ever wake up here again, Cinnamon Toast Crunch is my favorite food ever."

"Okay," he said carefully. "I'll remember that. In case you ever wake up here again."

Did that mean he wanted me to wake up here again? Was this a one-night-stand or the first of many? Should I ask him?

He seemed pretty normal, definitely not as nervous as I was.

Jake thought the best part of a relationship was the beginning, when both parties were only showing their best cards. I disagreed. There was too much uncertainty at that time. Everyone was at their best, yes, but they were also on their toes. No one ever relaxed. I wished I could just loosen up with Jake and eat the pizza and not worry about what was coming in the future. Instead, I was tense and uncertain, and my muscles were starting to ache. I didn't know what he was thinking, or how he felt, and I didn't like it at all.

When we finished our pizza, he took the empty pizza box to the kitchen to throw it away. When he came back to the bedroom he opened up the top drawer of his dresser and pulled out a new pair of boxers.

"I'm gonna take a shower," he told me.

"Okay," I said with a little jealousy. I'd wanted to take a shower since I woke up that morning, but didn't want him to think I was too comfortable there, so I didn't ask.

Like that scene in *Top Gun* when Tom Cruise went to Charlie's house for their first date and he asked if he could take a shower. I couldn't sleep at someone's house for the first time and just be like, "I'm getting in the shower." How strange.

"Do you want to come?" Jake asked, interrupting my random thoughts about Tom Cruise.

"Yes, please," I said eagerly.

And I did. More than once.

Jake Odom was fucking amazing.

"Damn," I said as I towel-dried my hair in the bathroom after our shower. I had another towel wrapped tightly around my body. "You'd think we'd been doing that for years." It was true. If our kisses seemed choreographed, the rest was a complete dance routine. We were like professionals.

He was standing in front of the sink shaving with an electric razor. He had a towel wrapped around his waist. My comment made him pause, the buzzing of the razor stopping as he thoughtfully tilted his head to the side. He was choosing his words wisely.

"We have," he said quietly, looking at me through the reflection in the mirror. "In my head anyway." He smiled at me in the mirror before he turned the razor back on.

What was he saying? That he'd been fucking me in his mind for years? If I were being honest with myself, I'd have to say the same was true for me. But I was feeling too cautious to admit it. He wouldn't be safe for very long if I started talking about my feelings or any mushy garbage like that.

"I'm glad you got in so much practice," I told him. "It's definitely paying off." I changed the subject before anything got icky-feeling. "I guess I should get home so I can get ready for work." I had to be at work in two hours.

"Do you want to wear something of mine?" he asked. "So you don't have to put your old clothes back on?"

That was considerate of him.

"Okay," I said quietly.

I followed him into his room. He pulled open a drawer and grabbed a gray t-shirt and a pair of black gym shorts and set them on the bed.

He selected a different outfit for him to wear and let his towel fall to the floor with no modesty at all. Thud.

He pulled on a pair of boxer shorts before he realized I was still standing there next to the bed, gripping my towel closed tightly.

He looked at me impatiently.

"When are you gonna cut this shit out?" he asked. "Do you really think, as many times as we've had sex today, that I haven't seen you naked?"

That was completely different. Didn't guys get it? When you were in the throes of passion, no one was paying any attention to stretch marks or cellulite or dry skin or pimples or anything else undesirable. It was a completely different story to stand naked in front of someone when sex was not in play.

I glared at him, tightened the knot on the towel, and grabbed the t-shirt off the bed. I could get dressed without showing him a thing! So there!

I had the t-shirt over my head, and couldn't see anything but gray cotton, when I felt his hands at the top of my towel, threatening to remove it. In a panic I hurried and pulled the t-shirt over my head so I could see again. He gave me a shit-eating grin and pulled the t-shirt I'd just put on *back* over my head and threw it to the side.

He held my shoulders and moved his face close to mine to drive home his point. "I saw everything," he said. "And there wasn't a single part I didn't like. So stop trying to hide from me."

He pushed my shoulders back to nudge me closer to the bed. I felt his comforter touch the backs of my knees. It had been only twelve hours since we moved out of the friend zone, but I already knew enough to recognize that look in his eyes.

"You can't be serious," I said.

"I'm sorry," he said, not sounding sorry at all. "But when I'm done with you, you're going to need another shower."

He pulled my towel open. I didn't fight him as it fell to the floor.

I pushed the elastic band of his boxers down until they dropped to the floor, too.

I'd never been with a guy with this much stamina before. One after another like that? I'd be damned if I was going to be the first one to tire out.

He reached over to his nightstand and opened up the drawer to get a condom.

"This is the last one," he said. "I'll get more after I drop you off."

Why did he need more? Did he need to replenish his stash for the next chick he brought home? Or did he need more because he planned on using them with me? I wish I knew. I wish I knew what he was thinking, but we hadn't exactly stopped having sex long enough to have any kind of conversation. Not that that was a bad thing. At least I knew he wanted me. That was a good thing, right? It had to be a good thing.

IN THE END, I put my old clothes back on since I was going to need to shower again anyway. By the time we got into Jake's truck I had a very small window of time in which to get myself ready and get to work. Being in the daylight, outside, I started to feel awkward again. This whole thing was like being on a rollercoaster. When we were naked, everything was good. It felt right. It felt normal. It felt comfortable.

But as soon as we were dressed and in a non-sexual setting, I started to feel nervous and tense and uncomfortable and ... just weird. I didn't like it.

We drove about a mile in silence. It was the longest mile of my life.

He cleared his throat.

This was it. The gentle let-down speech he'd been rehearsing in his mind.

"So I was thinking," he said, "that it would be best if we didn't –"

Yep. Just as I thought. I looked out the window so I didn't have to see his face.

"If we didn't," he repeated, "let anyone at work know about this. It's not because I'm trying to hook up with other girls, so don't think that. But I know Zeke wouldn't approve. And there are certain people there who wouldn't make it easy on us, especially on you. I've seen it happen before. They get into your business and it turns into a he said-she said disaster."

"Okay," I said with a nod. I didn't want them in my business either.

"And it would be great if your brother and your parents didn't know either. At least not right away. Not until we figure out what this is."

"I agree."

"Good. So I'll get more condoms, and you can pack an overnight bag for tonight if you want. We both have tomorrow off, and Adam won't be home 'til around dinnertime."

"You want me to come over again tonight?"

"Well, yeah ... I mean, if you want to. If you don't, it's okay. I'll just go home and think about you while I jerk off."

I laughed out loud and shook my head. "Of course I want to."

"Good."

"I guess this means I'm your secret."

"Yeah. Just for now."

"I'm your dirty little secret."

"Say it again and watch how fast I pull this truck over."

"Do not pull the truck over. We don't have any condoms."

"I don't need a condom for what I want to do to you."

"Okay. Pull the truck over."

"Ha! Nope. You'll have to wait. I can't have you late for work. I'm your boss, remember?"

"I remember. But make sure you remind me tonight, okay?"

He pulled into the driveway, and I put my hand on the door handle. I didn't kiss him goodbye. That would be weird. That would be like a boyfriend and girlfriend thing to do. And we weren't boyfriend and girlfriend.

I opened the door and hopped out.

"See you at work, Little Girl."

CHAPTER 13

I WAS GLAD I'd worn my work clothes home because my parents were in the kitchen having dinner when I walked in the back door. I knew they had to have seen Jake's truck pull up. Coming in the house wearing yesterday's clothes made it look like we'd been out partying all night, which they were used to. Coming in wearing a guy's clothes would have given me away for sure.

"Hi, Mom!" I said cheerfully. "Hi, Dad!"

I felt like Michael J. Fox in *The Secret of My Success* during the "Walking on Sunshine" scene. I was happier than a bird with a French fry. I wanted to throw my arms in the air and say, "Can I get a hell yeah?"

"Hey," Dad said. "We cooked brats on the grill if you want one."

I grabbed a potato chip from the open bag on the kitchen island. "No thanks," I said, trying to be casual and not too giddy. "I'll eat at work."

"Do you need a ride?" Mom asked.

"Yes," I said. "That would be great. I'll be down in a few."

Because I was short on time, I couldn't spend as long getting ready as I usually did. I put my hair in a French braid while it was still wet and did my makeup – very carefully – in the car while Mom drove me to The Bar.

I was bouncing around the place like a bundle of nerves for the first few hours. *Can they tell?* I wondered about my co-workers. I also wondered what he was doing. Had he changed his mind about wanting me to come over tonight? Maybe he had some time to think about it after he dropped me off, and realized we'd made a mistake and now he was trying to figure out how to tell me. Maybe I was just being paranoid. Hopefully I was just being paranoid.

He got there at eight. I was so hyper-aware of my surroundings that I was pretty sure I knew of his presence as soon as his slip-resistant shoe hit the tile inside the back door.

In my peripheral vision I watched him walk over to the bar and make himself comfortable behind it. I was busy taking an order at a table and unable to give him any kind of greeting.

It had been a good thirty seconds since I'd asked the customer what kind of potato she wanted with her steak. It wasn't a life or death decision. She wasn't a doctor weighing the pros and cons of a risky surgery. She wasn't the president of a dying country trying to decide on a stimulus plan. She wasn't even a judge on *American Idol* trying to pick the top twelve contestants, because even that might have made a difference in someone's life. This was just a potato, and it wasn't going to change the world.

"Are the fries seasoned?" she asked.

"No."

I was starting to feel awkward because we were now going on a full minute since I'd asked the question. I had four other tables to attend to, and I wasn't trying to spend ten minutes waiting on an answer about a freaking potato. Not only that, but the customer's rack was the size of bowling balls. Her v-neck was so tight and low-cut that I hoped to make an exit before there were any wardrobe malfunctions like last year's infamous Nipplegate at the Superbowl.

She picked the lemon slice off the rim of her glass and squeezed it into her water. A drop of lemon juice spattered up and right into my eye. I gasped, backed up a foot, and wiped my eye, hoping I didn't smudge my eyeliner. She didn't apologize. I wasn't even sure if she'd noticed.

"How thick are the fries?" she asked while chomping on a tortilla chip. She'd asked me to bring a bowl of chips to her table immediately because she claimed her blood sugar was low and she was about to pass out. Yeah. Sure. A few more of those chips and I feared her shirt might actually rip in half like a scene straight out of *The Incredible Hulk*. "Are they like steak fries or shoestring fries or what?"

Once I'd given her the approximate width of the fries, she still seemed unsure. "Should I give you a few more minutes to think about it?" I asked, with a glowing smile on my face to disguise the fact that I was totally being sarcastic. I didn't know if she bought it.

"I guess I'll try the fries," she said with a sigh, as if all that thinking had exhausted her. "But make sure they're hot."

Did that mean everyone else in the restaurant wanted cold fries?

"And for you?" I asked her friend, the one who had been licking salt from the chips off her fingers so loudly I could barely hear the Outkast song coming from the speaker in the ceiling.

"Um," she hesitated as she broke a chip in half. I cringed at the site of her blinged-out acrylic fingernails. Then I looked at my short, pale pink nails and felt like an outsider. I really hoped short, natural fingernails would come back in style someday.

"Are your oysters local?" she asked.

"No," I answered, trying harder than ever to keep my cool. *Where the fuck are there local oysters in Ann Arbor? Was someone farming oysters in their yard?* "They're from the Gulf Coast." I didn't mention that I recently read an article on the internet about a high percentage of oysters from the Gulf Coast testing positive for Salmonella. It was up to her to do her own research.

"I guess I'll have the scallops then."

I bet those were local.

"And would you like fries or a baked potato with that?" I asked.

Suddenly I heard a sound louder than the smacking of her lips as she licked her fingers. It was her cell phone, and it was blasting the latest Timbaland track. Ordinarily I wouldn't mind the intrusion. I was a fan of Timbaland myself. Everyone knew the guy had the best beats in the biz. What I did mind was that she answered the call. As if I wasn't standing there waiting (with a glowing smile) for her order! Oh hell no!

"Hey" she said into the cell. "Can you hold on a sec?" Then she looked at me. "What are my choices again?"

As I walked toward the computer to place their order, I heard a voice behind me. "Hey, lady!"

It was The Incredible Hulk calling for me. Calling me lady. Oh no she didn't!

"I changed my mind," she said when I turned around. "I'll have a baked potato instead."

When I finally got to the computer at the bar to put in my order, Jake was standing there, arms crossed on top of the bar, smiling in a creepy ventriloquist kind of way. He must have witnessed the whole miserable scene.

"Hey, *lady*," he said with a huge smile.

I shook my head as I punched their order into the POS system.

"It could be worse," he told me.

"How is that?"

"We could work at a restaurant that makes the servers do line dances."

I smiled at him. Because he was right. That *would* be worse. And because he was gorgeous. And because I loved the way he kissed me and I couldn't wait for him to do it again.

ALL GOOD THINGS

My "Walking on Sunshine" attitude lasted about three more hours. I felt his eyes on me constantly and there were many secret smiles exchanged. I felt like the prettiest girl in the bar. Until all of a sudden I wasn't.

A woman had been sitting by herself at the bar since shortly after Jake started his shift. She looked older than us, probably at least thirty. She had the two-toned blonde hair over dark hair look that Christina Aguilera made popular during her *Stripped* days. I had loved the look then, and I loved it still, but I was too much of a chicken shit to try it on myself. Maybe that was why I was already a bit annoyed by her. The fact that she was wearing white capris with her summery tank top, and actually looked good in them, might have added to the annoyance. I mean, come on, who really looked good in white pants?

Even though the bar was busy, I managed to keep an eye on her. She seemed to be doing a lot of drinking, a lot of laughing at whatever Jake was saying, and a lot of touching his arm whenever she had the opportunity. I was irritated, but managed to keep my cool. We'd only had one night together. I wasn't his girlfriend, and I wasn't trying to get all psycho-jealous on him. I had enough sense to know that was never a good look on anyone.

I saw her write something on a napkin and slide it over to him across the bar. I wasn't an idiot. The only thing people ever wrote on bev naps was phone numbers. Jake accepted the napkin with a smile. Of course he did. He did everything with a smile. I could deal with that.

But then she stood up to leave and he gave her a long once-over, from her face, all the way down, and then all the way back up. Intentional and obvious. He finished off the once-over with an appreciative half-smile, the kind with droopy eyes, bedroom eyes. His face said he liked what he saw, and he'd definitely use that phone number.

That was when my pot boiled over. I wasn't going to say anything to him about it, because I didn't want to be *that* girl, but I wasn't going to take it quietly either. They said if you couldn't beat 'em, join 'em. I could play this game, too.

The baseball game was over and The Bar was starting to go from mostly dinner crowd to mostly drunk crowd. I had a group of college-aged baseball fans in my section who had started with beer earlier in the night and then progressed to shots. My original plan had been to flirt with them shamelessly, but when one of them asked if he could take the lemon with his lemon drop from my mouth, I saw an opportunity I couldn't pass up.

The Bar didn't blatantly encourage such activities, but Zeke trusted us to make the right decisions based on the crowd and the ambience. He wanted three things: to make money, to make the customers happy, and to make sure no one got hurt. So dancing on the tabletops was out. But an occasional body shot was okay if the crowd was appropriate (pretty young), the customer asked for it, and the server was willing. Ordinarily I would find someone like Shannon to take care of the request, but Jake had given me a reason to handle this myself. I wasn't going to let him lick sugar off me, because licking was just gross, but I could pass him a lemon.

ALL GOOD THINGS

My section was directly in front of the bar so I knew Jake would have a great view of the shenanigans. After the first one, everyone else in the group decided they wanted a lemon drop, too. That meant more money for The Bar, more money for me, and happy customers – a win/win. It was just a bonus that Jake would get to watch.

I punched the order for six more shots into the computer and watched Jake as he pulled the ticket from the printer and started lining up shot glasses along the bar. His face looked tense as he filled them up with vodka.

"Thanks," I said sweetly, as I set the shots and lemons on my tray.

"You're welcome," he said just as cheerfully.

OKAY. I ADMIT. It wasn't entirely a win/win. I had way too many yucky mouths way too close to mine. It was something I would absolutely never do again. But I'd gotten this far, and I couldn't stop the charade without making my point.

I went up to the bar after close to get my drink and let Jake know I didn't need a ride home. I told him one of the guys from that table had invited me to an after-party and I'd accepted the offer. My plan was to count out my money quickly, go outside like I was leaving, and then beg the first person that came out the door behind me to drive me home. It wasn't exactly genius, but it was all I had.

I threw my apron up on the bar and pulled my money out to count it, acting nonchalant about the whole thing. I even bobbed my head to the music.

Jake was unaffected. He set my drink in front of me like nothing was at all out of the ordinary. But then he leaned closer, close enough so Katy or any other coworkers from the nearby table wouldn't hear him, and said, "Dude, that is not cool." His voice was even and calm, but his expression was of disappointment. "Instead of getting a ride home from one of the girls, and pretending you went to an after-hours just to piss me off, how 'bout we throw some snowballs around right now?"

I knew what he was referring to. I had replayed that morning, and the kiss the night before, in my mind dozens of times – maybe hundreds. But I didn't want him to know that, so I rolled my eyes instead.

Sometimes I wished I could bitch-slap my own self in the face.

"What are you talking about?" I asked. "There's no snow."

"It's an expression. One that you made up a few years ago, remember? When things get weird we're supposed to have a snowball fight. So let me hear it. What's the issue here?"

The conversation was dangerously close to being overheard. For someone who was intent on keeping this thing a secret, he sure wasn't acting very discreet. I knew the discussion needed to end sooner rather than later, so I simply said, while clenching my teeth, "There's no issue."

"We will talk about the issue when *I* drive *you* home tonight," he said as he mixed up a drink for another server.

"Fine," I replied quietly, as not to let the argument progress any further. I didn't really want to pretend to go to an after-hours anyway. Besides, it was pretty sweet that Jake remembered something so insignificant all these years later.

"ALL RIGHT," HE said when we got into his truck. "What was that lemon drop shit about?"

I shrugged. There was no way I would ever admit I had done it to make him jealous. No way. "What lemon drop shit?" I asked innocently.

"Please," he said. "You've never acted anything but classy in there. Now all of a sudden you're acting like you're on *Girls Gone Wild*, and I'm supposed to believe there's no reason behind it?"

"Are you saying I didn't act classy tonight?"

"Yes. That's what I'm saying." He didn't even sound apologetic about it.

I knew I deserved it, but my first instinct was to react defensively. I tightened my grip on my tote bag and looked out the window. I needed to take a few deep breaths and think about what I was going to say before I said it. I was hurt and angry, but I knew better than to blurt out a quick and easy eff-you. That wouldn't solve anything.

We reached the turn toward my parents' place, and I was surprised when he drove past. I'd expected him to take me home since I was such a tramp. I would have taken my ass home if I were him.

"Where are we going?" I asked.

"To my apartment," he said, as if it was a stupid question, like we would go anywhere else.

"If you think I'm so trashy, why don't you just take me home?" That wasn't a whole lot better than an eff-you.

Disclaimer: Forgive me for acting like a spoiled child here. I didn't always know the right thing to say, and I definitely didn't always say the right thing. But I was only twenty-one. I had time to learn.

Current Lesson Plan: Learning when to shut the fuck up.

Current grade: C-

Hopefully I could get my grade up before I made a royal mess of things with Jake. I had a feeling I was going to need to put in some extra credit.

The fact that we'd hooked up for the first time only twenty-four hours ago, and were already having our first fight, was alarming and scary. This could easily get out of hand. I didn't wait all this time for him just to throw him in the trash at the first sign of trouble. He was worth fighting for. He was worth admitting I was wrong. He was worth swallowing my pride. And he was also right. Classy would be the last word I'd use to describe my actions tonight. Instead of acting like a snot, I should be begging his forgiveness.

He stopped the truck at a red light. "Come on, Roxie." It was a plea. "Why are you being like this? Is this the part of the movie where there's some big misunderstanding that drives the characters apart for the remainder of the second act?"

I snapped my head over to him quickly. He compared us to characters in a movie. *I* did that. That was *my* thing.

And he knew it. He knew *me*. How could I stay mad at him? How could I ever be mad at him at all?

"Is this what you really want?" he asked. There was a hint of sarcasm in his voice. "You want a misunderstanding montage? You, walking along the street with your hands in your pocket and looking at the ground because you're so lonely without me? Or having a *care-uh-mel* latte at our diner while a little tear slides down your cheek?"

My face broke into a smile. I could tell he was trying not to laugh, but his mouth turned up in the corners a little. He was doing a bad job hiding his amusement.

"And me," he continued, "sitting at the bar, crying into a glass of whiskey? Or wiping tears away while I fold my own laundry?"

"When we finally make up," I said, joining in, "can there please be a slow-motion run to each other while the *Chariots of Fire* song plays in the background?"

He put a hand to his mouth and looked away to hide his snicker.

I coughed to hide mine.

"But really, Rox, you're going back to school in two months. I don't want to waste time on any grade school bullshit."

I felt like a real douche. Even if he did take the woman's number with an intention to call her, I had no right to be mad. Like he'd just pointed out, I was going back to school in two months. I couldn't really expect him to sit at the diner crying into his toast. Puh-lease.

We drove the rest of the way in silence. When we pulled into a parking spot at the complex, he got out and started walking around to open my door. I opened it first. Without a word he held out his hand and I took it. Even though he was not very happy with me, he still wanted to hold my hand. All the way to his apartment.

He opened the door and gently led me inside. When he let go of my hand, I hated it. I wanted it back.

I closed the door and took off my shoes. He set his keys on the kitchen counter and opened the refrigerator. When he closed the refrigerator door, he had two bottles of beer between the fingers of one hand. With the other hand he popped the caps off. Bartender Jake. Sexy Jake. He handed one to me.

He sat down on the reclining end of their sofa, put his feet up, picked up the remote, and turned on the TV.

I stayed near the dining room table, confused. Were we going to watch TV now? Did this mean the whole lemon drop psycho-jealous-slut-bag moment was forgotten? I seriously doubted it.

He patted the couch next to him. He wanted me to sit down. The spot he patted was *thisclose* to him. I sat down in the middle of the couch instead. He stuck his finger into the waistband on the side of my shorts and pulled me closer to him, close enough that our hips were touching. I put my feet up on the recliner next to his feet. Damn, that shit was comfy as hell. I totally needed to get a recliner for my next apartment.

Jake had joked about the misunderstanding montage before, but I knew the lemon drop debate wasn't over.

Being quiet was his way of letting me know the ball was in my court. I could hold onto it and watch some TV, or I could hit it over the net and hash it out once and for all.

I used my thumb to push droplets of condensation down the sides of my beer bottle. The little drops fell from the bottle and hit my bare thighs. I didn't know what was on TV, but Jake seemed engrossed in it.

He touched his beer bottle to my thigh and I jumped from the cold. I could tell he wasn't mad at me, but I knew I owed him an explanation.

"I was feeling insecure," I said, breaking the silence.

He turned the volume down on the TV.

I looked down and kept pushing drops off my beer bottle.

"I saw that girl, the one with the Christina Aguilera hair, give you her number and I just thought ... I don't know. It was stupid."

He explained that bartenders were notorious for being flirts, and I needed to get used to it and know it didn't mean anything.

"This can't turn into anything messy," he said. "We've been friends too long to screw it up over some dumb shit. I'm telling you right now that my intentions are not to hurt you, piss you off, screw you over, or anything like that. I just like being with you, Roxie. And I'm not going to like you any less if you tell me what's on your mind. If you ever have something to say, say it. If there's something you want to know, ask me. If you're mad about something, tell me. It doesn't have to be complicated.

"Okay."

"No mind-games, no secrets, no lies. Promise me."

"Promise," I said.

He held his beer bottle up. "Let's drink to that."

We clicked our bottles together and then he took my other hand in his. Hand holding. It was such a juvenile thing to get excited over. In middle school, handholding didn't even count as getting to a base. But when he touched his fingers to mine, it didn't feel juvenile. It felt intimate and special and sweet.

And I was a dork.

"Have you ever seen *Entourage*?" he asked.

"No."

He shook his head slowly, dramatically. "Now *that* is a real problem."

"You didn't really invite me over to watch TV, did you?"

"No. I'm just relaxing for a minute while I decide where I want to fuck you first."

He got my attention with that line. My nipples perked up in my bra. They were curious to know where Jake was going to fuck me as well.

"Shit," he said. "For a minute I forgot you're still my friend's little sister. I shouldn't say things like that to you."

I stood up to set my empty beer bottle on the coffee table. Then I slid on top of him, one knee on each side of his waist. I put a finger under his chin and lifted his face up to look at me. It was still him. Still Jake. I had to keep reminding myself that this wasn't just some guy I worked with. It was fucking Jake. And I wanted him more than I ever thought I could.

"I want you to," I whispered.

"You want me to say things like that?"

"Yeah." I brought my face down to kiss him but stopped just before our lips touched. "And I want you to fuck me."

Any other guy would have been putty in my hands by this point, but he was holding strong. "We won't be able to do this in the apartment anymore when your brother comes home. So where do you want it first? The bathroom sink? The kitchen counter?"

"I don't care, Jake!" I said a bit desperately. "I just want it now!"

"Okay, okay," he said as he pulled my tank top over my head. "Right here is fine. Should we close the blinds?"

I reached between my thighs to undo his belt. "Nope."

"BUT SERIOUSLY," HE said later while we were in his bed watching an SNL rerun, "we won't be able to do this here when Adam comes home."

I laid my cheek on his chest and sighed. Was this it? Was this when he'd tell me he was done with me? Was it just a weekend thing? "I know," I said sadly.

"We'll have to get creative," he said. "And learn how to be very quiet."

So that meant he wanted to keep hooking up? I should ask him. He told me to be honest, and if I wanted to know something, just ask him. Could life really be that simple? Could people really go around saying what they were feeling all the time? As effortless an idea as it seemed, in actuality, it was extremely difficult to change the way you'd been living your whole life. I'd always been the person who said what I thought people wanted me to say, did the things I was supposed to do, never wanting to be the nuisance with the annoying questions. Could I really just be me, with no apologies? And would anyone like me if I was? Would *he* still like me?

Standing naked in front of someone was scary enough, but full exposure ... it was like cutting a line down my chest, pulling it open and saying, "Here. This is me. I hope you like it. And by the way, I'm about to bleed to death on your floor. Sorry 'bout the mess."

"Jake?"

"Yeah."

"I told you I don't have flings," I started cautiously. "I'm not really sure what the rules are, or how long they're supposed to last, and you know how I am. I like things to be organized."

"I know how you are," he said. "You need structure. And rules."

"Yes. And I'm not sure what your intentions are. You told me your intentions weren't to hurt me, and that's good to know. But I am curious what you do intend on doing with me."

"I thought I made it pretty clear what I want to do with you," he said with a sly grin.

"Yeah. You did. And that's great. I guess what I'm asking is, for how long do you intend on doing this with me? I've been looking back on girls you've hooked up with in the past, and it seems like they were always out of the picture in a week or two. Should I expect the same kind of expiration date? And it's okay if that's what you want. I just like to know what's coming."

He sighed. "First of all, you shouldn't compare yourself to other girls."

Ha! I shouldn't eat Reese's pumpkins on Halloween either, but I do. And Reese's trees on Christmas, Reese's hearts on Valentine's Day, and Reese's eggs on Easter. If they created a Reese's sunshine for the summer season, I'd eat those, too. It was just what I did. It was a part of who I was. I compared myself to others. Like crazy. And I liked Reese's.

"This is completely different," Jake said.

"How is that?"

"I already know you. The other girls, I had to get to know them. It doesn't take very long to realize we aren't right together. But I already know I like you." He turned onto his side so he could face me. "Rox, this isn't ... it's not just some random hook-up. I have been thinking about this, and waiting for this, for years."

"Really?"

"Don't act like you didn't know. I kissed you when we were in high school, remember? That time I got busted with the rolling papers?"

"Of course I remember. I just thought you were trying to make out with everyone back then."

He laughed. "I kind of was. But then I kissed you again at Central."

"And you were trying to hook up with everyone back then."

"Yeah. I kind of was. Everyone *but* you. That was why I went downstairs that night. I didn't want you to be everyone else. I knew if anything happened between us that night, I would have screwed it up the next day. I would have."

"But you won't screw it up now?"

"No. But I do think we have an expiration date. You're going back to school in the fall."

"That's two months from now."

"Yeah."

"So you think you're gonna want me for two whole months?"

"I'll want you a lot longer than that."

"But you're committing to two months?"

He took a moment to truly think about it before he answered, "Yes. I promise you two months."

"So what you're saying is that you can listen to the same radio station for the rest of the summer without getting bored?"

"You say it like it's a bad thing. This isn't a sacrifice I'm making here. I *want* to stay on the same station all summer. I *want* to be with you."

Sigh. "Promise? No matter what?"

"Yeah. No matter what."

"No matter how many MILFs give you their number?"

"Yes. I'll wait until September to call them," he said with a smirk.

"Fair enough. What if you get mad at me?"

"How is that a problem? I can have sex when I'm mad."

Now I had the urge to make him mad just to see what it was like. But I couldn't think of a time I'd ever actually seen him seriously mad, so I had a feeling I would never find out.

"It's one summer," he said. "It's not like you're going to start embroidering Jake and Roxie pillows for my bed. You want structure, I'm giving you structure."

"I already feel better about it."

"Good. So that means no matter how many people flirt with me at the bar, you're the one I'm going home with. Are there any other terms to this agreement that we need to discuss?"

"Ummm ... no, not that I can think of. Just that you're mine, to do with as I wish, for the rest of the summer. No matter what."

"Nah. Fuck that. You're *mine*."

"Yes. I'm yours, Jake."

CHAPTER 14

NEITHER OF US had to work on Sunday. I'd envisioned a lazy day of love with my boy toy. And by love, I meant the naked kind, not the red roses and doves flying overhead kind.

I was not disappointed. I got exactly what I'd hoped for. And some Cinnamon Toast Crunch, too.

But all good things must come to an end. Adam was on his way home. Our romantic weekend in our cozy hideaway was nearly over. Real life was turtle-heading. We showered, dressed, and headed to my parents' house to do laundry.

I felt a million times better after our talk the night before. I wasn't a sacrifice. I wasn't a mistake where he was trying to dig his way out. He *wanted* to be with me. That was what he'd said. And if Jake said something, he meant it. Of that much I was sure. Because of that, there was nothing that could wipe the smile off my face.

ALL GOOD THINGS

Like every Sunday of the summer thus far, my parents had gone to brunch with friends, and then to the golf course. I hoped I had as active a social life when I was pushing fifty.

He put his first load into the washing machine while I went out back and got comfortable in a lounge chair by the pool. The last few Sundays, after we'd had breakfast at the diner, we'd hung out by the pool and read my mom's *People* magazines while his clothes dried. I figured we'd do the same thing this Sunday, so I kicked off my flip-flops, grabbed a magazine, and plopped into a lounge chair.

This Brangelina stuff was driving me bonkers. How could he? Seriously. How. Could. He? And TomKat? What the hell *was* that? No! Joey could not marry Tom Cruise! It would ruin everything! She belonged with Pacey!

Jake surprised me when he asked if I wanted to go to the store with him. I had gotten used to being kept in hiding when I was with Jim.

"Where are you going?"

"Best Buy."

"Oh. Okay. Sure."

"We'll go as soon as I put this load in the dryer." He nodded toward the magazine. "What's going on with your friends?"

I shook my head sadly, thinking of poor Jennifer and Katie. "Nothing good."

JAKE DIDN'T REACH for my hand while we walked from the parking lot to the store, and I didn't reach for his. Boyfriends and girlfriends held hands when they were shopping. Friends with benefits, or whatever we were, did not. FWBs usually didn't go shopping together at all, so I was lucky he was willing to walk next to me in public. I didn't need to push my luck.

He found what he was looking for quickly, holding up *Entourage: The Complete First Season* DVD, his face beaming. "Will you watch it with me?"

Wow. A whole season of a TV show. Now that was a serious commitment. Of course I would watch it. I would watch videos of women giving birth with him. If it meant I got to be close to him and touch his fingers again, I would watch anything. I almost shrugged my shoulders and said, "Sure," in an I-really-don't-give-a-shit voice. But then I remembered the honesty thing I'd promised him.

"I'll watch anything with you, Jake," I said instead.

His smile got even bigger. And so did mine. I could get used to this way of life for sure.

The washer and dryer were in the attached two-car garage. I helped him fold the first load while he threw the second one into the dryer. Honestly, I was just folding clothes. It was totally innocent. Until he grabbed me by my hips, pushed me up onto the dryer and stuck his head under my skirt.

"Jake!" I reached my hands down to stop him. It was too late. He'd already pulled my panties down to my ankles. I grabbed his face by the cheeks to pull him up. "My parents will be home any minute!"

"Not true," he said, looking up at me innocently. "They usually get home around six. We probably have at least twenty minutes."

"*Probably?* You don't risk my parents finding you with your head up my skirt based on a probability! That shit needs to be fact or nothing!" I closed my thighs together tightly to keep him out.

He laughed and tried to pry them open. "At least we'll see *them* before they see us."

"I can't concentrate under this kind of pressure. We can go to my room if you want."

He looked up at me and shook his head. "We won't hear your parents come in if we're upstairs. They could walk into the middle of a screaming fit. If we stay where we are, we'll hear the garage door opening way before they see us."

I thought for a second. He was right. It was a foul-proof plan. Sounded like he'd thought this through.

I sighed and released the tension in my thighs. "Okay then. Carry on."

I WAS COLLAPSED in a heap on top the dryer when I heard the garage door start to open. My parents were in their car on the other side, waiting to pull in. I could see the tires. I had to find my underwear, get off the dryer, and try to act like *that* didn't just happen. And I needed to do it *now*. Shit!

Jake had his ventriloquist smile on his face when I hopped off the dryer. He knew I was squirming, and he was enjoying it.

"Where did you throw my underwear?" I whispered frantically. I knew I didn't have time to put them back on, but I was hoping to throw them into Jake's laundry basket before anyone saw them. Even in the laundry area of the house, a pair of panties strewn in the garage would raise some alarms. We did not leave clothes in the laundry room, whether dirty or clean.

The door was halfway up. I saw my mom's Taurus behind it. There was nothing obstructing their view. They could see us.

"Relax," he said quietly, folding a t-shirt like nothing was out of the ordinary. "I've got them in my pocket. Now start folding."

"I really can't bend over and grab clothes out of the dryer," I said between gritted teeth. "I have on a skirt with no underwear, and my parents are behind me."

He laughed out loud while he bent over, grabbed a handful of laundry from the dryer, and set it on top. He was absolutely enjoying this. I would get him back for this one day. The next time he was on the phone with his mom, game on.

I heard the car pull in and the engine turn off. A door opened and closed. Then another.

"Oh good," Mom said. She was generally a little tipsy after an afternoon at the golf course. I hoped this day would be no different. "You're both here. Adam just called. He's bringing over some pizza for dinner."

"Um … hey," I said. "Yeah. Pizza is good. We haven't had dinner yet."

We? What the hell was that?

"I mean," I continued, "*I* haven't eaten yet. I'm not sure what's going on with this kid here. I'm just helping him fold clothes because there was nothing on TV."

I should have stopped when I was ahead, though I'm not sure I ever was. I definitely took several steps back with my unnecessary disclaimer. My face grew hot and looked down at the pair of jeans in my hands to avoid the eyes of everyone else, especially Jake. He would make fun of me for this later. I was sure of that.

Dad went around to the trunk to remove their golf clubs and put them away until next weekend. I prayed he was distracted by the clubs and didn't notice my embarrassing rambling or my red face.

Mom had already flipped open her cell phone and was pressing buttons. I assumed she was calling Adam to tell him to bring enough pizza for us.

"Hey, sunshine," Dad said to me when he walked past us to get into the house. He playfully punched Jake in the arm.

I didn't think he knew. If he did, the punch would not have been playful.

As soon as both parents were in the house and the door was closed, Jake burst into laughter.

"You are the worst liar ever," he told me.

I also punched Jake in the arm. "Gimme back my underwear."

He shook his head. "Not a chance."

I rolled my eyes. "Fine. I'm going upstairs to change."

I headed toward the door, but he grabbed my hand from behind and twirled me around like a dancer. He secured our hands on the small of my back, pushing my body into his.

"I can't wait to get you alone again," he whispered.

That made two of us.

ONCE I'D GONE up to my room to change into a pair of sweatpants, I came downstairs to find Jake helping my parents get the dining room ready for dinner.

Mom set Parmesan cheese and hot pepper seeds in the center of the table.

I pulled a 2-liter of Coke from the fridge and grabbed five glasses from the cupboard.

Dad grabbed a roll of paper towels and set it on the table.

Jake set five plates.

For the last few days, ever since our first kiss, I'd had this bizarre feeling that my life was choreographed. Every move was a dance. Every sound was a beat to a song. It was like living in a real-life musical. If my parents had suddenly started singing about setting the table, I wouldn't have been all that surprised.

I guess that was what life was like when you were content, when everything fell into place. There was a rhythm to it – a happy pulse.

Adam arrived with pizza, and the five of us sat down to have a meal together for probably the first time in years.

ALL GOOD THINGS

Mom was sentimental: "How nice it is to have everyone together when we have the chance. You know, we took dinners for granted when you were younger, because they happened every night. Now I know to appreciate times like this. They seem to happen less and less every year." Yeah, she was tipsy.

Dad was nostalgic: "Remember when Rox would try to cook for us and the kitchen would look like something had exploded?"

Everyone laughed at my expense.

"But it always tasted good," Jake chimed in, sticking up for me.

I smiled at him across me. His bare toes met mine under the table. I'd always thought playing footsies was something only creepy people did. It was along the same line as winking, and the idea of doing either gave me the heebie jeebies. But I didn't have the heebie jeebies when Jake's foot touched mine. I liked that it was a way for us to connect without anyone else at the table knowing a thing.

There Mom and Dad were, trying to have a special family moment, and all I could think about was when I could touch Jake again.

I had it bad.

"Can you believe your sister has never seen *Entourage*?" Jake asked Adam.

"Does that mean we have to watch the first season again?" Adam asked, pretending to be inconvenienced.

"I got the DVD today," Jake told him. "You guys want to watch it after dinner?"

"For sure," Adam said. "Janelle hasn't seen it either. I'll invite her, too."

Great. This should be interesting.

ADAM LEFT AFTER dinner to pick up Janelle while Jake and I finished up his laundry before we headed back to their apartment.

When we got there, Adam and Janelle were already looking comfy on the reclining part of the couch, the same part Jake and I had cuddled on last night. And had sex. Yeah.

Jake put the DVD in and sat down on the other end of the sofa. I wasn't sure where to sit, so I sat in the armchair.

It was disappointing to be so far from Jake. But luckily *Entourage* was entertaining enough to distract me for a little while.

We watched three episodes before Adam and Janelle stood up and said they were going to bed. Together.

When his bedroom door closed, I gave Jake a disgusted look and stood up. "I guess you should take me home now. I'm not gonna stay here and listen to this shit."

"Yeah. Okay."

HE PULLED IN front of my parents' house instead of using the driveway. We didn't use the driveway late at night because the headlights would shine into their room and might wake them up.

"I missed you tonight," he said quietly.

"How could you miss me? I was *with* you. All day."

"No, you weren't," he said, shaking his head sadly. "Your panties were in my pocket all night. Which was awesome, by the way. Especially during dinner. But you were across the table, and then you were in the chair. You were too far away. I hated it."

"I hated it, too," I admitted. He made me feel like a teenager. And yeah, I knew it wasn't so long ago that I *was* a teenager, but I felt like a young teenager, like thirteen or fourteen, when kids got so giddy with attraction that they grabbed onto their crush's belt loops, tugged the sleeves of their shirt, and did anything to touch them so they could feel close to them. That was where I was at with Jake. Sitting five feet away from him had been painful. I needed a piece of him, any piece of him, to make me feel good again. I was starting to feel like a drug addict. I needed a Jake fix.

I took his hand from across the bucket seat and pressed my fingertips to his. His touch removed my anxiety and tension. My body started to relax from head to toe, covered up with an imaginary blanket of content.

"My parents usually have some drinks at the golf course," I told him. "And I saw my mom opening a bottle of wine before we left."

"Yeah? What does that mean?"

"It means they sleep really well on Sunday nights."

He nodded. "I like where this is going."

"Do you want to come in?"

"Can you be quiet?"

"Can *you*?"

"We'll see."

We got out of the truck and closed both doors quietly. Like cat burglars, we crept around to the backyard hand in hand. I felt pretty safe back there since my parents' bedroom was in the front of the house. The chances of my parents catching us in the backyard were slim.

Jake came up behind me as I stuck my key into the patio door, and pulled my hand away, leaving the keys dangling in the lock. "What's wrong with the backyard?" he asked. He lifted my hair up and kissed the back of my neck. "No one will ever hear us out here with the air conditioner running and the windows closed."

I turned and gave him a quick kiss and a sly smile. "Where's the fun in that?"

"Oh, I see. So this went from *having* to be sneaky, to *wanting* to be sneaky?"

"Guilty."

What could I say? He'd turned me on to the idea of a secret romance. Now I was a devoted enthusiast.

"Just remember," I whispered as I pushed open the French doors that led into the kitchen. "You created me."

I would never again look at that kitchen island without thinking of Jake.

"YOU WANNA GO to the Tigers game tomorrow night?" It was Monday night, and Jake and I were the last two in The Bar. I munched on snack mix while he worked on his closing side-work. "I thought since we're both off tomorrow it would be fun to get away for the day. Just the two of us. The game starts at four, and we could have dinner and drinks after. Kind of like a date."

He turned from his liquor bottles looking uncomfortable. He ran a hand through his hair – a bad sign. "I can't tomorrow."

"Oh," I said. I didn't try to hide my disappointment. Honesty, right? "Okay."

"I have something I have to do."

He had *something* he had to do? What the fuck was that? That was intentional vagueness right there. You didn't say you had "something" to do, unless you didn't want *someone* to know what that *something* was.

I trusted Jake. I trusted him as much as I was able to at this point in my life. But hearing him say something like that didn't make trusting him easy. What was he keeping from me? Was he going out with another girl? I thought our talk about radio stations had meant we would not see other people for the rest of the summer. Maybe he'd thought differently?

Images flashed in my mind like a movie trailer. He and Shannon. At his apartment. Naked. On the couch. In the shower. In his bed. Right in front of the picture of us on the bookshelf.

My stomach twisted in knots. I dropped the pretzel I was holding. I wasn't hungry anymore.

He said he had something he had to do. Maybe he meant he had some*one* he had to do. It was possible I wasn't enough for him. Or maybe I was too much for him and he needed a break. Maybe I was getting on his nerves.

I'd like to say I wasn't always the kind of girl to jump to such conclusions based on a single statement. I'd like to blame that on Jim. But it wasn't entirely his fault. I did sometimes grab onto a sentence and run across the planet with it.

One year for Halloween I should dress as Worst-Case Scenario Girl. I could put a bunch of words and phrases onto colored cardstock and pin them to my body. *Car accident. HIV. Kidnapped. Shark attack. My boyfriend has a teenage pregnant girlfriend. My husband left me for someone ten years younger and fifty pounds lighter. Jake is still fucking Shannon. Jake has been fucking Shannon this whole time. Jake has been fucking Shannon this whole time, and they have been laughing together at how easily I was fooled into thinking he liked me.* Oh God. Total nightmare.

When my mind wandered to Worst-Case Scenario Land, it seriously got up and walked away. Left the room. Left the building even. I had to wait for it to get back before I noticed Jake staring at me, waiting for me to come out of my trance.

"Whatever you're thinking right now," he said, "stop. That didn't come out right."

The knots in my stomach paused.

"I'm taking a class this summer, a photography class on Tuesday and Thursday afternoons."

The knots loosened up and began to unravel. I looked at the pretzel I'd abandoned. Maybe I was hungry again.

"I bought myself a nice camera for Christmas last year and still haven't figured out how to use it. So I signed up for a class. Tomorrow is the first day."

"Oh. Okay. I thought maybe you were sick of me or wanted to hook up with someone else. Like maybe someone blonde. With a nice tan."

He looked annoyed. "Baby, I told you it's just you and me for the rest of the summer. I promised. Does my word not mean anything to you? I don't understand what I did to make you this suspicious of me."

"It's not you," I said quietly. "I'm suspicious of everyone."

"I wish you wouldn't be. Worrying about things isn't going to change whether they happen or not. Like all the worrying you do about disasters. Car accidents and STDs and serial killers. I'm not saying you should stop wearing your seatbelt, or stop using condoms, or go out jogging at four AM with your hair in a ponytail and headphones on your ears. But there are certain things you can control, and certain things you can't. It'll be a lot easier to be you when you figure out which is which."

Well then.

"And what's this thing with Shannon? That's not the first time you've mentioned her."

"The way you're always flirting. And the way you guys were attached at Katy's that one night. It looked familiar and comfortable, like it wasn't the first time."

"Shannon is a flirt, and maybe I am, too. But there's nothing going on between us, not now, not ever. I don't go for the ones who throw themselves at me. I like a challenge."

That must be why he enjoyed the sneaking around stuff. It was a challenge. To find a place to meet up and then make sure we didn't get caught – it added another layer of excitement to our rendezvous. It took our chemistry from hot to off-the-charts. But I did find myself wondering what we would have if we weren't a secret, if we weren't a challenge. I guess I had my answer.

"Well, whatever. I'm done talking about this. Go to your class. I'll just hang out with Allison or something. Maybe go shopping. It's not a big deal." I wasn't being a spoiled brat. I meant it. We didn't have to spend every second together.

He leaned over the bar and took my face in his hands. He touched his lips to mine in the sweetest way. I actually smiled when our lips were together and he did, too. Then we both laughed at our lameness. Laughing while kissing – you couldn't do that with just anyone.

"I would love to go to a Tigers game with you and spend the whole day there," he said when he pulled himself back up. "Just the two of us. Like a date. We'll go to a game before the end of the summer. Okay?"

"Okay."

CHAPTER 15

WHEN I ASKED Allison if she might want to go shopping Tuesday afternoon, I expected an erratic, chaotic trip to the mall. You know the kind: three whiny kids terrorizing the place, ripping clothes off hangers, crawling under the dressing room doors to scare the hell out of the neighbors, and hiding behind the clothing racks to jump out and scare the other shoppers, all eventually resulting in a call to mall security to report a missing kid. Don't forget the messy faces and peanut butter sandwiches smashed onto their shirts. That *was* a typical shopping trip with three kids, right? I'd been to Wal-Mart during back-to-school season. I'd lived that nightmare before.

But Allison jumped at the opportunity to enjoy an adults-only afternoon and saved us all by asking her mom to watch the kids.

It was her idea to go into the sex store. Sweet and innocent Allison looking at anal beads? So strange.

"When you've been together as long as we have," she told me, "you can always use a little something extra. Or," she continued, "when you're not getting any at all, like you, you can always use a little something extra."

I didn't correct her. I liked keeping Jake to myself.

She showed me the vibrators and dildos. Correction: she showed me the *freaking gigantic* vibrators and dildos. Even if I weren't getting any like she assumed, I sure as hell wouldn't want anything to do with those! It wasn't the Panama Canal for Christ's sake!

I browsed a little while she tried on corsets and garter belts in the dressing room.

"Have you seen this?" the sales clerk asked me. She reminded me of a grown-up Rainbow Brite doll. Maybe that was because she was wearing a Rainbow Brite Halloween costume, complete with striped thigh highs and a flouncy skirt. All right, fine, Rainbow Brite *actually* looked like that. Whatever.

Rainbow held up a white bottle. "It's a revolutionary new product."

Of course it was revolutionary. Every new product was revolutionary. There was probably a website somewhere filled with testimonials. If I stayed up really late, I might even see an infomercial.

"What is it?" I asked.

"It's a flavored water-based lubricant that works well enough for anal-" She stopped when I grimaced at her use of the word anal, before continuing, "-and also works as a nipple, clitoral, or erectile stimulant. And it contains added pheromones. It's like a one-stop-shop sex gel."

ALL GOOD THINGS

I didn't think I really needed any of those things. Jake was a good lubricant and stimulator all on his own.

"We're giving out free samples today." She held the bottle out toward me like she was going to pump some into my hand.

What was I supposed to do with it? Go into the bathroom and rub it on? Or maybe I was totally off course, and she intended to apply it to me herself.

I backed up slightly and looked around. Was this normal? I hadn't spent enough time in sex toy shops to know the typical protocol. If this was it, I needed to get out.

She laughed. "Just kidding! You should have seen the look on your face! Love it." She opened her other hand where she held little plastic samples with twist off plastic caps. "Strawberry, pina colada, or chocolate?"

"Pina colada."

"Here ya go. Remember, it's water-based so it's perfectly safe for you, and for condoms."

I took the little sample and stuck it in my purse.

"Whatcha got there?" Allison asked, popping up with an armful of lingerie.

Rainbow went into her spiel again and gave Allison a strawberry sample.

"You don't want to try anything on?" Allison asked me. "Even if no one sees it, just knowing you're wearing it will give you a big confidence boost."

Did I need a confidence boost? I thought I'd been doing okay lately. I hadn't cried in weeks and hadn't even looked at my spreadsheet since the night of the broken dishes.

"No," I said, "but I *am* buying this." I gave her a wicked smile and held up a red heart-shaped lollipop that said *"Fuck Me"* in white letters. Jake would love it.

"I don't even want to know what you're going to do with it," she said.

Good. Because I wasn't going to tell her anyway.

JAKE GOT OUT of class at seven. I knew Adam's schedule by now and knew he would get out of class at nine. That meant Jake and I had a small window of opportunity.

"Where are you?" he asked when he called at 7:03.

"Allison and Braham's," I answered. I'd stayed for dinner. Hot dogs and hamburgers on the grill.

"Can I steal you away from them?"

I nonchalantly walked over to the grill and pretended like I was grabbing another hot dog so they wouldn't hear my conversation.

"Maybe I should walk somewhere and meet you."

He sighed. "Look, you know why I don't want our coworkers to know about us. And I'm still not sure about your family yet. But I don't see why we have to be a secret around your friends. Maybe I should start being as suspicious of you as you are with me."

"No. Definitely not. I just don't want her trying to tell me it's wrong." If I told Allison about us, she would find a way to bring me down from my flying carpet. She would be happy for me for having a fling, but that was just it. I didn't want anyone thinking of us as a fling. I didn't want Allison acting like he was just some guy I was wasting time with, like I could toss him aside without a second glance. That would make the time we spent together seem superficial.

On the other hand, I didn't want Allison thinking of us as a couple either. That might be worse than her thinking we were a fling. She would worry about me. She would warn me. She would ask the questions I was too afraid to ask myself. "Rox, are you sure you know what you're doing? What happens in the fall? What happens after graduation?" And all those other questions I didn't want to think about right now.

I already knew what would happen after summer if Allison found out about Jake. In fact, I could see the scenario play so vividly in my mind that I felt physically ill for a moment.

I'd be back in Chapel Hill trying to pretend like I didn't leave someone amazing back home. Allison would make a normal phone call to me, except she wouldn't act normal at all. She'd talk about the kids and Braham and electric bills and laundry and she might mention running into my mom at the grocery store or seeing Adam at Applebee's, but she would never, ever mention Jake. And then I would be left wondering why she hadn't mentioned him. Had she seen him? Was he seeing someone? Did she know anything? Was she feeling sorry for me right now? Was there something she wasn't telling me because she was reluctant to be the bearer of bad news?

Nobody wanted to be that person – the one walking around like everything was normal while everyone else avoided their eyes out of pity and embarrassment – because they knew something she didn't. I didn't want to be the last one to know. Shudder.

I wouldn't be able to ask Allison if she'd seen Jake. It would give me away. I would seem needy and pathetic and weak, and I was trying to move in the other direction. I was trying to be strong, carefree, and confident. Pining away for a boy I left behind (if, indeed, it went down that way), was something I needed to do on my own – not in public, not with friends.

And *that* was why I couldn't tell Allison. I didn't want that scenario to ever happen. If it was just the two of us, I could stay in our bubble and pretend September wouldn't ever come. And when it did come, I could pretend I was okay without anyone walking on eggshells around me.

"Why would she say you were wrong?" Jake asked.

"It's nothing personal. You know she's always trying to protect me."

"Yeah." I sensed a tiny bit of irritation in his voice. "I know. Since when does she need to protect you ... from me?"

I shoved a big bite of a hotdog into my mouth so Allison and Braham didn't get suspicious of me for hovering around the grill. "That's not what I meant," I tried to say with my mouthful. "She juh dun't wamme t'get hurt."

"You're digging a deeper hole here, baby."

I giggled and swallowed. "I'm putting down the shovel."

"Either way, we *are* allowed to be friends. Tell them I'm picking you up because I need help with my homework."

"I don't know anything about photography." That wasn't technically true. I started my freshman year as a film major. When I tried to learn about things like aperture and f-stops, my brain turned to mush. It was way too scientific for me. I dropped that shit faster than the fastest shutter speed.

"You don't need to. My homework assignment is to take a photo of something beautiful. That's all I need you for."

Butterflies! Wings flapping! Heart swooning! Body reacting without the help of a revolutionary stimulation gel!

"Okay. I'll see you in a few."

"Be ready," he said.

"Who was that?" Allison asked when I returned to the picnic table.

"Oh. That was Jake. He's going to come pick me up. He started a photography class today and wanted to know if I would help him with a homework assignment."

"Homework?" she asked, eyebrows slanted. "What the hell do you know about photography?"

"He just needs an extra hand to assist with props and stuff."

"Hmm. Well he's not taking you anywhere until he eats something. So make sure he comes around back."

It reminded me of the scene in *Adventures in Babysitting,* when the babysitter and kids were told, "Nobody leaves this place without singin' the blues." She could be a little bossy at times. I was partly to blame for that since I'd been letting her boss me around for nearly fifteen years. I'd learned long ago that it was faster and easier to do what she said rather than argue, so I texted Jake.

ME: Allison said you aren't leaving this place until you've eaten a hot dog. So come to the backyard when you get here.
JAKE: I was hoping we could get to my place for a bit before Adam gets home.
ME: I am hoping for that, too. So eat fast.
JAKE: Gotcha :))

"I went to a sex shop today," I told him as he drove us to his apartment.
"Oh yeah?" he looked intrigued. "Get anything good?"
I pulled the lollipop out of my bag and smiled sweetly when I put it to my lips with the wrapper still on.
"Very cute. I know what I'm taking pictures of tonight."
I put it back in my bag. "Ha. Don't think so, buddy."
"You'll see. What else did you get?"
"A free sample of some flavored stimulating lube."
"Sounds fun."
It probably should have been.

ALL GOOD THINGS

IT WAS AFTER eight when we got to Jake's. That left an hour or less to get in some quality time before Adam came home and busted us. Thanks to some dirty talk on the way home, we were ready to go before we got there. I had him stripped and tasting like pina colada in no time at all.

Everything was going fine. Great, even. I had fun teasing him with the *'Fuck Me'* sucker and even let him take a few pics.

"I'll need material to jerk off to after you leave," he said.

What kind of cruel person would I be to deny him that? Besides, I liked the idea of him thinking of me after I left. As for the possibility of the photo ending up online one day, I wasn't worried about it. There wasn't any nudity, and it seemed like everyone was doing provocative photo shoots or 'accidentally' leaking sex tapes lately. If Rachael Ray could pose for *FHM*, and still be considered a good girl, I could get over a photo leak, too.

So yeah. Pina colada-flavored foreplay, a heart-shaped *'Fuck Me'* sucker, a camera ... it should have been a great time. And it was.

Until it wasn't.

We were in the bathroom. Not the safest place for us to be. If Adam got out of class early, we were fucked in more ways than one. That was probably why Jake picked the spot. With us, it seemed like the riskier the activity, the more fun we had.

I was sitting on counter and he was standing between my legs. All was well until he stopped moving and leaned into me, his hands on the counter beside each of my hips.

"Baby?" he said quietly, his lips slightly touching my ear.

"Yeah? What's wrong?" I ran my hands down his back.

"It's the condom."

"Did it break? Don't panic. You know I take the pill just in case."

"It didn't break. It's gone."

I leaned back so I could see his face. "What do you mean gone?"

"I mean it's not there anymore." He pressed his right hand onto his forehead and closed his eyes. He looked disappointed. "I don't think you're supposed to use a lubricant *before* you put on a condom."

"She said it was safe for condoms."

"Yeah. Like it wouldn't eat through the latex. But we should have put lube on *over* the condom. Not under it."

Jake completed four years of college, and I'd finished three. Yet neither of us had the common sense to know you didn't put something designed to be slippery underneath a condom. I couldn't help but burst out laughing.

I was relieved when Jake laughed, too.

I waited until we'd recomposed ourselves before I asked the looming question. "So, where is it then?"

"It's inside you somewhere."

Oh jeez. "Somewhere? What are we supposed to do?"

"Get it out."

"How?"

"With our fingers, I guess. Do you want me to get it, or do you want to do it yourself?"

Uh, let me think about this for a second. Which scenario would be less embarrassing?

- Jake dropping to his knees to get up close and personal in a non-sexual way? I imagined him pulling up a stool and getting out a spotlight like my OBGYN. Anything but that, please!
- Jake watching me dig it out myself? I bet that would be attractive. He'd probably never get the image out of his head. Ten years from now we'd run into each other at Starbucks, and he'd see me digging for a condom that went swimming upstream.
- Jake leaving the room and knowing I was in the bathroom shoving a few fingers up my vagina?

It was a no-win situation.

"I'll get it," he said, taking charge.

He did not kneel down to get a better look *or* get out a flashlight. I said a silent prayer for that small victory. He stayed where he was and stuck his forefinger up there like an expert.

His assertiveness was a turn-on.

He pulled it out and, with a sigh of relief, tossed the useless thing into the trash.

"You were in there without a condom," I said quietly as it dawned on me. He had gone where no man had gone before.

He must have thought I was angry because he got defensive. He put his arms behind me to pull me closer and rested his head on my shoulder. "I'm sorry. I didn't mean to."

"I know. It's okay." I rested my head on his shoulder, too, and ran my fingers up his sides. With me up on the counter, we were at the same height and it was much easier to kiss him. I lifted his head off me, put my elbows up on his shoulders and kissed him. So often kissing became nothing but a means to an end, a routine, just another part of foreplay. I didn't ever want it to be that way with Jake. Kissing him was a complete act in itself. We didn't need sex.

But I did really, *really*, want it. I showed him as much by grabbing him by the hips and trying to pull him back. He resisted.

"It's just gonna fall off again, baby. We can't."

"Just do it," I whispered. "And don't stop kissing me or I might change my mind."

"I never have," he said quietly. "I've never had a serious girlfriend before, so I've always been real careful. I didn't want to end up like my parents. And I didn't want any kid to ever end up like me. So I just never..."

I ran my fingers through his messy hair. "Hey," I whispered back, "you don't have to defend yourself. It's not a bad thing. I think it's awesome that you've been careful. We'll just push pause for now. It's fine."

"You're really on the pill?" he asked.

"Yes. I have been since high school."

"I trust you," he said. "Do you trust me?"

"Yes."

"Then I'll kiss you the whole time."

"Okay," I whispered.

He kept his promise. Even when we weren't actively kissing, our lips touched the whole time as we shared the same breath. And I knew I would never, ever change my mind. Holy fuck! I'd seriously been missing out! I had no idea it would feel so different, so much better.

"That was fucking incredible," he said.

Our lips were still touching.

"No shit," I said, breathlessly. "When can we do that again?"

"Tomorrow?" he asked.

"Do I have to wait that long?"

"'fraid so. And Rox? No more revolutionary products, okay?"

I laughed so hard I snorted.

CHAPTER 16

FALL 1999

JAKE
Sixteen years old

SHE'S BEEN TALKING for about three blocks, ever since we left school (on foot, since I don't have my license yet, and Adam has to stay after school for football practice). Roxie is always a rambler, but she's chattier than usual today. I suspect some kind of energy pill. The girls have been lining up at the water fountain lately, getting all jacked up on whatever latest convenience store packet is popular at the moment. She's different than me in that way. I like to chill out and relax after class. She likes to do cartwheels on the way home from school.

"It was some kind of archaic alphabet, and the assignment was to write a sentence about ourselves using the alphabet. But it was missing letters. I wanted to write 'I love NSYNC,' and there wasn't a V. So I asked, out loud, in front of the whole class, 'Mr. Wilson, how do you make love?'"

"You didn't!" I say, even though I know she did. It was a rhetorical 'You didn't.'

"I did. Everyone thought it was funny. I guess it is now, but I felt really dumb when it happened. Then, I was in Typing when Nick Green asked if anyone wanted a piece of gum. I raised my hand. He threw one over to me, but his aim was, like, way off, and it landed in the aisle between the desks. So I tried to grab it and tripped over one of the computer cords. I landed on my face, Jake. In front of the entire class!"

"No!" I reply, even though I'm not all that invested in this conversation because I can't stop staring at her mouth long enough to pay attention to what's coming out of it.

I'd decided today, in fourth hour, today was going to be *the* day. I am finally going to kiss Roxie Humsucker. I've been thinking about it for four or five years now, but she was always too young. A guy in junior high can't kiss girls in elementary school. A guy in high school can't kiss girls who are still in junior high. And guys in college can't kiss girls who are in high school. (Okay, scratch that one. They *can,* and they *should*).

This is the first time since sixth grade that Roxie and I have been in the same school. And juniors *are* allowed to kiss freshmen. I checked.

I've been ready since the first day of school, but I've given her a few weeks to adjust to high school before I turn her whole world upside down. Or more like horizontal, I hope.

We're now two weeks into the fall semester and there's no time better than the present. I think.

If only she would stop talking...

"It's like I'm cursed. This has been the most embarrassing day of my life."

Roxie exaggerates ... a lot. I mean it's not like she shit her pants in class and had it dripping out of her pant leg under the desk. That scenario would qualify as the most embarrassing day of someone's life. That would be I-must-change-schools-immediately embarrassing.

"I'm just waiting for a semi to drive through a mud puddle and drench me."

There are no semis driving through this residential neighborhood. There is no mud anywhere that I can see either. But I don't correct her. No sense making her feel stupid when I'm about to kiss her.

Yep. I am going to kiss her.

Any minute now.

She switches subjects so fast it makes my head spin. Now she's talking about fall. She's making a list with me. She has a whole notebook filled with lists about the most random things: Best Teen Movies of the 80s, Best Icebreakers When I'm Feeling Nervous in a Crowd, Hottest Boy Band Members, Funniest *Friends* Episodes...

Best Things About Fall.

"New TV shows," she says.

I nod in agreement and add my personal favorite, "Apple cider."

"Oh! For sure. And the leaves. They're incredible." She's been on an 'incredible' kick lately. It's like her new word. I hope she thinks *I'm* incredible. I don't know what I'll do if she rejects me. I know I'll be embarrassed as all hell. I might even have to avoid the whole family for a few days. But she'll forget about it. Girls are like that, especially Roxie. She's like a butterfly. She lands on a topic, or some moment of drama, sniffs around for a bit (do butterflies even have noses?), and then flutters over to the next one, forgetting everything that came before. She gets upset about things, but she gets over them quickly. If she hates it that I kiss her, she'll probably yell at me and be angry for the remainder of our walk home. By tomorrow, it'll be old news.

What if she likes it that I kiss her? Will I still be old news tomorrow?

"Adam's football games," I add. I don't play, but Friday night football games are easily my favorite part about high school. When the air starts to get chilly, people start thinking about hooking up. The Friday night football game is usually where it all begins. The anticipation, the waiting, the nerves – it all adds up to a great time.

Roxie has always come to Adam's games, but it seems different this year, now that she's there as a student instead of a little sister. I've seen her, sitting in the bleachers with the other freshmen.

Just last week I saw her leaning back between the legs of the kid sitting behind her. She looked cool and comfortable with her elbows up on his knees, like it was so natural for her. I felt something unfamiliar stir inside me then and I found it hard to look away. It took a minute before I figured out what that pesky feeling was – it was jealousy. *I* wanted to be the guy sitting behind her. I wanted her elbows on *my* knees. I wanted to ask if she was cold and offer her my sweatshirt. I wanted to tell her she looked pretty in her purple Pioneer gear and buy her some popcorn.

Eventually she'd busted me staring at them. Of all the people in the bleachers, she'd found me. I didn't get embarrassed when she caught me looking. I didn't look away. I wasn't shy about the way I felt – or sorry. I would never apologize for caring.

"Yeah," she says, pulling my mind away from the football game and back to the sidewalk we were walking on. "I do like the football games. It just gets so cold sometimes."

She stops walking suddenly and turns toward me, her eyes big and bright, her smile wide and white. I know exactly what she's going to say.

"HOODIES!" We both say it at the same time.

She throws her head back and laughs. I can see a silver filling on her top row of molars, and a big, dark pink piece of bubblegum on her tongue.

She has her hands in the front kangaroo pouch of her pullover hoodie. She smiles at me in front of a backdrop of orange and red and yellow leaves. Even in the moment I know I have something special here. A lot of times we don't realize something special is happening until the moment is long gone. This time I know it. I hope I can find a way to keep this image with me until the end of time.

ALL GOOD THINGS

I grab her by the sides of her face and lean in. I take no time to pause to look at her and make sure it's okay. I just do it. I close my eyes and kiss her. Finally.

Her lips are soft, and she tastes like something sweet and fruity, maybe raspberries.

She gasps with delight when our tongues touch. I release my intense grip on her face and she gasps again. It sounds more like a squeal actually. She pulls her hands from her hoodie pocket and starts flapping her arms. Wow. She's getting really excited.

No. She's choking. Oh my God! She is seriously choking!

Her eyes plead with me to save her. She looks terrified. No sound comes from her anymore. Her throat must be completely blocked.

People always wonder how they'll react in an emergency. Fight, flight, or freeze. I'm proud to say I'm a fighter.

I hit her on the back a few times. No luck.

I think back to the photocopied sheets I'd seen hanging in kitchens and restaurants. I know the basic idea of the move – the Heimlich. I've never done it before, but I have no choice but to try. Her face is turning purple.

I get behind her, put my fist where I think it's supposed to go and pump. Once. Twice. The piece of gum shoots out of her mouth.

She collapses onto her knees in the grass between the sidewalk and the street. I can't see her face because she's looking down. I can hear her as she takes short, loud gasps of breath.

Oh shit.

She's breathing fast and shaking, too. She wipes an eye with the sleeve of her hoodie, and I see tears. At first I think her eyes are watery from the trauma, and that might have added to it, but she is definitely crying.

I kneel down on the grass next to her, but I am too afraid to touch her just yet. I think it's best if I give her time to recover and not smother her.

I give her a few moments to recompose, and I need those moments myself. My heart is pounding so fast I can hear it. I have never been so scared before. I feel incredible for saving Roxie's life. But then I remember what caused her to choke. It's my fault. Roxie almost died, and it's all because of me.

I almost lost the girl I've loved as long as I remember. All because I decided to kiss her. How selfish. Her parents, her brother, they would be devastated if anything happened to her. I would, too. I would seriously fucking die.

I put my head in my hands right next to her. I can't cry in front of Roxie. God knows she's seen enough of that shit. Hopefully God is the *only* one who knows she's seen enough of that shit.

I've got to keep my shit together and take care of her right now. I can't take care of her if I'm a bawling mess like a fucking pussy.

I see the tires pull up along the curb. I look up at the cop car, glad someone stopped to help.

He rushes to Roxie's side.

"Are you okay, miss?" he asks.

She looks up at him, her red face streaked with black from her eye makeup, and nods.

"Did he hurt you?"

She shakes her head.

"We got a call from a resident that there was some kind of domestic dispute."

I thought back to what had happened. The way I grabbed her by her head. It was kind of aggressive. And then when I smacked her on her back. I hit her hard. I was desperate. The Heimlich was obviously a life-saving maneuver, but whoever was watching us was probably already dialing 9-1-1 before it got to that point.

The good news is that Roxie is okay. The bad news is that I'd finished a joint on the way home. The cop smelled the weed and asked me to empty my pockets where he found rolling papers.

Roxie walked the rest of the way home by herself, and I got to ride in the back of a police car for the first time. Talk about an embarrassing moment. I think I got you beat, Rox.

I AM LUCKY to live in Ann Arbor where marijuana laws are so lenient. If I'd been caught somewhere else I could have been slapped with a felony. Instead, I get a metaphorical slap on the wrist and a phone call to my mother.

She isn't mad. We get into the car and she smiles at me and tousles my hair. "My baby's first drug bust," she says, like it's some kind of rite of passage, the first of many. I hope not. I like to chill out and get high sometimes, but I don't want to end up a loser who drops out of school to sit home, smoke weed, and play video games all day. I don't want to be the guy who delivers pizza for a few hours a night on a suspended license just to get enough cash for a forty-ounce and an eighth of weed while I live in my mother's basement and sleep ten hours a day. I'd like to land a little bit farther from the tree.

I'M ABOUT TO microwave a can of soup for dinner when Roxie calls.

"Jesus!" she yells. "Thanks for fucking calling me!" I love it when she swears. It's so naughty, and goes against her cute, good-girl face. "I've been worried sick about you. How long have you been home?"

"Uh, like five minutes. They called my mom to pick me up. That was it."

"I'm sorry, Jake."

"For what?"

"I feel like it's my fault. If you got arrested or something, it would be my fault."

I laughed. "Not even close to your fault. You don't even smoke."

She's quiet for a minute. I'm relieved she seems normal so far.

"Chili," she says. "We forgot about chili. I didn't think of it until I walked in the house after school. It's been in the slow cooker all day."

"Chili. Yes. That one should go above football and below apple cider."

ALL GOOD THINGS

"Agreed. I'm setting a place for you right now. Hurry up."

I OPEN THEIR front door without knocking. I haven't knocked on their door in about ten years. Adam is sitting on the couch in the living room playing Gameboy. He throws the gadget onto the couch cushion and stands up when he sees me enter.

"Dude! What the hell?" he asks as he comes toward me. He continues in a quiet voice, "Roxie said you got arrested."

"Not arrested," I say, also in a quiet voice. "Just a citation. They called my mom. That was it."

He slaps me on the back of my shoulder as Roxie enters the room from the kitchen.

"You really should stop smoking in public, man," he warns. "I've told you about that shit."

I look at Roxie. She didn't tell him. I smile at her, relieved. She smiles back, looking sweet and shy ... which makes me want to kiss her all over again.

AFTER DINNER I pull on my jacket and head out the door. I'm on the bottom step when I hear the door open and close behind me. I turn around. She's standing on the porch in her slippers. She pulls the long-sleeves of her thermal over her hands to keep them warm.

I climb back up to the porch, and as I do, I notice her freckles are starting to fade away with her summer tan.

I've always loved her freckles, sprinkled across her cheeks, not too many, just enough. I'll have to wait until summer to see them again.

"You won't tell your parents, will you?" I ask. I was disappointed in myself for barely escaping a criminal record. I would hate myself if I disappointed them, too. After all they've done for me ... they would be hurt. I would be ashamed.

"I won't tell them what?" she asks. "That you almost got arrested? Or that you kissed me?"

She remembers. I was wondering if the near-death experience had been so traumatizing that she'd forgotten what caused it in the first place. Guess I used up all my luck with the police officer, eh?

"Uh," I look down at the concrete and put my hands in the pockets of my coat.

She crosses her arms across her chest and shivers. I want to grab her and wrap her up inside me and keep her warm. But someone would probably call the cops.

"Neither. I hope," I say, while looking up cautiously to catch her expression.

She's smirking. She thinks it's funny. I guess it really is. It was scary as hell, but now that everything is okay again, it's some funny shit. I wonder how many times we'll laugh about this in the future.

She decides to start right now.

I can't help but laugh, too. Her giggle is contagious.

"Sorry I almost killed you," I say.

"Hey. You saved my life. Thanks for saving me, Jake."

"I will save you any chance I get," I say.

ALL GOOD THINGS

I don't know if she'll ever need to take me up on that again, but I know I'll never tire of it.

Roxie Humsucker, let me be your hero.

JULY 2005

CHAPTER 17

ROXIE

> FREAKING LOVE this kid.
> That is all.

AUGUST 2005

CHAPTER 18

SIXTEEN DAYS LEFT

Dear August, I fucking hate you.
Prior to the appearance of a pregnant teenager at my door, I'd had high expectations for this summer. I thought of it as my last summer of freedom. College graduation wasn't just about receiving a degree. It was a symbolic moment – a metaphorical line I would cross. On this side of the line was a (most-likely naïve) girl with hopes, dreams, and high, idealistic expectations for the future. I was the girl who drank 'til I puked, spent too much money on shoes, wore sweatpants in public, ate Kraft macaroni and cheese for dinner, and Taco Bell in the middle of the night. I wore heart-shaped sunglasses, sang out loud whenever I could, and have been known to make out with complete strangers when I was single. Basically, I was twenty-one.

Once I crossed that line in May, when I put on that cap and gown and accepted my BS in Social Work, I'd have to change. I had to grow up. I had to be a lady, a woman, not a girl. In a grown-up world, I needed to sip a glass of wine at dinner instead of throwing back shots at a bar. I needed to get up early in the morning and wear blazers and fashion scarves to a job that didn't require an apron. I'd be expected to make real meals with real ingredients, not those that came from drive-thru windows or cardboard boxes with packets of powdered cheese. Grown-ups had savings accounts, not maxed out credit cards. They slept on beds that didn't turn into couches during the day. They didn't wear sweatpants, miniskirts, bikinis, or heart-shaped *anything*. And when they met a guy, they made him take them out on a date before their first kiss.

Yeah, I had a lot of work to do in the next year. I was scared. Thinking about what was expected of me, and trying to become a person I didn't know how to be, it scared the shit out of me. I had a lot of growing up to do and this summer was my very last chance to be … well, *me*. And because of that, it needed to be the Best Summer Ever. Failure was not an option.

Except for my setback in the beginning, I'd gotten on the right track. With Jake's help, I'd had a great June. Because of him, July was perfect. This summer was better even than the Best Summer Ever list I'd made back in April (the one I never mentioned, because I tore it up and threw it away during a bitch-fit back in May).

In our endless summer there was no talk of school, classes, Tar Heels, fall. And there were no regrets. Our summer, The Summer of Jake & Roxie, was bonfires, barbeques, beaches, bikinis, baseball games, lots of sunscreen, and lots of sex, especially in Jake's truck. So totally tenth grade, yeah. But seriously, it was smoking hot – the urgency, the desperation, the thrill of being busted. This was definitely going into the books as my hottest summer on record. I couldn't have been happier. Honestly. I couldn't recall a single period of my life when I'd been as consistently happy as I'd been this summer.

And then came fucking August. Yuck. Now I had back-to-school shit shoved down my throat daily. It was making me gag. The Target commercials, the Abercrombie & Fitch catalog, the Wal-Mart billboards, the pencils and notebook displays smack-dab in front of every store. Could someone please tell them to back the fuck off? August was still summer!

Then there was Zeke working on his fall menu – a menu I would never serve. And Jake, researching apple cider drink recipes – drinks I would never serve. And Shannon, planning an End-of-Summer party that was going to be so great. "Other parties will be jealous," she'd told me.

Fuck all of you. And that was all I had to say about that.

I WAS A little testy tonight. I was pretty sure it had something to do with the email I'd received from UNC earlier in the week reminding me of my registration date. How was I supposed to keep living in our endless summer when I had to go online to register for classes?

The conversation I'd overheard between Zeke and Jake earlier hadn't helped my attitude any either. I shouldn't say I overheard it. It wasn't like I'd been eavesdropping on a secret conversation. I'd been standing right there at the bar waiting for Jake to get me a Corona. And I wished I hadn't been.

"Hey," Zeke had said to Jake, "would you mind putting a few wanted ads on the internet tonight? We need almost a whole new staff, trained and ready to go, in only two weeks. You know I'm not good with computer stuff."

Instead of responding to Zeke right away, Jake turned his head and looked at me. I think he wanted to see if I'd heard or not. We hadn't talked about the end of summer. We pretended it wasn't happening. I would be content to go on pretending, live out the next few weeks in blissful denial. But people saying shit like that made it harder to ignore the obvious.

"Yeah, sure," Jake said to Zeke as he set a Corona on my tray. He looked up to meet my eyes, but I turned away before he could say anything. I could pretend I hadn't heard anything. And we could pretend the end of summer wasn't near.

As if I wasn't already pissed off enough, a guy came in by himself, sat at a four-top in my section instead of sitting at the bar like most single people, and ordered a basket of French fries and a water with a bowl of lemons on the side. Really, dude? Taking up a whole table for a five-dollar tab?

Ordering water with dinner was not a big deal. I didn't even mind adding a lemon slice. But asking for an entire bowl of lemon slices, squeezing them into your water with a packet of sugar, and mixing, that's called freshly squeezed lemonade, and it's generally at least $5 at any pop-up carnival. It got on my nerves when people thought they were going to pull a fast one on us. We were on to you, buddy.

I huffed and puffed like a child and headed over to the bar to put in an order of fries. Rachel was watching Jake pour some kind of concoction from a cocktail shaker into a row of shot glasses.

"I've got one!" I told Jake and Rachel as I threw my fist in the air triumphantly. I had something great to add to the list. I'm talking about the mother of all lists. We'd been working on it all summer. By we, I meant the staff of The Bar.

What Your Drink Order Says About You

- PBR – I own a faded t-shirt that says, "I hate hipsters." Just to be ironic.
- Bud Light – I used to crush beer cans on my forehead when I was younger … and by younger, I mean an hour ago.
- Cosmopolitan – I shower right before sex.
- Screwdriver – I love the missionary position.
- Vodka rocks – I may have a drinking problem.
- Well vodka – I'll be crying myself to sleep tonight. Just like last night.
- Craft beer – I know what I'm doing. Bonus points if it's local.

- Jager bomb – I finally passed the GED exam! Let's party!
- A shot of Jameson – I'm a bartender.
- Anything with tonic – I want you to think I'm sophisticated and grown-up.
- Scotch – I wish it was socially acceptable for straight guys to drink Appletinis in public.
- Vodka Cranberry – This is my first time in a bar. My ID is fake.
- Orgasm or Blow Job – I'm totally flirting with the bartender.
- Whiskey neat – I carry my own flask to parties.
- Sex on the Beach (ordered with a giggle) – I once entered a wet t-shirt contest. I didn't win.
- Pants Down Party – I once entered a wet t-shirt contest. And won.

We were very proud of our list. But we'd forgotten something: the non-alcoholic drinks.

"Water with lemon," I said quietly to Jake and Rachel. I had to make sure the customers didn't hear. "It means, 'I have a small penis.'"

I looked over at the guy with the water. He had his cell phone sitting on the table next to him, like he was waiting (hoping) for a call. He seemed like a nice guy, maybe just a little lonely. I felt guilty for what I'd said, so I quickly added an amendment.

"But I'm a nice guy, so I get a lot of fucks."

ALL GOOD THINGS

"In that case," Rachel said, "a water with lime means, 'I have a small penis, and I'm also a douchbag. I get no fucks at all.'"

"Sounds good to me," I said.

I pulled my server's book out of my apron and wrote the two new additions down on my notepad. I would type it into the spreadsheet tonight. I thought we had something pretty good here, maybe even publishable. I would look into sending it out on the interwebs when I got back to school.

No! Stop! That wasn't happening. August was still summer.

I was in for a surprise when Guy-Who-Drinks-Water left a ten on the table for me. I felt awful. If you ever wanted to make a server feel lousy, leave a big tip after getting subpar service. It'll really get 'em in the gut. Stiffing them would make them hate you and hope those spicy wings you ordered would leave your asshole throbbing for a week. Leaving them money they knew they didn't deserve will have them lying in bed all night rethinking their entire lives.

My guess was that he wanted to watch the baseball game, but didn't have cable. He knew he couldn't afford dinner, a drink, and a good tip, so he'd saved money on food to make sure he had something nice to leave me. How could that not tug at my heartstrings a little? I felt guilty, again, for saying he probably had a small penis. Even if he did, I could tell he was a nice guy. If I weren't with Jake, I'd totally throw him a vagina.

WITH JAKE. I hated how serious that sounded. I used to roll my eyes at people who were afraid of labels, like the words *boyfriend* and *girlfriend*. Now I'd turned into one of them. He'd said the word girlfriend a few times, in the most casual of ways, like that time in the bathroom when we lost the condom. I never called him out on it. But it nagged at me. Girlfriends were serious. If I was his girlfriend, that meant we were a couple. If we were a couple, that meant we were going to break up – soon. And it made me want to vomit.

I FELT A vibration in my apron. I hid in the server's station and pulled out my phone to look at the text from Allison.

Shit. I forgot.

"Hey," I said to Jake later on when none of our coworkers were within hearing distance. "I totally forgot to tell you. Allison and Braham's annual summer luau is tomorrow night."

"I know," he said as he stocked margarita glasses in the overhead rack. "Why do you think we both have tomorrow off?"

"You knew about it?" I asked.

"Yeah. She invited me."

Oh. Okay. They'd known each other just as long as I'd known them, but Jake was more my friend than hers. She didn't usually invite him to parties. But I was fine that he had been invited. Now I didn't need to think of an excuse to bring him with me.

ALL GOOD THINGS

"What time do you plan on going?" I asked. "I want to make sure we don't arrive at the same time."

Jake rolled his eyes. "Whenever you want me to," he said. He looked and sounded a little irritated. I didn't think too much about it. I was sure I could make him forget he was angry later on.

And if I couldn't, it was probably for the best anyway.

"Wanna go to the airport?" he asked when we got into his truck after work.

When I was sixteen I'd found an old boarded-up restaurant near the airport right underneath one of the flight paths. I used to park my car in their vacant parking lot and do homework, watch planes fly overhead, and make lists about my perfect future as a film director in New York City.

A few weeks ago Jake needed to photograph lights in motion for a homework assignment, and I had the idea for him to take photos of an airplane overhead. I took him to the secret spot after work one night, and we lay in the bed of his truck, waiting for planes until he got that perfect shot.

The picture was badass. His teacher was so impressed she suggested he create accounts for himself at stock photo websites. He took her advice and sold three photos in his first week. He was very proud. I was too.

The restaurant in the lot was reopened now, but by the time we got out of work, they'd been closed for hours. We'd spent several nights since then lying in the bed of

Jake's truck, watching the planes, looking for shooting stars, and just being close to each other. One night we even fell asleep and woke up sweltering hot at eight in the morning with the sun beating down on us.

Finding a place to have sex was easier than you'd think, probably because it was over so quickly. Working together all night, it was hot. Imagine eight hours of foreplay every day. By the time we got to the main course, it was over before we could slow it down. We'd had a lot of fun in a variety of public places over the summer, even once in the beer cooler at work ... in the middle of a shift.

But it was a lot harder to find a place where we could hang out and just *be* together. I knew that sounded lame. But sometimes I just wanted to be around him and not have to stay five feet away. Keeping my distance was painful. The parking lot by the airport gave us what we needed to reconnect.

"Okay," I said. "Let's go."

We really needed a reconnection tonight. He didn't seem like himself; he'd been quiet and guarded. When other people were quiet, I felt like I had to talk a lot to make up for the silence. But tonight, I let us be quiet. I felt guarded, too.

It had been a really bad night for me. I knew time was going by too fast and I would be leaving him soon. I was torn in two. The soft side of me wanted to snuggle up and enjoy every last minute I had left with him. But the hard side, the side with the cement heart, wanted to distance myself a little more each day to make the separation easier. If I hadn't promised him I wouldn't play games with his head, I would have probably already started a stupid fight with him, just to get him to renege on our agreement.

Believe me, I'd thought about it. I'd thought of several ways to push him away. Any other guy and I would have done it already. But come on, this was Jake. He was too good for lies and games. He was too good for *me*.

We pulled into the empty lot, and he turned the truck off. It was the kind of quiet I loved: nothing but crickets and the occasional airplane. It was a lot louder during the day, but the planes were scarcer in the middle of the night.

I walked around to the rear of the trunk. It was chillier than usual. *August was still summer! Got that, Mother Nature?*

I'd gotten used to bringing clothes in my tote bag. I never knew where I'd end up after work. I pulled out a pair of sweatpants and put them on over my tiny shorts.

Jake joined me behind the truck with our favorite fleece blanket in his arms. He tossed the blanket into the bed and tugged at the front waistband of my pants.

"What's this about? You're supposed to remove clothes, not put more on."

I shrugged. "It's kind of chilly tonight."

"Sure is," he said dryly. I had a feeling he wasn't talking about the weather.

He lifted the handle of the tailgate and let it drop with a loud thud. I flinched. He seemed angry, but I couldn't figure out why. I had *thought* about doing something to make him mad, just to push him away. But I hadn't actually gone through with it. Had I?

I thought back through our night at work, from beginning to end, and tried to figure out why he was so pissed. I honestly had no idea, but I wasn't going to play the "What's wrong?" game either. If he had something to say, he should say it. Wasn't that one of the rules?

He walked back up to the front of the truck and opened the driver's side door. He came back with another blanket and tossed it in with the first.

I reached into my bag and grabbed a thin cotton pullover hoodie. While I was pulling it over my head he decided to say what he needed to say.

"Why didn't you tell me about Allison's party?" he asked.

I pulled the shirt down over my stomach. "Is that why you're so moody tonight? Because I didn't tell you about the party?"

"No, not originally. I figured you forgot. But when I told you Allison invited me ... you seemed ... disappointed."

"Jake! I was not disappointed. I was surprised because Allison has never invited you to the luau before. But even if you weren't invited personally, I would have brought you with me anyway."

He took a step closer to me. When I stepped back in defense, my butt hit the tailgate.

"*Would* you have?" he asked. "Or would you have been afraid she might find out your dirty secret?"

"Jake, really? You know you're not a dirty secret. It's not like I'm ashamed of you."

"Sometimes I wonder if you are."

"Are you serious?"

If he really felt that way, if I ever did anything to make him feel that way, I would hate myself.

"What else am I supposed to think? I thought we were keeping this to ourselves out of necessity. You act like you prefer it this way."

I didn't know what to say. He was kind of right.

"I know we agreed on the whole summer," he continued, "but if you want out early, just say so. You have a few weeks left here, and you don't need to keep sneaking around with me if I'm not what you want."

What? He couldn't be serious. Just thinking about being without him made me ill. I wouldn't trade him for anything. "You are *all* I want. You have to know that. But this was your idea. You're the one who said we should keep it to ourselves."

He slid his arms around my waist and rested his hands on the lowest part of my back. "Yeah. Two months ago. Because it was new and felt fragile. I was trying to protect us. You know, let us get a little stronger before we threw ourselves to the wolves. But I'm tired of sneaking around. It takes so much time and energy. Sometimes I just want to chill out without worrying who is around. I want you in my bed, not my truck, or your parents' backyard, or the beer cooler ... well, maybe the beer cooler. But I'm tired of not being able to touch you in front of anyone. I'm done with it. If our coworkers want to start shit, let them. If your family is disappointed, they'll get over it. We can take whatever they throw at us now. We're not fragile anymore. You and me, we're tight enough to make it. Don't you think?"

What I thought was that that could be the nicest thing anyone had ever said to me – *would* ever say to me. *Tight enough to make it*, I repeated to myself. Unbreakable.

"You think we're unbreakable?"

"Yes. Unless I'm wrong," he added. "Unless you *are* ashamed of me. I can't think of any other reason you'd keep me a secret from your best friend this long."

"I wish I could explain to you why I haven't told her. I just don't know the right words."

He stuck his hands into the back of my sweats and pulled me even closer to him. "Why don't you try?"

"I guess it's like a defense mechanism," I said, thinking of Sigmund Freud's theories. I had to stop talking for a second because I felt like I might cry, and I did not want that. Crying was serious, way too serious for us. We were about having fun, not crying or pouting.

I put the back of my hand on my forehead and took a deep breath. When I continued, I spoke calmly and evenly so I wouldn't break down. "I'm going to miss you. A lot. And it'll be easier to get through it if no one knew about it. I won't have people – like Allison, or my mom – asking me how I'm doing, if I'm okay. I know it sounds totally psycho, but I'm just trying to protect *myself*. We might be unbreakable together, but I'm not unbreakable without you. Not even close. Does that make sense?"

He didn't answer me. He just hugged me. It was exactly what I needed him to do.

Then I asked if he could take me home with him.

ALL GOOD THINGS

"You want to come home with me?"

It reminded me of the first night. It was only two months ago but it felt like forever. I couldn't even remember what it was like to *not* be more than friends with Jake. Did that mean one day soon I'd forget what it was like to be *more* than friends? Pretty soon this summer – the right now – would be just a memory, and a fading one at that. I wanted them to be happy memories. I wanted him to be happy. So if he wanted to take me home, he could take me home.

"Yes. I want to go home with you."

"And if Adam sees you there?"

"He'll get over it."

ADAM WAS ALREADY in bed when we got to the apartment, and he left before we woke up. I was relieved. I wanted to make Jake happy, and it was awesome sleeping in his bed with him, just like that first weekend. But I would still prefer for people not to know about us. I wanted to be able to mourn the end of our relationship in privacy. That was all.

Jake dropped me off at home the next afternoon and I told him I'd see him at the luau. I even kissed him goodbye. In my driveway. My parents totally could have seen. That was a girlfriend thing to do, but I figured, we had two weeks left at this point, so did it really matter? No. We were what we were, with or without a label.

I GOT TO the luau a little early to help Allison and Braham get everything set up. Allison's parents had had a summer luau every single summer since we were children. When Allison and Braham got their own place together right after high school, they took over as hosts of the party.

I looked forward to it every year. They served drinks in coconut shells and roasted a pig. The girls wore grass skirts and flowers in their hair and practiced belly dancing. The guys wore Hawaiian-print shirts and embarrassed themselves playing the limbo. And everyone got lei'd. It was a good time.

I wore the same outfit every year: a grass skirt (I'd splurged on a nice one, not one of those cheap plastic ones) and a brown triangle bikini top in place of a coconut bra. I brought a brown hoodie with me for later, in case it got cold.

Allison had on the same outfit. I knew she would. We'd bought them together a few summers ago. Three kids and she could still show her belly. It was sickening. To be fair, though, she did Pilates and kickboxing. It wasn't like she sat around eating ice cream and Butterfingers all day.

She put me to work in the house, cutting up fruit and assembling an antipasto tray with olives, cheese, and sweet baby gherkins. I hadn't yet decided which was the better pickle: the sweet gherkin or the bread 'n butter. All I knew was how blessed I was to live in a world with both. The party guests would be lucky if there were any pickles left by the time I was done.

ALL GOOD THINGS

I could see the backyard from the kitchen window. When people started to arrive, I kept a close eye out for Jake.

"I have a surprise for you," Allison said, bursting through the back door with her hands clasped in front of her in excitement.

I was intrigued. "What?"

She grabbed my hand and pulled me out of the house, down the back steps, and toward the little fire pit. I made sure not to look over at the pig when we walked by. It always grossed me out. Poor little guy.

"What's going on?" I asked as I let her pull me through the backyard.

"A guy," she whispered. "Remember when you said you needed to find a summer fling? I just realized that you never found one. So I found one for you."

Before I could argue, she pulled me in front of a guy in an emerald Hawaiian-print shirt, jean shorts, and deck shoes without socks. He was older, at least thirty. He looked like a grown-up, someone who probably had a 401k. Even if I was single, this guy was not my type at all. I was twenty-one! I didn't even really know what a 401k was!

"Clint," Allison said, "this is the one I've been telling you about! My BFF-for-life. Roxie."

His face brightened, and he gave me a quick and appreciative, but subtle, onceover. At least he had some tact. "Hi there, Roxie."

Hi there? Who said that? Old people, that was who. People in their thirties.

"See?" Allison said, cheerfully. "Didn't I tell you she was hot?"

Funny, because she didn't tell me anything about you, Clint. Even if I wasn't seeing someone, I would be completely humiliated to be set up so obviously and without a warning. What was wrong with her? She knew I would hate this.

"She's only here for a few more weeks until she goes back to school," Allison told him. "I wish I could have gotten you guys together sooner, but things kept getting in the way."

What things? She'd never even mentioned him.

I gave her the dirtiest look I was capable of giving. She acknowledged it, but smiled at me in return. If I didn't know her any better, I'd think she was enacting some kind of revenge scheme on me.

Wait a minute. I did *know her. She* was *getting revenge.* I rubbed my forehead, so confused.

When she walked away I didn't want to be rude to Clint. He started asking me questions about The Bar and North Carolina. He told me he was a Blue Devils fan, but he wouldn't hold it against me. Typical small talk stuff.

I didn't even have a chance to figure out a way to gracefully exit the conversation when I heard Allison, in a dramatic display, calling out for Jake.

"Jake!" she said in a louder voice than she'd greeted anyone else. "I'm so glad you could make it. It's so nice to see you. How *are* you?" Wow. She was laying it on thick.

ALL GOOD THINGS

I stayed near Clint and watched the scene between Allison and Jake play out just inside the gate. She hugged him, and he looked as confused as I felt.

"Roxie told me you were trying to find her a guy for the summer."

"Umm..."

"Look no more! Braham has a friend that is just perfect for her! I know summer's almost over, but there's still time for a quick fling. I've just introduced the two of them." She waved her hand in our direction. "His name is Clint."

Oh. My. God. I couldn't believe she was talking that way, loud enough for other people to hear, including Clint, *and* her parents, *and* her children. A quick fling? She was making me sound like a total slut. I was completely, utterly horrified.

In the middle of my mental meltdown, Jake caught me looking at them and smiled at me. It was the ventriloquist smile. The smile so exaggerated I knew it was fake as hell. He thought this was hilarious? Great. I would kill them both.

Instead of coming to my rescue, he went over to the picnic table to get some food. I wasn't sure if the smoke I saw above me was coming from the fire pit or my ears.

Clint made a few more snippets of small talk, and I listened patiently. I was too polite to tell him he was wasting his time, that I was already more dick-whipped than Pamela Anderson had been over Tommy Lee ... or was it Kid Rock? Either way, dick whipped, me, Jake, yes.

"Would you like me to get you something to drink?" Clint asked.

Jake finally appeared by my side.

He handed me a pina colada in a coconut shell, decorated with a pink umbrella and a blue straw.

"I know how you like your pina coladas." He nudged me with his elbow and stood to the side holding a paper plate and gnawing on a chicken leg. "Who's your friend?" he asked with a smirk. "Maybe he would like to hear about how much you like pina coladas."

I swallowed hard, hoping to get some of the anger out of my throat so I could speak clearly. I wanted to stomp on Jake's foot.

"Clint, this is my friend, Jake. Jake, this is Braham's coworker, Clint. He was just telling me how much he loves Duke basketball. You should talk to Jake about that. He totally loves college basketball," I said sweetly. "Why don't you guys chitchat while I go get a drink? Pina coladas aren't really my thing."

I made a quick exit, furious with both of them.

I dumped my pina colada (I didn't think I could ever drink one again after the lube incident) into the trash bin by the back porch and refilled my coconut shell with a mai tai from the punch bowl, tossing it back in one gulp. I took a few deep, calming breaths before I poured another one. When I felt slightly less mortified, I looked around to see that Jake had gotten away from Clint and taken a seat in a lawn chair to eat the rest of his food. I was on my way toward him, about two feet away from his chair, when Allison stopped me. She stood in front of me and pointed a finger toward my belly.

"What is *that*?" she asked loudly.

ALL GOOD THINGS

I looked down at my stomach, thinking I had spilled something on myself or had a bug on me. I didn't see anything. "What?"

She grabbed a piece of fat about an inch thick, just above the waistband of my grass skirt, and pinched it between her fingers. So I had a tiny belly bulge. Did she really need to point it out in front of people? In front of *Jake?* I didn't think my humiliation could grow any larger today, but I'd underestimated Allison.

And I was wrong if I thought she was done punishing me for the day.

"I know what this means," she said in a knowing voice.

"It means I ate too many chicken wings at work this week," I said dryly, my face probably permanently red by this point.

"No." She paused dramatically and looked around. She wanted to be sure people were listening. They were. "It means you're in love."

I gasped and looked at Jake. I shouldn't have. He was looking intently, right at me, awaiting my response from his lawn chair.

"Yes," she said, sounding completely sure of herself. "It wasn't there when you came home this summer. You were miserable and sad. You weren't eating. You looked ill. Now you're happy. You're glowing. And you have a cute little piece of belly fat. No one goes from miserable to glowing that fast unless they fall in love."

I looked away from her, away from Jake, away from Clint ... I looked at the freaking pig. That was how desperate I was to be out of this situation.

"Who is the lucky guy?" she asked.

She was being a bitch. She was doing this on purpose. Somehow she had found out about Jake and she was making me pay for keeping secrets.

"Why are you doing this to me?" I asked quietly.

"Why didn't you tell me about Jake?" she asked just as quietly. Not so quietly that Jake couldn't hear everything, but quiet enough that the rest of the party went back to whatever they'd been doing before she pinched my belly.

I shook my head. "How do you even know?"

"I didn't. But I guess I do now."

This was crazy; she was acting like a total crazy person. I was afraid of what she might do as an encore. I just wanted to get the hell away from her house as soon as possible.

"I understand why you wouldn't tell your family. But I don't understand why you thought you couldn't tell me." She didn't sound angry. She sounded sad. "This is a big deal. I've been waiting for it to happen for years. So have you. So has he, I'm sure. And I've never seen you this happy. How could you keep something so good a secret?"

"You did all this? Why didn't you just ask me?" Talk about a drama queen. Was she going stir crazy or what? "I've never known you to be so vindictive and manipulative. I don't have to tell you everything I do. It's not like it's the law."

"Do you even know what you're doing, Roxie?"

"This. This right here is why I didn't tell you." I turned to go.

ALL GOOD THINGS

"You know I was just messing with you about Clint," she said behind me. "He's married. His wife is going to be here later. I'm surprised you didn't notice the ring."

I turned around for a second. Her smirk made me want to punch her. "I'm going to go now. I don't really feel like partying anymore."

"Rox! I'm sorry for what I said about your belly. I think it's cute. But you really are in love. I just hope you know what to do with it."

I kept walking without looking back. I went inside, grabbed my hoodie, and walked out the front door.

I was opening the door to my mom's car when I felt him behind me. He put his arms around my waist and kissed the side of my neck.

"So who put the psycho salt in the mai tais?" he asked.

Psycho salt? Of course Jake would find a way to make me smile.

"I'm glad you don't feel like partying tonight," he told me.

"Why?"

"Because we both have the night off." He slid my hair over and kissed the back of my neck. "And it's only six." *Kiss.* "And Adam has class until ten." He reached his hands around my chest and cupped my brown bikini top in his hands. Yep. Right there in front of Allison's house, in broad daylight. I loved it. "And you're wearing a grass skirt. Do I need another reason?"

I giggled and turned around to kiss him on the lips. When he pressed me into the car, I was glad I didn't feel like partying either.

I was also glad he didn't bring up that love stuff.

CHAPTER 19

SIX DAYS LEFT

F UCKING END-OF-SUMMER PARTY. Fucking Shannon. I wished she would stop talking about it already.

I was having a bad day again. Lately, I'd been having a lot of bad days. The new people had started training. I had to look at the people who would be working with Jake, and maybe even hooking up with Jake, after I left. The images were playing on repeat in my head.

The fem-bot was Ashley. You know the type: tiny, blonde, tan, and tight. Fem-bots were usually the kind seen on MTV Spring Break specials, the kind of girl you saw on TV or in a magazine and thought, *no one in real life is that pretty. It must be the cameras. It must be the hair and makeup crew. It must be Photoshop.*

Imagine that one popped up in real life; not at a hair salon, a tanning salon, or at Hooters, but as your boyfriend's new coworker! Imagine the horror. Just for one second, imagine it.

Then imagine this:
"That bartender is hot."
Yeah. *That* happened.
"I bet he's good in bed."
And that happened.
"Um, get in line," Shannon said. "I was here first."
There was a line now? There was a fucking line?
"I have a boyfriend," Rachel told Ashley. "So you have no competition from me. But if either of you see success, make sure you report back. I want all the details. And any photos or video you might take as well." (Insert stupid giggle.)
"As soon as the girlfriend leaves for school, I'm all over that shit," Shannon said.
"There's a girlfriend?"
"Yeah. The waitress over there with the dark hair."
Huh. How long had they known?
"Oh, the fat one?"
That part didn't really happen. I'd just had a fat complex since the luau. What she actually said was, "Oh, the cute one?" The word *cute* could be taken as a jab if I wanted to over-think it. Cute was the funny best friend, the supporting actress. Cute was not the star, but part of the ensemble. Saying, "Oh, the hot one?" would have been better. But I'd take someone describing me as cute over fat any day. Cute was a compliment coming from her.

I had forgiven Allison for embarrassing me at her party. I'd always forgiven Allison of everything, and she'd always done the same for me. It was kind of a silent agreement. She forgave me for my moments of thoughtlessness and selfishness and my tendency to overreact. I forgave her for her controlling, manipulative schemes. Luckily, they only happened very rarely. If she was to go off the deep end one day and start resembling Lady Macbeth, I would intervene. But a harmless knock on my belly fat, I could get over.

IT WAS A Monday, the night of Shannon's End-of-Summer party. She'd picked the slowest workday for the party so less people would be on the schedule and more people could be at the party. Jake and I worked together on Monday nights. We weren't going to make it to the party until way later, if at all. Boo fucking hoo.

It was always slow on Mondays, but even slower than usual tonight. Zeke came in to work on the new fall menu with Jake and Paul, the head chef. Paul cooked up the new menu items, and Jake took pictures for the website. The few people working got to taste everything afterward.

Jake also mixed up some of his new fall cocktails and shots for Zeke to taste. Zeke insisted that everyone else taste them, too. *Just a sip.* I might have taken more than a sip. By the time the kitchen closed and everyone had left except Jake and me, I was pretty tipsy. He added fuel to the fire when he set my shift drink in front of me. By the time the drink was gone, so was I.

"I'm really fucking drunk, Jake."

He leaned across the bar and kissed me on the lips.

"You're also really fucking beautiful," he said.

Thud. Beautiful was better than cute. Beautiful was even better than hot. "Thanks."

"I might be kind of drunk, too," he confessed.

"So you only think I'm beautiful when you're drunk?"

He laughed out loud. "I have always thought you were beautiful. You know that."

"Even if my belly is fat?"

"Would you stop? Your belly is not fat. I could kill Allison for even saying that."

"I could kill Allison for a lot of things." But I wouldn't. Everybody said things they didn't mean sometimes. I would get over it. Really. I would. Someday.

It was two AM when Jake locked the front doors and turned off the red OPEN sign.

"We probably shouldn't drive," I said. "We can see if Adam is still up. He could come get us."

"Or we could just stay here, and I could fuck you all over this bar."

That sounded like a great idea, but ... "There are cameras."

"We can turn the lights off."

"They could have night vision, like in Paris Hilton's sex tape."

"How do you know there was night vision in Paris Hilton's sex tape?"

"I saw the highlight reel."

"There were highlights?"

"Ha ha. I guess so."

He turned the lights off.

"Jake!"

He reached for the button on my black shorts. "Drunk people don't care about cameras. Either we have sex all over this bar, or we call Shannon's to see if anyone is sober enough to come get us."

"When you put it that way..."

WHEN WE WERE done working off our buzz "all over this bar," we went to Shannon's after all, just to make an appearance. It was a mixture of the summer staff and the new people who were still training. Everybody was drunk.

There was a beer pong table, a flip-cup table, and a two card tables set up in her garage.

Jake and I walked over to the corner of the garage where Shannon had a makeshift bar area set up. Liquor bottles, mixer bottles, a huge tub of ice, cocktail shakers, stirrers, straws. She even had a garnish tray with lime wedges, cherries, and olives.

I could hear all of the other parties talking about this party behind its back.

"What do you want to drink?" Jake asked me. He nudged me gently with his elbow. "You wanna do a shot with me so we can catch up to these fools?"

I could feel eyes on us as we stood there assessing the situation. I now knew they were onto us after hearing that conversation between the girls. I didn't have to pretend anymore around them.

"Yes, please. I'd like a screaming orgasm."

"Haven't I given you enough tonight?"

Never. I could never get enough of him.

I took a long, slow look at him – his warm brown eyes that were filled with light even in the darkest times, his bright smile that made me feel like I was on my way to the top of a roller coaster, the soft lips that sent me over the highest hill every time they touched mine, the stubble on his chin that made me hurt in the best way (and let's not even talk about the other body part that made me hurt), the biceps that begged to be squeezed, the tattoo sneaking out of the sleeve of his t-shirt. He was really fucking beautiful, too. And inside his gorgeous shell he was kind, devoted, determined, witty, smart, and faithful. He was crazy if he thought I was ashamed of him. I couldn't have been prouder to be by his side. I couldn't have been more frightened either.

I was safe with Jake. I knew that. He would never intentionally hurt me and I knew he would do anything he could to make sure he never unintentionally hurt me either. And that was probably the very reason I would hurt so badly when it was over. Safe did not exist. The safer we were, the deeper we fell, the harder we hurt.

"I'm the luckiest girl," I said to him quietly.

He smiled down at me. "Why? Because your boyfriend makes a good screaming orgasm?"

That word again. The roller coaster. The butterflies. The free-fall.

"No," I said quickly. "I mean, it helps. But I can get a screaming orgasm from a lot of bartenders."

He looked hurt, not sure if I was speaking literally or about the drink. I think I was talking of both.

ALL GOOD THINGS

"I'm the luckiest girl because my boyfriend makes me feel beautiful and loved, all the time, no matter what."

"Yeah? Who is this guy? I'd like to thank him for being so good to my best friend."

He smiled and handed me a shot. I could have taken offense to that comment, but that was just the thing – I knew he meant it in the nicest way.

We clicked our plastic shot glasses together. After we took the shots he threw his cup onto the table, wrapped his arms around my waist, and slammed my body into his in that rough, aggressive way I liked so much.

"You *are* beautiful and loved," he whispered. "All the time. No matter what."

Have you ever had a moment so sweet you forgot you were in a crowded room? Yeah. That happened.

When he kissed me in front of everyone, I let him.

"HEY!" IT WAS Chris calling from the card table. "Why don't you two quit making out and come play cards with us. Ten dollars per person, per game. Let's see what ya got."

I took Jake's hand and led him over to the table. Chris and Ashley were the winners of the last game. They sat there smugly, challenging us. Wrong move.

"What are you playing?" I asked innocently.

Ashley giggled.

"Euchre," Chris said.

"I've never been very good at this game," I lied.

Jake sat down at one side of the table and smiled up at me. "I got your back, baby. Sit down. It's only ten dollars if we lose."

We'd been playing this game together since childhood. We never lost. *Ever.*

We finished the first game with a high-five across the table above Chris and Ashley's pouting faces.

After that, it was one challenge after another. Everyone seemed to want their turn to lose. We ended up winning $80 all together. Jake gave it to Shannon for hosting the party. She'd earned it. It really was a party to make all other parties jealous.

"You guys make a really good team," Katy told us as we were leaving.

"Yeah," Jake said, smiling at me. "We do."

WE WENT BACK to his apartment and snuck quietly into his room. It was six in the morning, and the sun would be rising soon. I hated being awake when the sun came up. It made me feel like I'd done something wrong. Even though I'd only been playing some cards with a few friends, I had that hating-myself feeling, like I'd been blowing through lines of coke all night. Sunrises were depressing to me. A lot of things were depressing to me lately.

I snuggled up to Jake under the covers, knowing our time was running out too fast. I'd been thinking about what would happen to us. I *had* to go back because I was about to graduate. You couldn't change schools in your senior year.

But he didn't have to stay here. I knew he had a good job that he loved, but he could be a bartender in Chapel Hill. And we could come back together in May. Zeke would let him come back. I knew he would. What I didn't know was if Jake cared about me enough to make such a sacrifice. He'd promised me the summer, nothing more. I couldn't expect him to pack up and move his whole life just for nine months. But what would happen if he didn't come? Would he meet someone else and forget me? Would I meet someone else and forget him?

I was waiting it out, waiting for him to say he was coming with me. He hadn't yet.

"You okay?" he whispered.

I rested my head on his shoulder. "I was just watching the light come into the room, knowing I'm another day closer to leaving. And it makes me sad."

"Yeah. I know. Me too."

"What's going to happen when I leave?"

Dun-dun-dun. The verdict was in. The elephant in the room raised his trunk and said, "Thank you for noticing me."

Jake sighed, long and loud, like he'd been dreading this conversation the same way I'd been. He turned onto his side so he could face me. "I'm going to miss you, if that's what you're asking. I'm going to hate not having you around."

That wasn't exactly what I was asking, but it was nice to know. "I mean, are we still going to talk ... or not?"

Jake and I did not usually talk on the phone during the school year. I saw him at parties and stuff between semesters, but that was about it. He and I had always followed that 'out of sight, out of mind' rule.

"I think that might just make things worse," he said. I could tell by the look on his face that it wasn't easy for him to say that.

It wasn't easy to hear either.

I winced. The cement cracked. So much for unbreakable. So much for my safety net. It hurt like hell, but I knew he was right. I appreciated his honestly.

"So we go cold turkey then."

"It's probably the best way, Rox. No drama, no long-distance shit, no worrying what – or who – the other person is doing. No messes. Don't you think it would be best that way?"

No. I didn't. I thought he was worth the worry. He was worth the mess.

The one thing he'd asked of me this summer was to be honest at all times. But I couldn't be honest now. I couldn't tell him he was worth it if he didn't feel the same way about me. And clearly he didn't.

"Yeah," I lied. "It's the best way. Definitely."

I rolled over so he wouldn't see my tears.

CHAPTER 20

JAKE

It *is the* best way.

I have seen the long-distance thing play out in the past with friends of mine, and it was pretty much the same scenario each time.

Phase One: – I miss you sooooooo much. I am counting the months until we see each other again. I enjoy the sexting between classes and the surprise care packages you send me filled with Pringles, juice boxes, and naughty scratch-off tickets. I live for our nightly phone calls so we can make kissing noises into the phone and whisper I-love-yous. You hang up first – No, *you* hang up first – *No*, you hang up first. "Why don't we just stay on the line until we fall asleep? It'll almost be like we're sleeping together." I love you – I love you more – No. I love *you* more!

Phase Two: – I haven't received a text or call from you in ten hours! When I call, it goes straight to voicemail! You're cheating on me. I just know it. Sometime since last night you met someone else and forgot about me. Just like that. I never meant anything to you, did I?

Phase Three: – Last time you said your battery died, and I believed you. This time it's been an entire day. There's no excuse for that. You *have* to be cheating. That is the only possible explanation for this. Yep. The only conclusion. Well, you know what? Two can play this game. I'm going to a party tonight. I'm going to hook up with the first person I see.

Phase Four: – What? You were in the hospital with pneumonia, and it was a total dead zone, and you couldn't get any bars on your phone? Omigod! I feel awful! Are you okay, baby? (Oh shit! I am such a douche. I hate myself. I am the worst person in the entire world).

Phase Five: – The guilt is killing me. It is eating me from the inside out. It started with my heart. When I heard you say you loved me, I felt a little piece of it break off. Then it moved down to my stomach. When we get off the phone, I go to the bathroom and throw up. It gets worse each time we talk. When I hear your voice, your sweet, trusting voice, I die a little bit inside. I feel like the only way to stop the pain is to confess, but I know that is the easy way out. That is the selfish thing to do. The nicest thing I can do for you right now is keep this secret.

Phase Six: – Patty told Amy that Jason told her Max said you weren't in the hospital at all! You were at a party! I was right all along. You *were* cheating on me. And guess what – You weren't the only one.

Phase Seven: – I fucking hate you – I hate you more.

ALL GOOD THINGS

I CAN'T HAVE some shit like that go down with Roxie. And that's a pretty realistic hypothesis there.

She's got some trust issues going on. Not that I blame her. I know what Riley did to her back in high school, and it sounds like the guy from UNC may have been even worse. It's normal for her to be skeptical and a little bit insecure after her negative experiences. Roxie lives her life looking over her shoulder, waiting for someone to pull the rug from under her. She's feisty and quick to panic. She gets anxious over ... well, a lot of things ... *most* things. She can also, at times, lean a little bit toward the neurotic side. Don't take that the wrong way. It's all part of her charm. Roxie's crazy in only the most lovable ways, and I love each and every one of them.

But when you mix insecurity with anxiety, throw in a couple of exes who destroyed her trust in guys, and send her eight hundred miles away from me, where my coworkers (according to her) look like they came straight from the *Sports Illustrated* swimsuit issue ... and we become a recipe for disaster. Disaster would occur. Mark my words.

I meant what I said when I told her we were tight enough to make it. But she was also being real when she said we were only unbreakable together. If we're not together, we're in trouble.

It's going to suck. But it's only nine months. It'll give us both a chance to miss each other, meet some other people, and figure out if this is really what we both want. Because next time she comes home, there won't be an expiration date. If we pick up things where we left off, that's it. It's for real, and it's forever. I want to make sure she's ready. I need to make sure I'm ready, too.

She thinks this means I don't care about her enough. She's wrong.

CHAPTER 21

ROXIE

THURSDAY WAS MY last night at work. It was a good thing I wore waterproof mascara because I had to dab a bev nap to my eyes throughout the night. When people asked, I told them I had allergies.

It was the last time I would wear my uniform, the uniform Jake had lots of fun taking off me all summer. It was the last time we'd share a secret smile at the server counter when he handed me a drink. The last shift drink he would ever make me.

We stayed after everyone left. The last rendezvous in the beer cooler.

"I've had more sex this summer than I have in all the years of my life combined," Jake told me when we got into his truck. The last time he would drive me home from work.

"You haven't been having sex all the years of your life. At least I hope not."

"No. Only the past," he counted on his fingers, "seven years. Since I was sixteen."

"You were sixteen when you kissed me the first time."

"Yeah."

"Was it before or after that?"

"After. I was hoping it would have been you, but when you choked I thought the universe was trying to tell me to back off. So I did."

"Huh." I thought about how different life might have been if I hadn't choked. Maybe he would have been my first. Maybe I would have gone to Central with him instead. Maybe we'd still be together. Or maybe he would have cheated on me just like Riley and I would hate his guts. It was always best not to question what might have been. All that really mattered was what was. Anything else was a waste of time.

He rolled the passenger window down. He was going down a 45mph road. There wasn't a lot of traffic at this time of night, but there was potential for danger. In my mind, there was always potential for danger.

I looked at him and smiled as I pressed the button to unclasp my seatbelt.

I pushed myself out of the window. I was still too shy to throw my arms out like a sorority girl, but I was getting closer.

THE LAST NIGHT

ALL GOOD THINGS

IT WAS ALLISON'S idea to have a Going Away Pub Crawl for the girls. When I say 'the girls,' I'm referring to about a dozen girls we went to high school with. We were spread out in different parts of the country during the school year, but we tried to get together a few times every summer. Most of them had been at my Welcome Home party, and I was sure they'd shown up to Allison's Luau after I left.

I wasn't really in the mood to party. Drinking when I was feeling down was a meltdown waiting to happen. I would much rather stay in my room and make a list of the things I would miss most about Jake, while listening to 3 Doors Down and taking shots of Jameson straight out of the bottle.

1. His smile.
2. His laugh.
3. *Entourage.*
4. His truck.
5. His bathroom counter.
6. The way he stares at my ass when we're at work.
7. The way he grabs my ass as soon as we're off work.
8. The way he makes fun of me for saying 'soda' instead of 'pop.'
9. The way he makes fun of me for saying "care-uh-mel."
10. The way he makes me do the dog.

I could go on. I could fill an entire five-subject notebook with the greatness that is Jake Odom. But I didn't. It wouldn't do any good.

And I changed my mind about 3 Doors Down. I wouldn't be able to handle "Here Without You" when I was there without him. I could handle it with Jim because that was more anger than sadness. Not being with someone because he was a dickwad was a lot easier than not being with someone because he was in a different state.

I was leaving tomorrow. To-fucking-morrow. The rental car was packed. Jake still hadn't changed his mind. He already told me he wasn't interested in carrying this into the school year. But as a girl, I couldn't help but hope for that pivotal climax like the girls always got in romantic comedies, when the guy showed up at the airport or chased her car down the street. I would be holding out hope until the last minute, probably even longer. Because how many times had the girl actually left, only to have the guy show up weeks later? It's happened! I mean, in movies. I didn't know about real life.

Jake was at work. It was a Saturday. He always worked on Saturdays. We always worked on Saturdays.

Allison had arranged the party bus to pick us up at a popular martini bar. Braham dropped the two of us off. I was immediately annoyed when I walked into the bar and found my friends. It was like they had all emailed each other and made plans to dress alike. They wore their hair in high, bouncy ponytails (mine was down), faded jeans (mine were a dark wash), and really long sweaters that tied around the waist like trench coats (I had on a tank top because – hello – it was summer). August was still summer! It was 85 degrees outside! Where was the memo about the long sweaters, and why was I not on the mailing list? And what was it with girls wearing sweaters in summer and tube tops in winter? Annoying...

We had one drink before we moved on to a karaoke bar. I didn't think karaoke was the best place to go after only one martini. I figured we'd all be too sober to sing.

I was wrong.

The girls took turns passing the songbook around and writing down their choices to give to the DJ. I put in a slip to sing Jessica Simpson's "With You." In the meantime, I decided to rush my buzz with a lemon drop while I watched the shit show before me.

Paula went first. Yeah, *that* Paula, the other half of *The Shining* twins. She walked up onto the stage with a hip-swaying strut, grabbed the mike with confidence, and sang "Redneck Woman" by Gretchen Wilson. You would have thought she was a country star on a world tour with all of that hair flipping and winking.

Next up was a song by The Dixie Chicks. I wasn't a country fan, but those chicks weren't so bad.

Then Tina was called up and the familiar music began to play. She was singing "Redneck Woman" too? For real? Huh?

The DJ made a joke afterward when he called up Amber. She giggled when she heard her name. "I can't believe we all picked the same song, he he he."

What? Again?

Another shot, please.

Luckily the party bus arrived before the DJ called my name. I would have had to slur and sob my way through that Jessica Simpson song.

WE ENDED THE night at The Bar, and we couldn't have gotten there fast enough. These girls were making me feel like an outcast and I needed Jake. I *needed* him.

It was nearly 1:30AM when we arrived. We'd probably only have time for one drink before last call.

Jake's eyes lit up when he saw me standing at the bar. I didn't even have to ask for a drink before one was set in front of me.

The last song of the night was always a slow song. It was the DJ's way of calming things down at the end of the night and making people feel lovey-dovey instead of fist-fighty.

I was standing at the bar, moping into my redheaded slut, when I realized Jake had disappeared. He'd already finished last call. He'd probably gone to the beer cooler to stock the bar. I scanned the room to make sure both Shannon and Ashley were visible. Of course they were. Jake would never do that. Not right in front of me. I knew that.

Just as I heard the music switch over to "True" by Ryan Cabrera, I felt his hands around my waist.

"He's playing this for us," he told me when I turned around. "Dance with me."

As he took my hand and led me to the dance floor, I felt the inside of my heart turn into liquid and drip through the crack in the cement. He wrapped his arms behind my waist. I wrapped my arms around his chest. It wasn't the typical high-school dance pose, but it was the closest I could be to him. I rested my cheek to his chest and breathed in the laundry smell that would haunt my dreams each night I was away from him.

I found it strange to think we hadn't danced to a single end-of-the-night slow song all summer long. Why? Because we were a secret.

What a waste. I'd had a great summer with Jake, easily the best of my life, but now that it was over, I could see all of the wasted opportunities, all of the time we lost together by being a secret. I didn't beat myself up over it because it was too late to change anything, but if I ever had a second-chance romance with Jake, I would know better than to keep it a secret. At least I hoped I would. It was always easiest to say, "Lesson learned," and move on. We all hoped not to repeat mistakes. But did we always learn? No.

Jake pressed his forehead to mine. "You're my favorite radio station," he said to me. "I could keep you on forever."

I didn't reply. I couldn't speak unless I wanted to cry. I stayed quiet instead and appreciated the fact that, for right now, I could still feel him.

WHEN THE BAR closed and my girlfriends went on to their booty calls, boyfriends, or, in Allison's case, husband and kids, Jake and I got into his truck to head to the airport. Our last time at the airport.

I was glad when I got into the truck and saw my Carolina Blue Tar Heel hoodie on the seat. I left it there by mistake. Boyfriends and girlfriends leave clothes in each others' cars.

It wasn't cold in the stillness, but when he was driving with the windows rolled down, it would get chilly. I put it on.

Tomorrow. I would be in Chapel Hill tomorrow, or maybe even today depending on what time I left and how many times I stopped on the way. I would resume my NC life. Like someone pressed pause, I would pick up where I left off. I'd go to classes, I'd go to parties, I could even go to Prohibition because Jim was far from my head these days. I would have fun, and I would feel good about myself. Being independent and getting good grades always made me feel good. That was one thing I didn't feel around Jake – Independent. I had voluntarily given up my independence to him and I had no regrets about it. But it was something I would be happy to get back. I was always the person looking for a silver lining, and that was as far as the positive thinking was going to go right now.

When we parked the car and the air got still again, I got hot again. As we walked to the back of the truck I peeled off my hoodie and threw it into the bed, kicked my heels onto the pavement, and peeled off my jeans. Did I mention I was a little drunk?

"You're not wasting any time tonight," Jake commented, with an amused grin.

I shrugged. "I'm hot."

"Yeah you are."

ALL GOOD THINGS

I pulled the tailgate down, pushed myself up onto it and crawled into the truck bed on my hands and knees.

"Stop right there!" Jake said.

I paused and turned my head to look back at him, but he was already in the cab. When he popped his head around back I realized what he'd been doing – getting his camera.

He clicked before I could stop him.

"Jake!" I yelled. I hurried to the front of the bed and sat down with my back against the cab.

"Sorry, baby. When I get a view that good, I have to preserve it."

At least I was leaving him with a couple of interesting photographs.

"Can I put this away now?" he asked, holding up the camera. "Are you done with stripper moves for the night?"

"Not even close," I said with a sly smile. "But I'm done with stripper moves you're allowed to photograph."

I pulled off my tank top and tossed it toward the tailgate. I did the same with my bra.

"I feel way overdressed," he said, kicking off his shoes.

"Get in here," I ordered. "I want to take them off."

The last time I took off Jake's clothes.

He joined me in the truck bed, and I went straight for his shirt, tearing it over his head as soon as he was close enough to reach.

"Damn, baby, what's your hurry?" he asked. "Not that I'm complaining."

"I just don't want anything between us," I said quietly. More like desperately.

He kneeled in front of me, put his hand under my chin and lifted my face up to meet his lips. *God, I love him.*

"Oh, hey!" I said loudly, stopping the kiss in action.

He jumped back a little, startled by the outburst.

"I have something for you," I said. I turned around and stuck my hand through the open window behind us to grab my bag from the cab. I pulled my tote bag through the window and set it in my lap. It took a little bit of digging around in there, but I pulled out a small gift box. I'd wrapped it in yellow wrapping paper because yellow was supposedly the color for friendship.

"You got me a present?"

"It's not a big deal," I said shyly.

He unwrapped the paper pretty neatly for a guy.

I tensed up. I'd said it wasn't a big deal, but it was a huge deal. The way he reacted to this gift could change a lot of things. I pulled my house keys out of my bag and pointed my mini flashlight at the box so he could see.

I bit my bottom lip as he lifted the lid from the small box and pulled out his gift.

It was a silver key chain shaped like a heart, the actual organ, not the Valentine's Day shape you'd expect. I thought that would be too girly for him.

"A heart?" he asked. It was a little hard to see in the dark, even with my light.

"Yeah. Remember that night I said you were my best friend and you asked if I was going to give you half a heart?"

"Of course I remember. I will always remember that night."

I shrugged. "I thought it would be funny if I gave you half a heart. But then I decided I wanted you to have a whole one. My whole heart."

He held the heart in the palm of his hand (how is that for irony?) and ran his thumb over an artery.

"I mean," I said shyly, "you do have my whole heart. I just wanted to make sure you knew that before I left."

"This is really funny," he said.

"That wasn't exactly the response I was going for."

He looked up at me and smiled. "I mean, it's really funny because I have something for you, too."

He reached into the back pocket of his jeans and pulled out a small piece of tissue paper. I pulled apart the paper to find a thinly braided leather bracelet with a little silver charm hanging from it. I held it up to the light to get a look at the charm. It looked like a Monopoly piece.

"Is it a dog?" I asked.

"Yeah. Get it?"

I laughed out loud. Yes. I got it. It was perfect.

I didn't mean to cry.

He wiped a tear from my cheek with his thumb.

"Are you upset? You don't like it?"

I shook my head. "I love it. It's perfect."

"I love my heart, too. Or your heart. Thank you for giving it to me."

I nodded.

He sighed. "All right, baby, we need a mood change. Maybe you should start taking off my clothes again?"

The last time we ever had sex. And it was sad. But sweet. It always was sweet with Jake. Even the dirty times when he was throwing me around and calling me a cock-loving whore. He'd always said it with such kindness. And he always, always, kissed me like he loved me.

Afterward, he said he could drive me down to Chapel Hill tomorrow. But I said no. This last night was just right. A few more days with him would be great, but that was only putting off the inevitable. It was like drinking alcohol to fend off a hangover. The hangover was going to come as soon as we stopped drinking. It was time for my hangover.

WE WERE DRIVING home when the song "Summer Girls" by LFO came on. Yes! At least the radio stations knew it was still summer.

I knew every word to the song and wasn't too proud to sing along. Most guys made a big display of their boy band hatred whenever a song like that came on, but Jake knew a catchy tune when he heard one. He turned it up and bobbed his head to the music.

When it was over he turned the volume down and looked at me. "You know what scares me the most, Rox?"

"What's that?"

"Thinking that one day, like ten years from now, this song could come on and make me think of you."

"Why is that scary?"

"The scary part is thinking of you as being my summer girl, the one who got away. I don't want to ever feel that way about you. Whatever happens in the future, I hope it's what's best for both of us. I don't want regrets. I don't want you to be the one who got away."

"I know an easy solution for that."

"What's that?"

"Don't let me get away."

When he stopped at a red light, he smiled at me and reached across the bucket seat to take my hand in his. The last time he held my hand.

He pulled the truck in front of my parents' house and turned the car off.

Awkward silence.

"Can I see your phone?" he asked.

"Sure." I handed him my Sidekick curiously.

He played around with it a bit before handing it back.

"What was that about?" I asked.

"I set an alarm," he told me. "It's going to beep every day at four-twenty. I set the same alarm on my phone. I thought that was a good time for both of us. It's before I go to work, and it's between your morning and evening classes."

I nodded.

"When the alarm goes off, you'll know that no matter what happens, no matter where we are, I'm thinking about you. Okay?"

I bit my lip. Couldn't cry now.

"This has been the best summer of my life, Little Girl. Just so you know."

"Mine, too, Jake," I whispered. I took a deep breath and tried to swallow the lump in my throat. "So I guess I'll see you in May. Or maybe at Christmas."

"I'll walk you to the door."

We walked to the front door. It was a chilly, dewy morning, and I put my hands into the sleeves of my hoodie to keep them warm. It reminded me of another time, a long, long time ago, when Jake and I stood on my porch together.

"You won't tell your parents will you?"
"I won't tell them what? That you almost got arrested? Or that you kissed me?"

Jake took my hoodie-covered hands in his and pulled me close. "You won't tell your parents, will you?" he asked.

He was thinking of the exact moment I'd been thinking of, at the exact moment I'd been thinking it! I smiled my biggest smile of the night. "I won't tell them what?" I asked quietly.

He leaned forward, his lips an inch from mine. "That I kissed you."

Our last kiss.

EPILOGUE

ONE YEAR LATER

Have you ever looked at yourself in the mirror and wondered who the hell you were and how the hell you got there?

As I sat in the gigantic arm chair in the church's bridal lounge, I caught a glimpse of myself in the mirror along the back of the door. I saw the expertly crafted updo, the baby blue earrings my mom bought for me, the necklace his mom let me borrow, the dress I'd finally chosen after trying on over fifty gowns. And I asked myself those questions.

Who was that girl in the mirror? She didn't look like me. The make-up artist used concealer to cover my freckles. She'd made my thin eyebrows big and bold. She'd added fake eyelashes that were driving me bonkers.

I looked like I could be on the cover of a bridal magazine. And that was great! Every bride wanted to look amazing on her wedding day.

I just wished I looked amazing as myself, not this girl I didn't recognize.

But then I guess my wedding look symbolized the last year of my life. *It wasn't me.*

I barely understood how it all happened. It was so fast.

It was Sera who dragged me to speed-dating night at the end of September. Her dance team was organizing the event as a fundraiser. They had one too many men on the registration list and she needed to even the playing field.

"Sera, I'm not in the right frame of mind for this," I whined. "I'm bitter, bitchy, and sarcastic. No guy is going to like me."

"Are you kidding? *Every* guy is going to like you. Guys love bitchy, uninterested women. They like the challenge. Besides, I don't need them to like you. I just need another body."

She opened my closet, pulled out an outfit for me, and pressed the ripped jeans and UNC t-shirt into my chest. "Here, this outfit screams 'I'm not trying.' They'll love it."

I rolled my eyes but put the outfit on.

"You know," Sera said, as she applied her makeup at her vanity, "it wouldn't be so bad if you *did* meet someone. The fastest way to get over one guy is to hook up with another."

Said the girl who'd been with the same guy since seventh grade.

"Maybe I don't *want* to get over him," I said quietly as I snatched an eyeshadow compact from her train case. I didn't like missing him. I didn't like feeling like half a person. But I liked *having* someone to miss. I liked my daily reminder that someone missed me too. And the school year would be over before I knew it. There was no reason for me to rush into someone else's pants to help me get over Jake. I liked being *on* him, as painful as it was.

I had no intention, none at all, of getting involved with anyone else.

THERE WERE TWENTY-FOUR daters registered in the speed-dating event: twelve guys, twelve girls. Add to that the members of the dance team organizing the event, and a few hangers-ons, and the lounge was filled with over thirty people.

But there was only one I couldn't seem to tear my eyes from.

He leaned back in a gold armchair with the casual manner of someone who didn't care about anything going on around him. His dark jeans were faded in just the right spots, and he wore a gray short sleeve Tar Heel t-shirt over a long-sleeve navy blue t-shirt. The layered look had always been my weakness. *Oh, you have two shirts on. Here's my vagina. It's all yours.*

His UNC baseball cap was pulled low over his face, so I couldn't see much, but I could tell he was wearing book-nerd glasses. A mysterious geek. Loved it.

It looked like he was talking to himself because his lips were moving. But I knew better. He wore a black earpiece that fit his ear like a cuff. I'd heard people call this Bluetooth, and I was pretty sure it was a way to talk on a phone without holding a phone.

I'd never been one to be on top of the technology game. I felt like the only person on campus who didn't have an iPod. I wanted one, but I didn't know how to get the music from the computer to the device. Sera had tried to explain it to me once, but anytime someone started talking about computers, my eyes glazed over, and I felt like I was missing part of my brain. So I let it go and walked around campus singing to myself instead. Nobody could hear me anyway. They were all listening to their iPods.

This guy must not have had any issues with technology because, while I'd heard of Bluetooth, I'd never known anyone who actually used it. He was ahead of the game, maybe even on the very top of it. Seeing him talking into his earpiece, it made him seem important, like a director, like a boss.

I liked being bossed around. Especially by guys who looked like *that*.

While Sera and the other dance members tried to get everything set up, I let my eyes rest on his lips as they moved. They were soft, thick, like pillows. They looked moisturized. He must use lip balm. I wondered if it was flavored. Vanilla or strawberry? Maybe peppermint. Yes, I wondered what his lips tasted like. But I did it in a nonchalant, *I wonder what it's like to jump out of burning building* kind of way. I didn't actually aspire to find out.

But, you see, Sera had been right. Guys *did* want the girl who showed no interest. When Bluetooth Guy sat down across from me during speed-dating, he gave me that confident, I'm-going-to-own-your-body smirk, and I didn't swoon – it was game on.

His nametag said Caleb. "I'm only here because my buddy didn't want to come alone. I'm playing wingman."

Uh-huh. "Of the four guys I have met tonight, you are the fourth to say that."

"Ah, a girl with an attitude. I love it." He held his hand across the table to shake mine. "Caleb Golightly," he told me. His voice was deep and in control. "Finishing my MBA this year and moving back to New York. You coming with me?"

He: Smiled an I-know-I'm-sexy smile. He seemed confident, without being arrogant. His swag was enough to make me think he owned the university, but not so confident that I didn't think he'd share it with me.

Me: Resisted the urge to roll my eyes while I ignored the fact that he had turned me on with his cockiness. I hadn't had sex in three weeks. I could be turned on by a baked potato right now. This meant nothing.

But wait, did he say Caleb *Golightly*? As in Holly Golightly, my favorite fictional character of all time? Did he mean New York as in New York *City*?

"Hey," he said, "what do you say we get out of here? I don't need to meet anyone else. Neither do you. If you'll be my Jackie, I'll be your JFK." That was a bold statement for someone to make after spending twenty seconds with me, but I was intrigued nonetheless. He'd just compared me to one of the most beautiful, revered, classiest, and beloved women of all time.

For one of the few times in my life, I was without a sarcastic comeback.

But the truth was, the speed-dating – listening to a guy talk about himself until the timer went off in seven minutes, and then having to do it all over again a dozen times – was dreadful. If we both left, there wouldn't be an uneven amount of people, and Sera couldn't get mad. "Okay," I agreed.

He took my hand and we ran from the Morehead lounge giggling like little kids. We spent the next two hours walking around campus. He was funnier than I'd expected. He was also smart and ambitious. We had a good night together. When he walked me back to my car and asked if he could take me out on a proper date sometime, I said okay. It was just a date. Just one date.

But Caleb was a guy who was used to getting what he wanted, and he wanted more, more of me, all of me. There were lots of flowers, gifts, and grandiose gestures. One date turned into two, turned into ten, turned into a public proposal that I'd seen coming from weeks out, and eventually, a sad-looking bride who was twenty minutes from walking down an aisle.

None of this meant I'd stopped thinking of Jake. I missed him every single day. It was against the rules to contact him. Cold turkey, we'd said.

I did hear from him once. It was five days after my mom had sent out the invitations. I received a text with a smiley face. That was it. I took it to mean he was happy for me. And if he was happy, he didn't want me. And if he didn't want me, I was doing the right thing by moving on.

I'd told him not to let me get away. But he did.

He sent the RSVP back with a checkmark next to the word *Regret*. There were so many ways I could take that. Did he simply regret that he was unable to attend? Did he regret that my mom insisted on inviting him, even though I hadn't had his name on my guest list? Did he regret that we'd created a world in which we could not communicate?

I did. I wished things could be as light and easy between us as they'd been before last summer. I wished I could text him right now and tell him I was shaking in my white stilettos. He would appear at the door in minutes, probably with a bottle of whiskey.

But there was no Jake to rescue me this time. I was on my own.

The alarm on my phone still beeped every day at 4:20. I told Caleb it was a reminder to take my birth control pill. I couldn't cancel it. It would have meant I was letting him go forever. I wasn't ready to do that.

I *should* have been ready to do that. I should have absolutely been ready to do that before I put a ring on my finger from another man. But, hey, I'd never claimed to be the brightest bulb in the chandelier. Or maybe I had ... Oops.

Caleb was so attentive to me, so giving; he was "all-in" from the start. After the proposal, and the rock that sparkled from across a room, he took me to New York for the very first time so I could "get a feel for the place." And I felt it. Whatever it was. Anticipation, contentment, achievement, even love. I felt a future. In New York, everything was right in the world, everything was right with me.

He took me to the New York Public Library, Tiffany & Co, the Central Park Promenade and, finally, to a lovely brownstone on the Upper East Side. I nearly shit my pants at the sight of it. It was Holly Golightly's apartment building! See? Caleb was a good guy. I got to sit on the steps of Holly Golightly's building. I got to be Holly for a day. How many other girls could say that?

And I loved the way he kept calling me, "The Future Mrs. Golightly."

Six months later and here I was, back in Ann Arbor, about to say, "I do." Our Manhattan apartment would be ready for us to move in right after a honeymoon in Cabo. His family loved me, my family loved him, and he spoiled me rotten. I should have been the happiest I'd ever been.

Instead, I felt nauseous. I couldn't stop staring at the back of the door. I was waiting for someone to burst through it, drop to his knees, and beg me not to do this. But the door remained closed.

Allison stood behind me, trying to get my hairpiece on correctly, like the stylist had shown her.

"I know every maid-of-honor says this, but you really are the most beautiful bride in the world."

I gave her a tiny smile in the mirror. "Thanks."

"You also might be the saddest."

I immediately tensed and sat up straight in defense. "I'm not sad. I'm just nervous. I'm sure every bride is nervous on her wedding day."

"I saw him, you know," she said quietly as she fixed a curl above my ear.

My chest tightened. I needed my cement. I didn't want to listen to this, whatever she was going to say. I was so tense I was starting to resemble a porcelain doll. The tiniest bump could break me.

Luckily, the moment was interrupted when the door finally opened. It was my mom. She came in to hug me and say goodbye before she had to be escorted down the aisle by one of the groomsmen.

The ceremony coordinator from the church came in next to let Allison know it was just about time for her to go.

Allison stood in front of me and gave me a long look. She wasn't checking my dress for wrinkles or making sure my necklace clasp was in the back. She was looking at my face. She knew how scared I was. She knew how unsure I was. But what could she do? She couldn't stop me. I'd made my bed. Now I needed to lie in it. Wow, the words were killing me.

"I love you," she said.

"I love you, too."

She hugged me and left the room.

I was on my own to stare at the unfamiliar face in the mirror for a few more moments until the coordinator came back to let me know it was time.

I stood up and moved my shaky ankles toward the door.

And then I heard it.

Of course.

It was 4:20.

I walked to the vanity where I'd left my Sidekick. I picked it up and clicked the alarm off. I went into the settings and, with a shaky thumb, I canceled it. Forever. It wouldn't go off again.

"You ready?" the coordinator asked with a patient smile.

I smiled and nodded. "I am."

THE END

You can read more about Roxie's story in *The Good Life*.

AVAILABLE NOW ON AMAZON.

ABOUT THE AUTHOR

Like Roxie, Jodie Beau was a film student who changed majors three times. After eventually receiving her degree in Media Arts from Wayne State University in Detroit, she moved to Wilmington, NC, to pursue a career in TV. Instead, she met a boy and got "distracted." A few years later came another boy, this one even cuter. The three of them are now living happily ever after in suburban Detroit.

Jodie loves hearing from readers. You can find her on the following sites:

www.facebook.com/sweetbutsnarky
Twitter: @goodlifelist
https://www.goodreads.com/author/show/6926288.Jodie_Beau
http://www.pinterest.com/authorjodiebeau/
booksbyjodiebeau@gmail.com

THANK YOU

It seriously takes a village to publish a book. In a way, it's kind of cool. It makes me feel like I have an entourage like Vincent Chase. In another way, it keeps me grounded. It reminds that I wouldn't be *anything* without ALL OF YOU. And that's the truth.

Thank you, Village:

My husband, for still believing I can achieve the unachievable. I love you for that. I love you for lots of things.

Ian, the little boy who turned my cup half full – thank you for cheering me on while you sat on my lap and made me type most of this story with one hand.

My parents, for being my biggest fans, always.

My family, friends, and coworkers, (if you're reading this – I'm talking to YOU), for not being afraid to throw The Good Life in everyone's faces.

My cover designer, Michelle Preast of Indie Book Covers. The airplane in the sky made my heart do swirlys.

My cover models, Lindsey Wickenheiser, and Lon Meehan.

My editor, Madison Seidler, for not being afraid to say, "Uh uh, you can do better."

My proofreader, Lee Darrow.

My beta-readers: Laura Wilson (for encouraging more cursing), Kami Madison, and Sally Bouley.

My Master-Beta, Kelly Moorhouse. I could not thank you enough for all you have done! Not just a beta, but a cheerleader, captain of the "modesty ship," tour organizer, playlist-creator, sounding board, and most of all, a friend! I'm so glad I know you.

My author friends: Melissa Brown – you're always willing to help me when I have no idea what I'm doing (which is often). And Beth Ehemann, for being there to tell me when I've gone too far, which she hasn't done yet. If you find this book offensive, blame her ☺

The blogs and bloggers who have helped with tours, cover reveals, written reviews, and spread the word. I don't think anyone would know about The Good Life series if not for you guys.

Thank you to EVERYONE who has written a review, shared a post, or recommended The Good Life series to others. It takes a small amount of time, but can make a giant impact, so thank you!

And I can't forget Jacki, for helping me with the mother of all lists; Cas, for being my unofficial PR rep; and Debbie, for telling me I looked like a dead body in a casket.

Much love...